THE
RULES

FOR
BREAKING

THE RULES FOR BREAKING

ASHLEY ELSTON

HYPERION

Los Angeles · New York

First Edition
1 3 5 7 9 10 8 6 4 2
G475-5664-5-14060
Printed in the United States of America

This book is set in Bell Regular.
Designed by Marci Senders

Library of Congress Cataloging-in-Publication Data
Elston, Ashley.
 The rules for breaking/Ashley Elston.—First edition.
   pages cm
 Sequel to: The rules for disappearing.
 Summary: "Just when it seems that Anna Boyd's family has finally escaped Witness
Protection, the normal life she has attempted to rebuild comes crashing down"—
Provided by publisher.
 ISBN-13: 978-1-4231-6898-0 (hardback)
 ISBN-10: 1-4231-6898-4
 [1. Witnesses—Protection—Fiction. 2. Family life—Louisiana—Fiction.
3. Love—Fiction. 4. Adventure and adventurers—Fiction. 5. Murder—Fiction.
6. Natchitoches (La.)—Fiction.] I. Title.
 PZ7.E5295Ruj 2014
 [Fic]—dc23   2013049641

Reinforced binding
Visit www.hyperionteens.com

SUSTAINABLE FORESTRY INITIATIVE   Certified Sourcing
www.sfiprogram.org
SFI-00993

THIS LABEL APPLIES TO TEXT STOCK

For my boys—Miller, Ross, and Archer

THE RULES

FOR

BREAKING

Chapter 1

"CAN you teach me how to shoot a gun?"

I've been putting off asking Ethan this question for a week. It's now or never. We're in his truck, headed to the farm, and there is a practice range there that Ethan and his dad use to sight in their guns before hunting season. If he agrees, I won't have time to back out before the turnoff.

Surprise flashes across his face. "Are you sure?"

"I'm ready," I answer, hoping it's the truth.

I can tell he doesn't believe me, and I don't blame him.

"I'm not sure I'm ready," he says in a teasing voice.

It wasn't that long ago that I blacked out when I saw him shoot a hog that was attacking his dog. That shot brought back memories so horrible that I had repressed them for months. But I remembered everything now, and I was determined not to cower behind a couch the next time I came face-to-face with a killer. Not if there was anything I could do about it.

"What brought this on?" he asks.

I shrug, not meeting his eyes. "I don't like being scared of anything." And that much is true. I'm terrified of guns, but I'm more scared of returning to the life I led just a few short weeks ago. "I'm ready and we're here. Perfect timing."

My family has only been out of the Witness Protection Program a month and I'll do anything to avoid going back. Our short time in the program nearly destroyed my family.

He reaches for something near my feet and I automatically snatch my purse from the truck floor. The last thing I want is for him to see what I'm hiding inside. He grabs the remote control that works the gate to the farm, which must have fallen out of its usual spot in the cup holder, and gives me a strange look.

Probably because I'm acting like he's a mugger.

"You're jumpy. You hiding another boyfriend in that bag?"

I return his smile with a weak one of my own. Have I been glancing over my shoulder way more than what's normal? Yes. Have I nearly jumped right out of my skin at every little noise? Yes. Do I want to tell him why? No.

Ethan turns serious. "Anna, you've been different ever since the Mardi Gras dance. You know you can tell me if something's wrong, don't you?"

"No! I mean yes, I know. Nothing is wrong. It's all good. Sorry for being weird."

I hate thinking about the Mardi Gras dance.

Hate it.

It was supposed to be the perfect night. I was back to using my real name—no more fake identities—and I had convinced myself it was all over. I no longer dreaded the suits showing up and pulling

4

me away from everyone I'd grown to love, like they'd done so many times before. I no longer worried every time I said good-bye to Ethan that it might be the last time I saw him.

And it *was* perfect—at first. I felt like the belle of the ball dancing in Ethan's arms, and the night was getting even better when the party moved to Will's house.

But that's when everything fell apart. That's when the man I thought of as Agent Thomas re-entered my life.

"I've just been a little stressed lately," I add nervously. And that's the truth.

"And you think now is a good time to shoot a gun?"

"Yes, I do." I drop my purse back down on the floorboard.

"Okay, then. If you really think you're ready, we can try," Ethan says.

I may be good at hiding things from my dad and my little sister, Teeny, but I can't hide anything from Ethan. He knows something isn't right. Gripping my bag, feeling for the hard corners of the journal tucked inside, I think about how much to tell him.

I'm not mentioning the bizarre return of my missing journal . . . or the single daisy that was left in the pages. I'm not telling him about the note that Thomas, fake agent and would-be assassin, left in the pocket of my coat—the note that I tore to pieces, then taped back together hours later. I've re-read that note a hundred times looking for some clue or hidden meaning, but there's . . . nothing. It still freaks me out that Thomas managed to get within a few feet of me and I never knew it. I'm not telling Ethan there may still be someone out there watching me.

Ethan clicks the button on the remote and the electric gate

starts to open. "How long have you been thinking about this?"

"For a while."

Ethan glances from me to the farm road, back and forth, like he's trying to solve a puzzle. Given that the majority of the time we've known each other I was lying to him about who I was, I don't blame him for being skeptical.

"I'm not buying that. I'll teach you, but you have to tell me what brought this on. Are you sure nothing's happened?"

I give him a big smile and scoot across the front bench of the truck to get closer to him. I can't tell him. He'll make me tell Dad and Dad will call the suits and I don't ever want to see them again. I fought too hard to get this wonderfully normal life and I'm not ready to give it up.

"Everything's fine. Stop overthinking this. I know I freaked last time but I'm prepared now. I want to learn. I don't want to be scared."

I hope I didn't oversell it.

He moves a hand from the steering wheel to mine, squeezing it tightly. "Just as long as you're sure. I don't know if I can handle it if you pass out. That damn near killed me, seeing you on the ground like that."

And I don't know if I'll ever get tired of hearing him talk in that slow, smooth Louisiana drawl or seeing that dimple dig deep into his cheek. This moment, in the truck with him, reinforces why I will not go back to the way things were. I want this life. I deserve this life. But I need to learn how to protect myself. I don't ever want to be a victim again.

"Does your dad know you want to do this?"

"No. But it's not like I'm hiding it from him. He wouldn't understand and I don't want to try to explain it. He won't get it."

The first twenty-four hours after Thomas returned my journal and left the creepy note, I was terrified. I stuck to Dad and Teeny like glue, not willing to let them out of my sight. And Ethan, he knew something was wrong, but I dodged his questions like the seasoned evader I am. There were a million times in that first day that I teetered on the brink of telling Dad everything, but I couldn't say the words that would surely bring the suits back into our lives. And what would they do, anyway? All they know about Thomas is that he's some sort of assassin, or killer for hire, or something horrible like that. But that's it. They would have no idea how to catch him—so they'd probably just toss us back into the program.

After that first day, when nothing else happened, I decided that maybe Thomas did mean exactly what he said in the note: He just wanted me to have my journal back. I know enough about Thomas to know that if he wanted me dead, I would be dead.

Ethan pulls through the front gate of the farm and I rub my sweaty hands down the front of my jeans.

I can do this.

I have to do this.

There are several tractors working in the distance and I spot Ethan's dad's truck parked at the barn. I was hoping we would be alone—I don't need any witnesses if I am, in fact, *not* ready to do this.

Ethan turns off the truck and pulls me in closer, kissing me gently on the lips.

"We'll start slow. You can hold the gun, load it, get a feel for it.

If that seems all right, then maybe we'll try to fire a few rounds. If you start feeling bad, tell me and we'll stop. Don't push yourself on this. You're safe with me. You just have to put all of the other bad stuff out of your mind."

I drag him toward me, away from the steering wheel, and crawl in his lap, kissing him deeply. He knows and understands me like no one else ever has and that is a serious turn-on.

It's not long before we're totally making out in the front of his truck.

We hear a four-wheeler approach and I jump off Ethan's lap and move back to my side of the truck just before his dad stops on Ethan's side. I'm sure the slightly fogged windows give a little clue as to what was happening inside.

Ethan chuckles as he rolls down his window. "Hey, Dad."

He nods, sneaking a peek at us when he says, "Hey, son. Anna." He looks as embarrassed as I feel.

"Hi, Mr. Landry." My face is on fire.

"Dad, I'm going to teach Anna how to shoot this morning."

Mr. Landry jerks his head to me quickly. He also witnessed my meltdown the last time I was around a gun. "Are you sure?"

I nod and Ethan says, "We're going to ease into it. No rush."

No rush. I hope he's right and I won't need this skill anytime soon.

Chapter 2

**RULES FOR DISAPPEARING
BY WITNESS PROTECTION PRISONER #18A7R04M:**

~~Live on the fringe of society. . . .~~

NEW RULE BY ANNA BOYD:
Screw that.

I try not to hyperventilate. Ethan's got everything lined up: the gun, the bullets, safety glasses, and even a pair of earmuffs to deaden the sound.

We're on the back part of the farm where they do target practice. There's a wooden structure that's used as a gun rest at different heights so you can either stand or sit while shooting. In front of us are targets at varying distances.

"First thing I want you to understand is this is a completely safe situation. We're far enough away that there is no chance you will hit anyone or anything other than the target or the hay bale behind the targets. It's just me and you, Anna. No one else."

I nod and stare at the gun. As much as I try to keep the memories away, my mind instantly fills with the images of dead bodies and pools of blood.

Taking a step back, Ethan sees I'm having trouble and wraps his arms around me. "Anna, we don't have to do this today. Or ever. It's okay."

I shake my head and answer, "No, I don't want to be scared anymore." He thinks I'm talking just about the gun, but it's so much more than that.

"Do you want to talk about it?"

Ethan knows all about my family's time in the Witness Protection Program, but he's only heard the cold, hard facts that Agent Williams laid out. I witnessed two murders—not only was my dad's boss killed in front of me, but so was his son, Brandon, the boy I'd had a crush on for years.

It was so traumatizing I blocked that night out completely, and had no memory of it for months. But that memory returned right here on this very farm when I rode along on a hog hunt with Ethan. His dog, Bandit, was hurt and he was forced to shoot the feral hog attacking him. The sight of the gun, the crack of the blast, and the smell of the smoke flooded me with memories of that night.

Until that night on the farm, I thought the reason we were in the program was because my dad had done something horrible.

But it was me all along. I was the one the suits were protecting. I was the reason we were forced to leave our home in Scottsdale, our friends, everything we'd ever known.

I was the reason my mom turned to drinking. She couldn't handle staying in the program indefinitely while everyone waited for my missing memories to return, the suits showing up in the middle of the night because our location had been compromised. I was the reason she nearly drank herself to death and is now recovering in a treatment facility in Baton Rouge.

I drop down on the small stool next to the gun rest and bury my head in my hands. Ethan crouches down beside me, running his hand over my head in slow, calming strokes.

"Talk to me," he whispers.

"I can still see Brandon on the floor in that room. When I shut my eyes, he's there. One leg was at an odd angle and his shoe was untied. And the blood. It was everywhere. The room smelled like gun smoke and blood. . . . His body was just so . . . still."

Ethan pulls me in closer.

"And then the man who shot them, Sanchez, found me behind the couch where I was hiding and I knew I was next. He put that gun in my face and it was like everything was moving in slow motion. I thought I was dead."

A broken sob escapes my mouth and Ethan brings my face to his.

"But you survived because you are strong and smart. Don't forget that part. You are strong and smart."

"The only reason he didn't kill me was because of those ledgers. What if I hadn't seen Brandon's dad put them in that wall safe? What if Sanchez hadn't wanted them back badly enough and he shot me on the spot? If the cops hadn't shown up when they did, I would have told him the location and then he would have killed me."

Those ledgers are what kept my family and me alive for months. The suits wanted me to get my memory back so I could testify against Sanchez. But the drug cartel that Sanchez worked for had heard from him that I knew the ledgers' location. Ledgers that showed all of the ways Brandon's dad, who was the head of the accounting firm where my dad worked, had laundered their drug money. It would have completely shut down their operation.

And that's how "Agent Thomas" came into my life. He wanted the ledgers and knew I could get them for him. He drew me in, making me trust him. I thought he was the only suit who really wanted to help me.

"You're safe now. Sanchez is dead, remember? He can't hurt you."

He's dead because Thomas slit his throat from one ear to the other. Once the cartel got the ledgers back, they cut Sanchez loose. Apparently there are no second chances in the drug cartel business.

Except for Ethan and me. Thomas could have killed us in Scottsdale, but he didn't and no one knows why.

"Anna, please tell me why you want to do this."

"I want to be able to protect myself." And this is the truth, even if it's not the whole truth.

I stand up and give myself a good shake. "Please help me, Ethan."

His expression is guarded but I know him well enough to see that he is struggling with this. He wants to help me, but he doesn't think this is a good idea. At all.

"First, pick up the gun. It's not loaded. Feel it in your hand. See how you do with that."

I run a finger over the handle. It's cold even though it's been sitting in the sun, and shivers race up my arm.

Taking a deep breath, I wrap my hand around it, lifting it from the gun rest. It's heavier than I thought it would be. My fingers fit perfectly in the grooves on the handle.

"This is a Glock. It's small and there's hardly any recoil, so I thought it would be an easy gun to start with. Let's practice holding it the right way and aiming before putting any bullets in."

Ethan moves behind me. His hands move on top of mine and he brings them up, pointing the gun at the targets in front of us. He repositions my hands until the right one is holding the gun, my pointer finger on the trigger.

"You fire a gun with the same hand you write with, so for you that's your right hand. Your left hand will help support the gun like this," he says, and positions my left hand around the underside of the gun.

Ethan's body surrounds me completely. His arms line up with mine, his chest and legs mold against me. As nauseating as it feels to have this gun in my hand, I can't help but feel safe. It is a strange sensation.

"How do you feel?" Ethan asks.

"Scared but not scared. I know nothing bad will happen while you're here with me."

"Do you want me to step away? Let you hold it on your own?"

I'm terrified for him to let go of me. I'm not sure my body will support itself once his moves. But then I think of the journal—and Thomas. He took it from me—I assume for the secrets he thought might be written in it—and then inexplicably gave it back. What reason would he have to bother me once he had the ledgers? I have no idea, and that scares me more than this gun.

"Yes. Let me try it on my own." My voice sounds shaky, but I can't help it.

Ethan peels his body away from mine and it's agonizing, like slowly pulling off a Band-Aid.

I stand on my own, still aiming the gun at the target, and try to control my trembling limbs. I concentrate on that pit of fear in my belly. It churns and spins and makes me dizzy so I push it down. It will not control me. I will not live in fear. I will not lose this new life I have.

"Show me how to put the bullets in."

Chapter 3

NEW RULE BY ANNA BOYD:

When you finally get the life you want, enjoy every moment of it, or what's the point?

WE'RE celebrating. Not only did I load the gun but I fired it. I could only handle pulling the trigger once, but it was a huge victory nevertheless.

It's the first time I've been back to Will's house since the night of the Mardi Gras dance after-party. Will is Ethan's best friend, who also happens to be dating my best friend, Catherine.

It's us plus another couple and we're hanging out around his pool, listening to music.

Normal. Just another normal night in this normal life.

Catherine drops down beside me. "So do I call you Annie Oakley now?"

I giggle and answer, "Yes. Consider me armed and dangerous."

Will and Catherine were also there the night I passed out, so I didn't hesitate telling them about conquering that fear this morning.

Catherine leans close and whispers, "Okay, I wasn't going to say anything but you're carrying around luggage again. You haven't let that bag out of your sight all week. Something I should know about?"

Oh, crap. She noticed, too. And just as the journal that's stashed safely in my bag pops in my head, I reach down to feel for the hard edges.

"It's just my purse. You carry yours everywhere, too."

She shakes her head. "Spill it."

The interest in my purse goes back to the go-bag. We were pulled from placements so often in the program that sometimes we didn't have time to pack. So I started carrying a bag with essential items for Teeny and me. I was never without it and it always turned up in conversation.

"It's nothing. I just got so used to carrying around my bag, it's a hard habit to break."

Thankfully, we're interrupted when Emma and Ben show up.

"I still can't believe we're all hanging out again," Catherine says to me in a low voice. "I keep waiting for her to do something to piss me off."

"I know," I reply quietly. Ethan's twin sister, Emma, was not my biggest fan when I moved to this town, especially when her brother and I started hanging out.

Emma moves near us, obviously nervous, and I nod for her to sit down in the chair beside me.

"Hey," she says quietly.

"Hey!" Catherine and I answer back, probably more enthusiastically than necessary. It's awkward at first but it doesn't take long before we're talking about school and who's hooking up and how we're all ready for high school to finally be over.

Well, I'm the only one not ready for that last part. I don't want all of us to be scattered to different colleges. Ethan and I have talked vaguely of our future plans but nothing has been decided.

The guys join us and Ethan lifts me out of my chair, and then sits me back down in his lap. If I'm acting different this week, so is he. It seems like the more nervous or distant I get, the closer and more touchy-feely he gets.

Not that I'm complaining.

Will sits on the arm of Catherine's chair. "Okay, so next weekend we head to the Gulf to hang at Pearl's cabin. I say we cut class Friday and get a head start."

Pearl is Ethan's aunt and owns the local pizzeria. Even though Dad said I didn't have to continue working for her once we got out of the program, I'm still there almost every day after school. And Teeny's usually there with me making pizzas in the back.

"Sounds good to me," Ben answers.

Catherine pokes her bottom lip out. "I can't cut any more days or I may not graduate."

Ethan leans me to one side so he can dig around in his pocket, pulling his keys out. "These are stabbing into my leg."

I realize a few seconds too late that he plans on putting his keys in my purse. The journal is on top so there is no way he won't see it.

"Wait!" I grab for my bag, snagging the strap out of his hand, but I leaned too far over and fall out of his lap.

The journal lands on the floor practically at Ethan's feet. I dive for it, but he beats me to it.

To make matters worse, the taped-up note Thomas left drifts to the ground right between us.

It's in his hands and he's reading it before I can even think about what to do. He is going to freak out. Big time.

Everyone is quiet.

Ethan's eyes find mine and he's not just freaked out. He's pissed.

"Is this what I think it is?" he asks.

Catherine moves to his side and peeks over his shoulder, reading the note.

Her eyes get big as saucers. "Is this the journal you lost? How'd you get it back? Who's 'T'?"

The rest of the group surrounds us, all wanting to see the note and journal and hear my explanation.

"Yes, it is and I don't know what the 'T' is for. That's just how the note was signed." It's a lame answer and Ethan, at least, knows it. Of course the T is for Thomas, the only name I knew him by.

"When and where did you get this?" His voice sounds a bit like a growl.

"Last weekend. Here, at the party after the dance." I finally meet Ethan's gaze. "I don't know if you remember this or not, but when we were sitting in that lounge chair," I say, pointing to the other side of the pool, "someone bumped into us. I think that's when he put it in the pocket of my coat. I found it there not long after that."

"*Here?*" Will yells. "That son of a bitch came to my house! Did any of y'all see him?" he asks our friends.

Everyone shakes their head.

"Did you see him, Anna?" Ethan asks.

"No."

Disappointment sets in his face. "Why didn't you tell me?"

I deflate next to him. "I knew you would make me tell my dad. And the suits."

"Well, of course you have to tell them," Catherine says and pulls me into a hug. "This guy is a nut job. Why would he give it *back*? I'm not buying that bullshit in the note. He wants something."

Ethan drops the journal and note back into my purse. "Anna, we have to go tell your dad. Right now."

"I'll come with you," Catherine offers. Will, Emma, and Ben offer to come along as well.

"Thanks, guys. But I don't want to ruin everyone's night." I nod at Ethan and walk toward his truck.

We don't speak to each other until we're both inside.

"I can't believe you've had this all week and didn't tell me. This is a big deal, Anna. And I guess that's what this morning was about—you think you're some match for this guy? He's a professional killer. You could barely touch that gun this morning."

He slams his hand on the steering wheel, letting out a string of curses.

I don't want to tell Dad. At all. But with everyone knowing about the journal, there's no way it won't come out now. The way this small town works, I bet it will be all over the school by Monday. Half the kids there still call me Meg—the last fake name the suits gave me. This will not help. If . . . *when* . . . I get back to school, no one will probably come near me.

"I'm sorry I didn't tell you. I just don't want anything to change."

He reaches for my hand and I grab on to his. As mad as he is, I know it's mostly because he's scared about what this might mean. Does Thomas want something else from me? And will the suits try to move us away?

So much for my normal life.

Chapter 4

NEW RULE BY ANNA BOYD:

If someone is always watching, don't bother hiding. You're just going to a lot of
trouble for nothing.

DAD did exactly what I thought he would do when we told him
about the journal—he got pissed then called Agent Williams, the
lead suit on our case.

The journal and note are in a plastic bag, as instructed, sitting
on the coffee table. Agent Williams is coming to Natchitoches to
get the journal.

Ethan paces around the room while Dad stews in his chair by
the window. Thankfully, Teeny is still asleep.

"You need to make a list of everyone you know who touched
your journal," Dad says in a quiet voice.

"Why?" I squeak out.

"Because Agent Williams is going to run the cover and pages
for prints, hoping to find some trace of . . . Thomas. There are other
prints there—mine, yours, Ethan's, and whoever else touched it—
and he needs to weed those prints out."

I'm curled up on the couch, trying not to be totally depressed.
And scared. Agent Williams is coming back and I don't know what

that means. "Teeny may have touched it at some point," I add.

"When will he be here?" Ethan asks.

"In a day or so. That's the soonest he can manage. Until then, I want both of you to be extremely careful." Dad holds up his hand, stopping me before I can interrupt him. "And I know what you're going to say, Anna. I don't care that it's been a week and nothing else has happened. This guy is a killer. I want you staying close to home. Maybe even stay home from school until Agent Williams gets here."

I burst up from the couch, pissed, and run to my room. It's already started. My freedom is slipping away and the suits haven't even gotten here yet. Throwing myself across my bed, I bury my face in my pillow.

It's only a few minutes later when Ethan knocks on the door and pokes his head inside. "Can I come in?"

I nod and turn my head away from the door. I feel the bed dip when he sits down beside me.

The silence is heavy.

I glance around the room, absorbing each little piece of my time here. Photos cover a corkboard next to my dressing table showing new friends from Natchitoches next to the old ones from Scottsdale that I don't have to hide anymore. A poster from a concert in Shreveport cozies up next to one promoting the Mardi Gras Ball I snagged from school. Mementos litter the dresser: a napkin from our favorite restaurant, tickets from the chick flick I dragged Ethan to, and a flyer from Pearl's Pizzeria. It's the room of a girl savoring every moment of freedom she has.

"I'm done running away."

Ethan lies down next to me, linking his fingers with mine. "You don't know that they'll make you leave." He pauses a moment before saying, "Would you have ever told me about the note?"

I turn around and face him, our noses just inches apart. "I'm not sure. I'd be lying if I said this doesn't scare me. It does. It scares me to death. I don't know what the suits are going to do. I don't know if this warrants putting us back in protection. But if that's what they want, I don't think hiding is the answer. He found us before, and he'd find us again."

Ethan whispers, "You have to promise me something. Don't do anything risky. Promise me you'll play this safe. We'll figure it all out later but you have to be safe now."

I want to give my word that I'll do everything he's asking for right now. But I can't. I don't know what the next few days hold, but I won't sit back and be a victim of my own life. I couldn't do it before and I sure as hell won't do it now.

"Okay. I'll try."

Dad is true to his word; he's not letting me out of his sight this morning. Even when I move from the kitchen to the den, he's right behind me.

Teeny watches him pace back and forth around the room, looking out of the window every five minutes. "Dad, you're acting like a freak this morning." She's lying across the couch, the book in her hand forgotten for the moment.

We haven't told her what's going on. She'll find out soon enough and she might as well enjoy the last day of freedom. For her, I want reality to wait.

I gesture for him to knock it off—act normal—but he ignores me.

"Sissy, can we stop by Georgia's house on the way to the store today? She's letting me borrow a book and I want to start it tonight."

Since today is Sunday, it's also grocery store day. On Sundays, I always make a menu for the week and shop for what we need. I found out really quickly that having a plan is better than winging it. I've been playing Mom for longer than I like to think about and this was a hard-learned lesson.

"The shopping can wait," Dad says from the corner of the room. "I thought, maybe, you both would like to come to work with me today."

We try not to look at him like that's the dumbest thing in the world he could have said. Dad still works at the factory where the suits stuck him when he first moved to Natchitoches. He's not on the assembly line floor anymore, he's in the accounting office, but I'm still really surprised he stayed since he could have easily gotten a better job. Maybe he felt uneasy working for another CPA firm after he found out his old firm was laundering money for drug dealers right under his nose.

"Are you serious?" Teeny screeches. "I only have two days off from school each week and there is no way I'm spending them hanging out in your little office at the factory. Please."

Even though Teeny sounds like a complete brat, Dad and I smile. She hid in her shell for the majority of last year and any emotion—even bratty—is welcome. It means she's back to her regular self.

I just pray she doesn't relapse when Agent Williams shows.

Teeny goes back to her book and Dad motions for me to follow him to the kitchen. I'm barely through the door when he says, "I need to take care of some work so I'm free when Agent Williams gets here. He just called and said he'd be here just before noon tomorrow."

"Dad, we can stay here. I'll lock the door."

He's shaking his head before I finish. "No. That is not acceptable."

"What if we hang out at Ethan's while you're gone?"

His face is unreadable while he considers this. "You go to Ethan's and you come straight back here when I call you and tell you I'm home. Nowhere else. Do I have your word?"

I nod. "I'll call him and tell him to come pick us up."

Ethan is more than happy for us to hang out. He's as worried as I am about what tomorrow will bring and it's hard not to think today could be our last day together for a while.

Teeny talks the entire way to Ethan's. She's sandwiched between us in the front seat and is going on and on about some drama in her class between her friend, Georgia, and the boy she likes named Jimmy.

It's a good thing it doesn't take long to get to Ethan's.

Teeny runs in the house as soon as she jumps out of the truck but Ethan holds me back. "For today, let's not talk about what's going on or try to guess what will happen next."

"Or act like this might be our last day together?" I ask.

"No matter what, this won't be our last day together," he answers, his voice full of emotion. "Let's try for a normal day, okay?"

"Okay."

I love the feeling I get when I'm at Ethan's house. Homey. Relaxed. Safe. I want a normal day more than anything else and I know this is the perfect place to get it.

It's not long before Teeny and Mrs. Landry are baking cookies while Ethan and I settle in for a movie marathon.

Later that afternoon, just after Mrs. Landry invites us to stay for dinner, my phone starts ringing. I have to dig past the plastic bag–covered journal in my bag to find my phone. I'm not sure why I brought it with me. Even though it makes me feel nervous and sick, I can't let it go.

I find my phone just before the call went to voice mail.

"Hello."

"Where are you?" Dad all but screams on the other end.

"At Ethan's. Why?"

"Did you come home at all after you left with him this morning?" He's frantic on the phone and it's terrifying to hear.

"No! We've been here all day. Just like you said! Why?"

"Stay there. Don't move. Someone's been here. In the house. I'm calling the cops," Dad says.

"What?" I scream.

Ethan's head is close to mine, listening to Dad, and Teeny sticks her head out from the kitchen. It's obvious something is terribly wrong. And I can tell by her face, she's heard more of this than I wanted her to know.

"It has to be him! Who else could it be?" Dad's voice catches when he says, "And the journal's gone. If there were any prints there to identify him, it's gone now."

My eyes dart to my bag. "No. It's not. The journal is with me, in my bag."

"Sissy, what's happening?" Teeny asks.

I pull her close to me and tell her what's happened in as few words as possible.

"I want to see Dad," she says.

Even though Dad told us to wait, Ethan, Teeny, and I run from the Landry's house to Ethan's truck parked outside.

Expecting Ethan to crank the truck, I throw on my seat belt, but he sits still in his seat, staring at the cup holders.

"My remote to the farm is gone."

"What?" I lift my bag from off the floorboard. "Maybe it fell, like before." I search under the seat but it's not there.

"No, I saw it in the cup holder right after we got out of the truck earlier." He turns around and surveys the backseat, too. "My backpack is still there but it's open and papers are hanging out."

Ethan is meticulous with his things. His bag never looks that messy.

"Do you think . . ." Teeny starts but clamps her mouth shut. I can tell she is trying very hard not to burst into tears.

Ethan is pissed. "I think someone has been through my truck."

He cranks his truck and we race to my house. Ethan calls his dad and tells him to change the code on the gate to the farm. By the time we pull into my driveway, cops are already there.

Teeny and I both run inside and launch ourselves at Dad the second we see him. He hugs us back, hard, and starts crying.

He mumbles the same sentence over and over. "What if you had been here? What if you had been here?"

"We think someone went through Ethan's truck, too," I tell him.

Dad leans closer and Ethan tells him everything that was out of place or missing in his truck.

I look around the house while they talk and it's not completely obvious someone had been there. It's the little things like drawers left open and the scattered stack of mail on the desk instead of the neat pile it was in this morning. It's not like our house was ransacked, it's just a little disturbed.

Just like Ethan's truck.

An officer approaches us and Teeny grabs my hand so hard I almost yell out.

"I need to ask you just a few questions. When was the last time you were here today?"

I glance back at Ethan. My brain has turned to mush and I can't even remember what the date is today.

"I picked them up around ten thirty this morning. Mr. Boyd was still here. We drove straight to my house where we stayed all day," Ethan answers him. I wait for him to tell the officer about his truck, but he stays quiet.

The officer jots his reply in his little notebook then looks back at me. "Can you walk around the house with me and tell me what you think is different from this morning, or if you notice something missing?"

"Yes. Of course." I follow behind him, feeling numb. There are officers everywhere. It reminds me of the house in Scottsdale after Thomas took the ledgers. Flashes pop and every surface is coated with a fine, black dust. If it was Thomas who broke in, my guess is they won't find a single print of his anywhere. I reach behind me for Ethan's hand and I feel better the second his fingers wrap around mine.

We're in the kitchen and I make a full turn around the room.

27

"Those cookbooks were in the cabinet, not out on the counter. I remember because I wiped down that counter after breakfast because it was sticky from the syrup Teeny spilled."

I move near the phone and I can't stop the chills that race through my body. "My school backpack was on the floor right here," I say as I point to the ground. "It's gone."

And so it continues around the house. Knowing someone— probably Thomas—rummaged through our house is nauseating. I hate knowing his hands were on our things, and I wonder if I will ever feel safe in this house again. Teeny and Dad point out a few things but everything is pretty minor. Nothing really looks out of place except to us.

When we're back in the den, the four of us crowd onto the couch. The officer looks torn when he starts speaking. "We've taken prints and will run them through the system. We could find no evidence of forced entry. And the things disturbed are only visible to you who are familiar with your home. We've had officers talk with your neighbors and no one has seen anything. At this point, I'm not sure if this wasn't just some kid or junkie looking for some loose money or pills or something like that."

"But what about . . ." Dad pinches my arm before I can finish, then gives a small shake of his head. Does he not want me to mention Ethan's truck, or Thomas . . . or the journal?

"We'll be finished up shortly and the report will be ready in the morning if you want to make a claim against your homeowners policy for the missing items."

Finally the officer walks off so I can ask Dad what in the world is going on.

"I called Agent Williams right after I called 911. He's on his way right now, flying into Shreveport then driving here tonight. He told me not to mention Thomas or the journal. He didn't say why but he was emphatic. He said he will handle things when he gets here. He should be here within the hour."

I deflate next to Ethan and he pulls me in close. Our good day is officially over.

Chapter 5

NEW RULE BY ANNA BOYD:
You should also listen to what the suits aren't saying . . . sometimes that's
where the real truth is.

THE ticktock from the clock on the mantel echoes through the
room, reminding me it won't be long before the suits swoop back
into my life. We've been waiting, just like this, for a few hours.
Ethan is pacing and Teeny is asleep in a ball next to me on the
couch. Dad's holding down his chair in the corner.

"He should've been here by now," Dad says.

And before he finishes his sentence, headlights flash across the
room. They're here.

Every other time the suits have shown up at our house, it's
been a team of at least four agents—I guess that's how things roll
in the Witness Protection Program. I can tell something's different tonight. Agent Williams isn't by himself, but there's only one
other agent with him. And it's the one suit I hoped never to see
again—the one who chopped my hair off just before we moved to
Natchitoches—Agent Parker. She stands off to the side and I can't
quit staring at her. She's prettier than I remember, but maybe that's
because I didn't pay that much attention to her before.

Ethan drops down next to me, linking his hand with mine, and I cling to it like a lifeline.

Dad crosses the living room to shake Agent Williams's hand, and then nods at Agent Parker. Ethan tries to do the same but I hold him by my side so he settles for an awkward wave. They both say hello to me and I just nod.

"Greg, thanks for coming so quickly," Dad says.

"I'm sorry it's under these circumstances."

Agent Williams and Agent Parker both look toward me.

"It's good to see you, Anna," Agent Williams says.

I snort. Whatever.

"And you've gone back to your natural hair color," Agent Parker adds. "That looks so much better on you than that darker shade did."

My jaw drops open a little. As if she wasn't the one who picked out that horrible dye and forced it on my head!

"Yeah, I'm sure I look fantastic," I answer back. "What color are we going with next time . . . bright red?"

"Anna," Dad whispers my name. I get the warning.

"Start from the beginning and tell me everything, Anna." Agent Williams sits in a nearby chair and I push deeper into the couch, dragging Ethan with me. I think about waking Teeny—she'll be pissed if she finds out we left her out—but her face is so peaceful that I let her sleep.

Agent Parker perches on the back of the couch. I can feel her hovering and it's hard to resist the urge to knock her off.

I quickly run through the events—the bumped chair at Will's, the journal and note left in my pocket.

"And there was something else in the journal—a single daisy," I add.

I feel Ethan stiffen beside me. I hadn't told him that earlier. It's the creepiest part, and I hated to even think about that, much less talk about it.

"A daisy?" asks Agent Williams.

"Like the little one tattooed on her shoulder," Ethan says, then jumps up from the couch and starts pacing the room.

"Did you see him, Anna? Or anyone suspicious?" Agent Parker asks.

"No. There were a lot of people there, but all of them were kids my age."

Ethan adds, "I didn't see anyone there who didn't go to our school either."

"And what about the break-in today?" Agent Williams asks.

Dad tells him what was missing or out of place, then Ethan explains having a similar incident with his truck.

Agent Williams turns to Ethan. "And your truck was parked outside your home all day?"

"Yes, sir."

Dad leans forward in his chair and asks, "Greg, why is he doing this now? If he wanted to harm these kids, he had every opportunity in Arizona. It doesn't make any sense that he'd risk showing up here knowing Anna and Ethan would recognize him."

Agent Williams shrugs and I notice the extra set of wrinkles that seem to have taken up residence in his forehead. "I don't know. We've had agents working this case for weeks and we've got nothing."

"I just don't understand how *no one else* ever saw this guy!" Dad's eyes jump to me when he asks, "How many times did he come see you when we were in the program . . . three . . . four times?"

"Four," I squeak out. "In that coffee shop on Front Street, twice in the laundry room, and once at Pearl's."

"Four!" Dad exclaims. I shush him, reminding him that he will wake Teeny, and he lowers his voice a fraction before continuing, "Four times and not one of your guys ever saw him!" And then he turns on me. "And I still can't believe you never mentioned he was visiting you, even if you thought he was an agent. You didn't think it was strange?"

This is a conversation we've had a ridiculous number of times. Dad always seems to bring this up out of the blue—at the breakfast table, in the car, just before I tell him good night—it's the one constant question. Why didn't I tell him Thomas was contacting me?

And it's a question I have a hard time answering. Do I get back into how awful Dad was acting back then—all secretive and silent? Do I remind him that Mom was falling down drunk all the time and my main concern was that she not kill herself with a bottle of gin?

But it's more than that. And way worse. Every time a suit showed up, I would get nervous and panicked and jumpy, almost like I was allergic to them. But Thomas was so different than the other suits . . . obviously. He talked to me like I was an adult, not some useless kid. And I felt like I could trust him. That's the worst part about this. I would have never mentioned him to anyone else because it never occurred to me that I should. He totally played me.

So I never really answer this question because I can't bear to explain my stupidity.

Luckily, Agent Williams presses forward. "When you called me about the journal and note, I was very concerned that he decided to make contact with Anna. And in such a familiar way. But since it had already been a week and nothing else happened, I was stumped. But now that you have experienced a break-in, probably two, it seems like whatever this is, it's escalating." He turns to me and asks, "Where's the journal now?"

I point to the small book in the plastic bag on the coffee table. The journal I once found so comforting now disgusts me. It was the only outlet I had when we were moved from town to town and it was devastating when I lost it. Agent Williams pulls a pair of gloves from his pocket and puts them on before reaching for it. I didn't let Ethan or Dad look through the pages, but I know I won't be able to stop Agent Williams. Or, it seems, Agent Parker—since she's peering over his shoulder now.

As he flips through, a hole opens in my stomach. I cringe at the thought of all the suits reading what I wrote since most of it is about how much I despised them. And I was particularly unkind in my comments about Agent Parker after my makeover. Every feeling, thought, emotion, bad hair day, and bout with PMS I had while wasting away in the program for almost a year is written about in great detail in that journal. I may as well be walking around naked.

Agent Williams skims the pages, but thankfully closes it quickly. "Where is the note?"

"Folded up in the back of the journal."

"And you received flowers last weekend as well?" Agent Parker asks.

Could that have been only a week ago—getting dressed with Catherine and Julie and greeting the delivery guy, wielding a huge vase of flowers, at the door?

"Yes. But I threw them out. After I got the journal, I realized they were probably from him."

"He sent you flowers, too?" Ethan asks. He throws his head back in either disgust or anger. Or maybe a little of both.

I silently plead with him to come back to the couch and he finally drops down beside me.

"Anna, why didn't you tell me this was going on?" Ethan asks me in a quiet voice.

I lean in close when I answer him back. "I don't know. I think part of me didn't want to admit it was really happening."

This may be the last time I see him—the white, windowless van that moved us from placement to placement is probably gassed up and waiting outside. My hand moves to Ethan's and I catch Dad's look. He's not crazy about how close we've become in such a short amount of time. And sometimes it feels weird to me, too, when I realize just how much I don't know about him. But I still don't pull my hand away.

Agent Williams pulls out the taped-together note and reads it out loud.

"'Dear Anna. I'm sure you have questions, and someday maybe I'll answer them for you. I thought it was important for you to have this back. I hope the nightmares that haunted you are gone. Maybe one day we'll meet again.' And he signed it with just a 'T.' 'P.S. Tell your friend the tracker was a clever move.'"

Agent Williams leans back in the chair, letting his head drop and his eyes shut while Agent Parker paces behind the couch. The clock's ticking seems louder than normal as we watch them.

Tick. Tick. Tick.

Just when I start wondering if he's fallen asleep or something, he sits up in the chair and says, "I've debated how much of this to tell you, but it's time for me to put it all on the table. The reason we didn't bring a full team is because I believe we have a mole in our program."

Dad comes in closer but still won't sit.

Agent Williams takes a deep breath before continuing, "For lack of anything else to call him, we'll just use Agent X. There's no other explanation for how Thomas was always one step ahead. Or how he so perfectly impersonated a U.S. Marshal. Or how he contacted your father at his work and knew where to find you."

"And the little details that were in your personal records, like the daisy tattoo," Agent Parker adds.

My hand automatically goes to my shoulder where the single daisy sits. Ethan brushes my hand away and rubs his thumb over the spot instead. The pit in my stomach grows bigger and I feel like it's going to swallow me up.

Agent Williams gets up from the chair and walks to the window. "I knew something wasn't right toward the end of your time in the program, but I couldn't figure out what it was. That's why I had Agent Parker come in when we were moving you to Natchitoches. I needed some fresh eyes on your detail. She has been in another division and has never been on a case with any of the other agents in question. Since Arizona, we've narrowed it down to one of three agents; men who were on your detail from the beginning."

"Which agents?" I ask.

Dad interrupts him. "Greg, maybe Ethan shouldn't be here for this. I mean, this is family business."

Ethan tenses beside me. I know it will be hard for him to be shut out of what's happening.

I start to argue, but Agent Williams stops me. "Richard, this involves Ethan now. He saw Thomas in Arizona. Spoke with him. And for whatever reason, Thomas probably went through his truck in broad daylight in front of his house. There is something he wants and he wants it pretty badly to take those chances. I understand wanting to keep this private, but I think he should stay."

Dad turns his back to the room; he doesn't like not getting his way.

I'm not expecting Agent Williams to tell us who the suspected agents are, so I'm shocked when he says, "Agent Mullins, Agent Hammond, and Agent Webb are the three agents in question. Do you remember them, Anna?"

With all the moves, there were so many different agents. I tried really hard at first to remember their names but it became impossible, which is why I called all of them "suits." But I do remember Agent Mullins and Agent Hammond. Agent Mullins was assigned to us in the first safe house and helped us understand how the program works and what we should expect. He was nice and patient, especially with Teeny. In the beginning, Agent Mullins was a common fixture when it came to ditching identities.

Agent Hammond was different. I'd seen him before but I didn't learn his name until he showed up in Florida to relocate us. It was the night I was waiting for Tyler to pick me up. I remember him because I hated that move the most. I'd finally begun to have a life I was content with there. It wasn't the same as Scottsdale, but I was happy—I had friends and a boyfriend, and life was starting to feel normal. I begged Agent Hammond to let me call Tyler, to make up some excuse of why we had to leave so he wouldn't wonder forever about where I'd disappeared to. But he wouldn't let me, and I hated him for that.

The only thing I have to remember Tyler by is the strip of pictures from a photo booth that I kept buried in my go-bag. It was months before I could look at it again without feeling sad.

"I remember the first two, but I don't remember Agent Webb."

"He was the agent on the scene with me the night your mother was taken to the hospital," Agent Parker says.

My stomach drops at the mention of that night. The night Ethan dropped me at home and my mother was unconscious on the front steps. The night I thought my mother had finally drunk herself to death. After they pumped her stomach at the local hospital, she was shipped away to some rehab facility where she remains today.

"So, what now?" Dad asks. He doesn't want to talk about that night any more than I do.

Any minute my death sentence will be handed down—that's exactly what it will be like to leave Ethan and everyone else here. And what about Mom? Witness Protection sucked the life right out of her last go-around. This is not the "positive home environment" the doctors at rehab are asking us to create for her.

"Well, Richard, that's the tricky part. Until I can figure out which one of these guys is the mole, we're gonna have to go off the books on this one. If I don't know who to trust, then I won't trust anyone."

Great. Way to inspire confidence.

Dad's face turns so red that I expect steam to pour out of his ears. "I want this bastard caught. He was right there, was within inches of her, and no one knew it. He put a damn flower in her pocket, for Christ's sake. He's been in this house. What's next?"

Dad smacks the coffee table with a rolled up fishing magazine and Teeny jerks awake.

It takes her a few seconds to orientate herself with where she is and what's going on. She seems fine when she notices Agent Williams but starts to panic when she sees Agent Parker.

"Oh God! We're moving, aren't we? Is she going to dye my hair again?" Teeny throws herself into my side and burrows under my arm.

"We're not sure what we're doing yet," I whisper.

Agent Williams gives Teeny a small smile. "Elena, we're going to try very hard to get this sorted out without moving you."

I stiffen. It's weird hearing Teeny called by her real name.

In addition to the extra wrinkles, the bags underneath Agent Williams's eyes seem double their usual size and his skin is all pale and splotchy. He opens his coat and pulls out a big plastic bag. With gloves still on, he drops the journal and note inside. "Who, that you know of, touched this book?"

"I did, of course, and probably Teeny at some point. Dad and Ethan, too," I answer.

"I have everyone's prints on file except Ethan's." His eyes move to where Ethan is pacing behind the couch. "Do you mind if I get a sample of your prints so I can rule them out as Thomas's?"

"Yes. Of course."

Agent Williams turns to Agent Parker and asks, "Would you get my bag?"

She returns a minute later with his black briefcase, and the way she's carrying it makes me think it's very heavy.

She drops it on the coffee table and Agent Williams gets out what he needs. I recognize the white-card and ink set. It's the exact same way they took our prints when we entered the program.

Ethan kneels down at the coffee table near Agent Williams.

"Just relax your hands, Ethan. That's the best way for me to get a good print without any smudges."

We all watch as Agent Williams presses Ethan's fingertips into the ink then rolls them across the card, one by one, making a replica of his prints. Agent Williams drops the card in a plastic bag once it's dry.

"I'll be back in the morning. Agent Parker will remain here with you tonight to ensure you don't have any more unexpected visits."

Agent Williams stands to leave. He looks tired. And old.

"Sir, why don't you let me take the journal to Shreveport," Agent Parker says. "I can ask the local police to watch the house tonight and you could get some rest. I'm not sure if you should drive."

"No. It's fine. Sheriff Pippin is picking me up. I already requested a patrol to be parked outside. The state police have offered their helicopter since I'm headed to their facility."

"Do you want me to come with you, then?" Agent Parker asks.

"No, not enough room. And I'd rather you stay here, just in case."

I can't help but ask, "If you're afraid of this Agent X finding anything out, why are you involving the local police?"

"Good question, Anna. I haven't given nor will I give the local or state police any details about what is happening here. All I've asked for is use of their lab and a squad car to be parked outside for the night."

A knock on the door makes us all jump. Dad opens it up to find Sheriff Pippin. The sheriff and Agent Williams got to know each other pretty well after everything that happened last month and they greet each other warmly.

"Lock up and I'll see you all in the morning," Agent Williams says as he turns to go.

An awkward silence descends on the room once we're left with Agent Parker. She forces a smile but she doesn't look thrilled that she is being left behind to babysit.

It's going to be a long night.

Chapter 6

NEW RULE BY ANNA BOYD:
After midnight can sometimes be the best part of the day. Just saying.

FOR the first time in my life, Dad is letting a boy spend the night with me. Well, not "with me" with me, but in my house. Dad talked to Mr. Landry on the phone for a long time, about the break-in here and the possible break-in of Ethan's truck. It was decided that Ethan would be safer here with Agent Parker and the patrol car outside just in case. There were many rules set down before Dad actually went to bed himself, but Ethan is here, sleeping in my room, while I'm bunking with Teeny.

Dad tried to give my room to Agent Parker, which totally creeped me out, but she declined, saying that she'd set up a spot in the den. I guess she's like our night guard or something now.

It's way past midnight and I've tossed and turned for the last hour. From the faint squeak I hear coming from the next room, so has Ethan. Inch by inch, I snake my way out of the bed. I creak open the door, listening for any sounds of Agent Parker, and I hear a faint snoring sound coming from the den. I can't think about how much trouble I'll be in if I'm caught.

42

Ethan jumps up in the bed as the door slowly opens. Even in the dim light, the smile that breaks across his face is hard to miss.

"Your dad will kill me if he finds you in here."

I don't answer, just tiptoe to the bed and crawl in under the covers. There's only been one other night we've shared a bed, and that was in a questionable Motel 6 outside of Phoenix.

"He won't come in here." I hesitate for just a second before cuddling right up next to him. My head goes to his shoulder, his arm wraps around my waist and our legs tangle together.

We fit just right.

Ethan brings me in for a kiss and I lose myself in the safety that I have always found with him.

This is not the first time we've made out, not even close, but just like every other time—I feel desperate for him. Like this could be the last time he touches me . . . or kisses me.

And that's the only excuse I have for things moving so fast between us . . . it always feels like he could be yanked away at any moment.

"Do you ever feel like this is too good to last?" I ask in a rushed breath.

Ethan looks around the dark room and laughs quietly. "Hopefully, your dad won't come in here right now."

I swallow hard and shake my head. "Not this exact moment . . . I mean us. This crazy thing between us." He's confused and I run a hand across his cheek. "I'm anxious when I'm not with you. I can't keep my hands off you when we're together. We haven't known each other for long, but no one has ever known me better. Everything that's been good in my life has disappeared and I'm terrified you're next."

My cheeks are red with embarrassment by the time I finish and I have to look away. But it's true. My naïveté that the world is a kind place and nothing bad will ever happen: gone. My confidence that my mom will always be there for me no matter what: gone. Even my home that should always be a safe haven: gone.

Ethan guides my head back until our noses almost touch. "I know what you mean. We didn't meet in the normal way. Hell, nothing we've done has been normal. But I'm not going to disappear."

And if I have anything to do about it—I won't disappear either.

Ethan wakes me up as the early morning rays start poking their way through my window. The last thing I want to do is leave him or the warmth of this bed, but the whispered reminder that Dad will be up any minute is all I need to get moving.

I tiptoe out of my room just as Agent Parker appears at the end of the hall. With an arched eyebrow, she shakes her head, then mutters, "I didn't see anything," before she moves out of view.

I race across the hall to the bathroom and start the water for a shower.

I'm making coffee when Dad and Ethan finally enter the kitchen. Dad looks like hell and probably didn't sleep at all. Teeny drags in a few minutes later.

Agent Parker sits down at the table next to Teeny.

Teeny stares at her for a minute or two. "So you were brought in before we moved to Natchitoches because Agent Williams thought someone on the inside was leaking information?"

Agent Parker nods, looking a little confused as to where this is going.

"If an agent was the bad guy, why did you make us cut and dye our hair? Wouldn't they know we changed our looks? We looked horrible like that, you know."

An awkward smile breaks out on her face. "I know. And yes, they would know that. But since you were being relocated at an alarming rate, much more than any of our other families, we were trying to rule out that you were being recognized."

Teeny seems to digest that then adds, "I don't think it was Agent Mullins. He was really nice to me."

Agent Parker sits down at the table across from Teeny and says, "I hope you're right. I think Agent Mullins is a very good agent, too."

An uncomfortable silence takes over the room. I think about how different things would have been if Mom could have held it together. She'd have thrown open the blue checkered curtains to let the light chase away the dark mood and made a strong pot of coffee to go with her legendary blueberry pancakes. Instead, we're passing around a half-empty box of Cheerios and rationing off what little bit of milk is left in the carton. After a depressing breakfast, there's not much to do except wait for Agent Williams.

The five of us settle in, occupying various spots in the family room. But the room feels empty—we've all checked out.

Teeny tugs on my sleeve. "Do you think we're moving?" her voice catches as she asks.

"Not sure," I answer.

"It's gonna be fine." Ethan keeps saying this over and over. Maybe at some point I will believe him.

She bats a few stray tears away and crumples against his side. "If we leave, we'll never see you again," she says to Ethan.

There it is—my worst fear spoken out loud. Even though I knew that was a real possibility, I didn't realize it would physically hurt to hear Teeny speak the words.

Ethan strokes her head and watches me. I press my lips together so hard they hurt—no telling what will pop out if I actually try to speak right now.

Overhearing our conversation, Agent Parker says, "Relocation is not the automatic answer here. Agent Williams very much wants you to have a normal life, and he knows how hard the program was for you last time. Plus, there's the situation with your mom. We would have to move her as well and that's not so easily done."

I take some comfort in her words but it's hard not to assume the worst is going to happen.

We see Sheriff Pippin's cruiser pull in the driveway and I brace myself for what's next.

Agent Williams barely gets in the room and I can tell he is really pleased with himself.

"We found a print! It matched a name in the system and I'm waiting for the file to be sent over."

I hadn't realized I was holding my breath until it comes out heavy.

"What is the name?" Agent Parker asks.

"Daniel Sanders." He looks at each of us. "Do you know anyone by that name?'

No one answers.

"Is that Thomas's real name?" I ask. It sounds so . . . ordinary.

"No. The age isn't right, but I believe this person can lead us to Thomas. This is the best break we've gotten. They didn't have his picture uploaded in the system so we're waiting for a copy to be sent over."

"What is the plan?" Agent Parker asks.

Agent Williams drops down in the same chair he occupied last night. He looks exhausted.

"We're going after Daniel Sanders and will hopefully have him in custody within the next forty-eight hours."

Dad doesn't look as confident. "How can I trust any plan that involves your agency? You think there's a mole in your program, Thomas came in and out of here without anyone seeing him. . . ."

"Valid points, Richard. I'm not going through my agency on this. I can't say any more than that but I have full faith in the people I've entrusted with this information. I'm trying to figure out what to do with all of you, though. I want you tucked away somewhere safe while this goes down, but I don't want to use any of our safe houses since, like you say, we still have not identified Agent X."

I don't want to leave, even if it is "just for a little while." That's what they told me when we left Scottsdale. The suits are known for telling you what you want to hear to get you to do what they want. "Agent Parker, what do you think about this?" I ask. She's been quiet and her expression is not overly confident.

She takes a minute, as if she's really thinking about how to answer me the right way in front of her boss. "Finding a print is wonderful news. I agree with Agent Williams that there is an agent passing sensitive information to Thomas and I think it is a good idea that you are out of the line of fire." She takes a deep breath and glances at Agent Williams before adding, "But I worry about doing any operation without the full support of the agency."

Dad surprises me when he asks, "Where do *you* think we should go?"

"I've been thinking about that. We need to be somewhere fairly close so we can get you there quickly but somewhere tucked out of sight. If Daniel Sanders is connected to Thomas in any way, he will go to great lengths to stop us from getting to him. Thomas went through this house so I don't feel comfortable leaving you here for now. I can't figure out what he wants. I don't think it's the journal, or he would have never given it back to Anna to begin with. For whatever reason, Anna is back on his radar and I just don't want to take any chances."

"We've got a place you could use," Ethan says.

He's been quiet up until now and I can't help wondering what he's thinking.

The new wrinkles on Agent Williams's forehead deepen when he asks, "That place near the Gulf where you sent your friend? Everyone in the department knows where that is and will probably be the first place they think of."

"No, it's in Arkansas. Dad just bought into this hunting club. I went up there with him to check it out. It feels like it's at the end of the world. It's on an island in the Mississippi River. It's very remote—the only way to get on the island is by barge."

"What does that mean—by barge?" I ask.

"A barge," Agent Williams says and looks at me like I'm crazy. He's got his hands out in front of him, twisting around, like if he can show the shape of it I'll get it. "You know, a boat that you drive cars on."

Ethan chuckles. "It will take us from the mainland to the island.

No one else will be able to get a vehicle on the island. And even if someone has a boat, the camp is miles from the bank. And that's only if they know where to find the island, which very few people do. And it's the off-season—should be deserted right now. It's just a couple of hours from here."

"When did you go there?" I ask.

Ethan squeezes my hand. "When you and Catherine went shopping in Shreveport."

The Dress. The one I dreamed about buying and dreamed about wearing to the Mardi Gras Ball with Ethan as a normal girl. But that's not why I got the hand squeeze. Catherine took me that day because I was so upset and she was trying to cheer me up with shopping. Dad was driving down to Baton Rouge to see Mom in rehab and I couldn't force myself to go with him. He even offered to take me to New Orleans as an incentive, since it's so close to where Mom is. I didn't want to see her because I was still so mad at her for falling apart when we needed her the most.

"Ethan," Agent Williams asks, "I really hate anyone else knowing where they'll be. Are you certain no one knows you have this place? And would your father be okay with this?"

"He hasn't told anyone about it because he knows everyone will be asking him to take them hunting when deer season rolls around. This place is just for us."

"What about Ethan?" I ask. "Shouldn't he go with us?" I hate to drag him away from here, but I don't want to be "tucked away" somewhere without him.

"That's probably not a bad idea. I'll have to discuss this with Ethan's parents." Agent Williams turns to Agent Parker and says,

"Let's try to kill two birds with one stone. I want to catch Agent X if we can. We'll say we've got an informant who knows Thomas and is willing to turn against him. Let's see if any of them take the bait."

"How will you know which one it is, sir?" Agent Parker asks.

"I'll run the order for three safe house locations through the normal channels, but make sure each agent in question is told a specific yet different location of where our informant is being kept. If they check, they'll see my name on the order. I've got some off-the-books guys who can watch these spots and they can let me know the minute someone shows up."

She nods. "Yes, sir."

This is moving so fast.

"What about Mom? Is she okay where she is?" I ask. A wave of longing washes through me, taking me by surprise. How can I still be so mad at her and want to throw my arms around her at the same time?

Dad's face drops and Teeny bites her bottom lip.

"Richard," Agent Williams says to Dad, "this is your call. I don't have any reason to believe she's in danger, but if you want to move her, I can see about moving her."

"I want her kept safe, but she *needs* to stay where she is. Moving her will ruin all the progress she's made. When this is over, my wife will be coming home. Healthy." We're all shocked by the passion in Dad's voice. "Surely, you've got some extra 'off-the-books' guys to watch her. Keep her safe but don't tell her what's going on. This would destroy her."

Agent Williams nods and says, "I'll notify the hospital and have one of my guys inside at all times."

Teeny breaks for a second then pulls herself together. She's struggling to be strong. "Can I talk to Mom before we leave?" she asks.

Dad nods. "I think that's a good idea. We'll *all* check on her."

All means me. I haven't spoken to Mom since she entered rehab, but I think I would never forgive myself if I didn't speak to her now.

For privacy, we go to Dad's room to make the call. It's hard for me to be in his room because it is so clearly his and not theirs. The bedding doesn't match the drapes and there are no pictures on the wall or dresser. Even at the beginning of our time in protection, Mom always took special care with her room. It's so obvious Mom has never set foot in this house or slept in that bed. We moved here after she went to rehab and there's not a trace of her anywhere. That makes her absence that much stronger.

It takes a few minutes to get her on the phone.

"Hi, honey! How are you?" Dad's voice sounds too animated and if she is truly getting better, she will pick up on that in a second.

"I know, we just wanted to talk to you. How are you?"

He's silent for a few moments and I get nervous about my turn.

When Dad tells her bye, he holds the phone out to Teeny and she jumps at the chance to talk to her.

"Hey, Mama!"

Teeny rattles on, talking about school and her friends and every little detail of her life before the disastrous turn a few days ago. And she makes it sound so easy.

I stare at the receiver when Teeny holds it in front of me. It takes a second or two before I reach for it.

Bringing it to my ear, I don't say anything at first, just listen to the hum of the distance between us.

"Anna, are you there?" She sounds anxious.

"Yes, Mom. I'm here."

"Oh, sweetie! It's so good to hear your voice! I've missed you so much! How are you? Please, tell me everything that's been going on."

Her voice is so clear and she sounds so happy to be talking to me. I don't realize tears are streaming down my face until they start dripping off my chin. Dad ushers Teeny out of the room and shuts the door. I curl up on Dad's bed, the phone cradled against my ear.

"I'm good. I've made some really nice friends and I'm doing well in school. Ethan and I are still together."

She sniffles and I know she's crying, too. "Oh, sweetheart. I'm so sorry about everything. I'm sorry that I was drunk all the time. I'm sorry you were the one who had to make sure we had food. I'm so sorry you had to see me like you did. No child should ever have to do what you did for me."

Mom sobs softly in the phone.

"Mom." God, what do I say to this? My eyes fill with tears.

Before I can think of something to say, she continues, "But mostly, I'm so proud of you and the young woman you've turned into. And I'm so honored to be your mother and I can't wait to throw my arms around you. I promise I'll make things up to you."

I'm bawling now, not even trying to hide it.

"I love you, Mom. And I'm so happy you're doing better. I can't wait for you to come home." And I mean it. Really mean it.

"I know; me, too. And it won't be long. I'm learning some really good skills here about how to handle things when I feel over-whelmed. I'm getting strong, just like you."

This crushes me because I don't feel strong at all. Ethan tells me I'm strong, too, but it's not true. I feel helpless and out of control and scared about everything.

"I love you, Mom."

"I love you, too. Now tell me about Ethan."

A smile spreads across my face. "He's so nice, Mom. And cute. And fun. And he really likes me and I really like him. Like more than I've ever liked anyone and I haven't known him that long. Don't you think that's weird?"

She laughs and the sound is music to my ears. She sounds nor-mal. Better than normal.

"No, that's not weird. Dad told me what happened in Arizona. You and Ethan have been through a lot together and I think it's very normal to have intensified feelings after something like that."

It's so good to talk to her about this, especially when Dad thinks we should spend less time together.

"Are you being careful?"

Oh my God. Is she asking me about sex?

"Ummm . . . Mom, I . . ."

"You don't have to tell me. I'm not in the position to demand anything from you."

And this makes me suddenly so sad.

"Well, I can't wait to see you and Teeny and Dad," she says in a happier tone. "And go with your heart, Anna. Your instincts are good. And sometimes you just know when you've found the right boy for you. That's how I felt about your dad. Couldn't keep my hands off of him!"

"Mom!"

She laughs again. "And I still feel that way about him today. He's a good man and he wants nothing more than to protect his family. We're all so lucky to have him."

"I love you, Mom. So much."

"I love you, too. Kiss Teeny for me and I'll see you soon."

I end the call and head back to the family room, drying my face on my shirt as I walk down the hall.

Dad winks and smiles when I enter the room and I smile back. Talking to Mom was just what I needed.

Agent Williams and Agent Parker leave with Ethan so they can speak with his family while we pack up some belongings to last us while we're gone. Dad calls work to tell them we're off to Scottsdale to tie up a few loose ends.

I call Catherine with the same story. She knows I'm full of crap but goes along anyway.

It shouldn't be this easy to leave everything behind.

Chapter 7

NEW RULE BY ANNA BOYD:

Okay, maybe that's not such a bad rule after all . . . even if the bitchy cheerleader isn't that bitchy anymore—that doesn't mean you *want* to be best friends.

AGENT Williams is finding that it's a little harder to get things done when he can't (or won't) use the resources normally available to him.

Because we're off the books on this, there is some debate on how to get us to Arkansas. Agent Williams is dying to go after this Daniel Sanders guy but doesn't trust us to leave town by ourselves.

We wait for Ethan at the farm. The Landry's farm is outside of town in a remote area. The land around here is flat, nothing but crop fields, with very few trees. If someone was following us, it would be very hard for them to remain unseen.

Ethan, Emma, and their parents pull up next to us.

What in the hell? I thought it would just be Ethan going with us to Arkansas.

The men shake hands while Ethan heads to where Teeny and I are sitting in Agent Williams's Suburban. Emma and her mom haven't gotten out of the vehicle.

I open the door and I know I look confused.

"The whole family is coming with us." Ethan rolls his eyes and says, "Dad said he's been meaning to work on our camp and this is a perfect time to do that and wouldn't it be nice to hang out there as a family."

Right.

"I really think the fact that Thomas was in your driveway, going through your truck, freaked your mom and dad out and he wants to get y'all out of town, too."

Emma and I have been getting along lately, but I don't know if we can survive being holed up together in some remote backwoods hunting camp.

Agent Williams finally decides that he and Agent Parker will follow us to the state line, make sure no one's tailing us, then let us continue on our way alone.

As we load our bags into the back cargo area of Ethan's dad's SUV, it's kind of embarrassing how much space I'm taking up with my bag. I refused to leave all my stuff behind, so instead of packing a lot of clothes, I grabbed every memento I've saved over the past couple of months in Natchitoches. No matter how many times Agent Williams says we'll be back, I have a hard time believing him.

Mr. Landry and Ethan throw several guns and plenty of ammo in the back of their SUV, including the small one I fired, and just like that we're off.

We're crammed in this SUV like sardines. Dad and Mr. Landry are up front, dissecting the last few days. Emma and her mom have the two captain seats in the middle and Ethan, Teeny, and I are squished into the back row.

"At least we're not in that stupid van this time," Teeny says. "I felt like we were convicts or something riding around in that thing."

"Ben was supposed to pick me up after lunch to go to a movie," Emma says to no one in general.

Mrs. Landry pats her arm. "That's why you sent him that text, sweetie."

"He'll never believe I'm going to the camp willingly."

She mumbles to herself and digs through her bag. Her mom gives her a wide berth.

Teeny curls up on my other side to read and Ethan seems lost in thought as he stares out of the window.

Agent Williams left us about an hour back and, admittedly, I've been scanning the road behind us ever since.

Everything that has happened over the past week or so has stumped me. I can't figure out why Thomas would give me my journal back then break into our house. Is there something else we're missing? Did he only want me to have it back if I didn't tell anyone about it?

The hardest part of trying to figure Thomas out is trying to reconcile the difference in how he was when I thought he was an agent and what I learned about him in Arizona. How did I completely fall for the "nice agent routine" when in real life he is a cold-blooded killer?

We've driven for four hours and Emma has bitched the entire time. We've heard about every event in the next week she was scheduled to attend (five to be exact), every TV show she'll miss (she almost flung herself from the SUV when she found out we wouldn't have cable), every person who will tear through Natchitoches looking for her (around twenty, but she says that's a conservative estimate), and how many items she forgot to pack since Ethan rushed her (current count is seventeen but it's expected to rise).

Teeny and I passed notes most of the trip on what would be the best way to evict her from the car. Teeny won hands down with the idea of Emma turning into vaporized mist then being sucked out of the sunroof.

"Pleeeeeease tell me we'll be there soon. I'm dying to get out of this car."

She's asked this about twenty times. Mr. Landry doesn't bother to answer her anymore. And this is what I was worried about—I can handle Emma in small doses, but I'm not sure I can stand being around her for several days.

We turn off an old highway and hit a gravel road. There is nothing around us: no houses, no farms, no gas stations. At every turn, Mr. Landry glances in the rearview mirror. There is no one within sight. We drive on this bumpy road in the middle of nowhere for miles until it dead-ends into the bottom end of a tall levee. Mr. Landry pauses a moment but then throws the Suburban in four-wheel drive and keeps on going. We're nearly vertical for a few tense seconds until the SUV plops on top of the levee, then we're driving faster than what feels safe.

The levee is significantly higher than the gravel road we just left. It's bare dirt on top, barely wide enough for our vehicle, then it slopes down dramatically on either side, which makes it feel like we're flying. Even with the aerial view, I can't see any other signs of life for miles.

Well, human life, that is. Ethan pokes Teeny and me to show us a mama deer and a baby deer just inside the woods at the bottom of the hill. Teeny scrambles across me to get to the window for a better view.

The levee makes a sharp turn and we're barreling through a tunnel of trees. Even in February, the trees are thick with leaves and it's instantly dark outside. As soon as we're back in full sunlight, we stop in front of a huge body of water.

Mr. Landry throws the truck in park. "We're here."

Here. I look around.

Nothing.

"Surely there will be a structure of some sort we'll be sleeping in." Emma sounds a bit panicked, but I get why she's asking. There is nothing but a tunnel of trees behind us and a body of water ahead of us. And it's close to dark.

Ethan can't help but laugh. "Of course. We just have to barge across."

And then I spot the barge partly concealed by a bank of trees. What in the world? He said something about a barge, but surely he didn't mean that.

The whole barge/SUV thing concerns me. The barge looks a hundred years old, and there's a little tugboat attached to it that isn't any bigger than a Volkswagen bug. The river is wide and the current looks pretty strong. And if this is the only way to get over to that little island right there, I guess Ethan wasn't kidding when he said this would be a hard spot to find.

It doesn't take long before we're all piling out of the SUV, hoping to get a better look at it.

Mr. Landry jumps in the little tugboat that's attached to the side of the barge and a loud boom fills the air when he cranks it up.

Ethan comes up behind me, wrapping his arms around my waist.

"How does this work, exactly?" I ask.

Ethan leans his chin on my shoulder. "Well, he'll push that barge around with the tugboat and line it up in front of the car. We'll drive on it and ride it across to the other side . . . why are you shaking your head?"

"There's no way I'm getting on that thing. What if it flips over? And then we're trapped in the car and sink to the bottom of the river."

Ethan chuckles in my ear and says, "We can ride on the barge, next to the car. We don't have to be in it." He squeezes me and whispers, "Anna, stop worrying about everything. We'll hang out here for a few days, then head back home after Thomas is caught."

I don't say anything—just wish I could feel as confident about this plan as he does.

Chapter 8

NEW RULE BY ANNA BOYD:
Disappearing isn't all it's cracked up to be.

THIS place is beautiful. The barge ride scared me, but it was worth it to get to the other side. We're on a meandering dirt road that weaves through a thick forest of trees where a thousand shades of green are on display. And there's a ton of wildlife. Deer, squirrels, and rabbits stop eating and stare at the car as we drive by. There's even a particularly nasty-looking snake stretched out across the road, I guess taking a nap or something, and it seems in no big hurry to slither out of our way.

As we drive, little pockets open up in the woods where a field or small pond hides.

Ethan and his dad are in heaven, based on the expressions on their faces. They're looking at the deer with a different kind of appreciation than mine, which concerns me a bit. Maybe there's a hog problem here to keep them busy and the sweet little deer alive.

"Won't be long now." Ethan's grin is a mile wide.

Dad visibly relaxed once we disembarked from the barge. The forest thins out and some cabins come into sight up ahead.

"How many people own a piece of this camp?" Dad asks.

Mr. Landry had explained most of it when we first got in the car. He said this was a private hunting camp and the island was owned by the members.

"Twenty-two including us."

Mr. Landry called the caretaker who looks after the place and arranged for him to deliver some food. He lives in the town we passed about thirty minutes ago. He also verified we'd be the only ones here since hunting season ended a few weeks back.

We pull into a campground area and there are about fifteen cabins all clustered together. A few are bigger and nicer than our house back in Natchitoches while others are nothing more than a house trailer with an attached porch.

Ethan points to a modest-looking camp, not big, but cute. The exterior walls are covered in old-looking bluish gray boards that are varied in width, making an unorganized but nice pattern. A porch stretches across the front, and black shutters frame the windows. Matching rockers stand guard by the door. "It's that one."

We can't get out of the car fast enough. Ethan starts unloading bags and only struggles physically with mine.

"Why is your duffel so big?" Emma squeals. "He told me a small bag for a few days. Mom!"

I grab my bag and haul it inside before she can say anything else. The inside is what I think a camp would look like: an old black stove thing with a chimney and mismatched furniture that looks really worn in and cozy. A small staircase anchored against the back wall.

Teeny runs upstairs and back down again before I can figure out where to set my bag.

"There are bunk beds upstairs! I call top bunk!"

Mrs. Landry walks through the place then assigns rooms. "Anna, Elena, and Emma can have the room with bunk beds at the top of the stairs to the left. Richard, you can take the one on the right. We'll stay in the room down here. Ethan you get the couch."

Emma is not happy when she discovers there is no cell phone reception on this island. Mr. Landry must have known and mentioned this to Agent Williams before we left, since he was given a satellite phone to be used for an emergency. Other than that we are cut off.

It's going to be a long couple of days.

Teeny must be thinking the same thing when she asks, "How long do you think we're going to be here?"

I watch her for signs of that sad little girl that defined her for the better part of the year. She seems to be handling this fairly well, so I don't lie.

"I don't know. Agent Williams seems to think this will all be wrapped up in a few days. We could survive a month if we had to with the stash of groceries down there, though."

Teeny climbs up to the top bunk. "I don't want to be around when Emma figures that out."

It's midmorning by the time I make it downstairs. Teeny puts on a strong front while she's awake but she woke up screaming last night. It took a while to get her back to sleep and then I was wired.

Emma evicted Ethan from the couch and he ended up on the floor in a sleeping bag.

"Did you catch up on some sleep?" Ethan asks me.

We're in the main living area where Ethan and his dad are checking to make sure the guns they brought are loaded before putting them into a cabinet. Emma picks up a rifle and starts opening and closing parts and lots of other things I don't understand. I've heard she's as good of a shot as Ethan.

I nod and rub my eyes. Teeny's in the kitchen eating a bowl of cereal, looking fresh and alert and completely normal, like last night didn't happen.

While the guys go outside to chop some firewood, Mrs. Landry decides to teach Teeny and me how to bake, since there isn't much else to do.

I should be peeved over the obvious gender stereotypes in play here, but chopping wood looks hard so I'm going to leave them to it.

It was actually fun at first. Mrs. Landry is like my old kindergarten teacher, Mrs. Wilcox—she has the same sugary sweet voice and explains everything like we're five years old—so it's not surprising when she starts in with the corny cupcake jokes.

"Why did the cupcake crash his car?" she asks.

I glance at Emma who rolls her eyes, but not in her normal bitchy way. She's giggly and answers her mother with an exaggerated *"Why?"*

Mrs. Landry waits a moment for dramatic effect and answers, "Because he was baked."

Emma, Teeny, and I laugh, and that is the only push Mrs. Landry needs to keep the jokes rolling.

"Why did the cupcake major in restaurant management?"

We all groan in anticipation of the answer.

"Why?" Teeny asks.

"It wanted to be a Hostess."

And they only get cornier.

Emma moves closer to me and whispers, "Dad got her this culinary joke-a-day calendar and we've been subjected to cooking humor ever since. Who knew there were so many jokes about a cupcake?"

We have a really nice afternoon and I'm glad to see Emma loosen up.

But watching Mrs. Landry and Emma makes me think about Mom and how this could have easily been a scene from our kitchen back in Scottsdale. Or maybe it's the hope of a scene we may have in the future in Natchitoches. Teeny must have been thinking the same thing, because she got quiet and wasn't interested in learning how to make roses out of icing.

By early afternoon, we'd made two cakes, twenty-four cupcakes, and three pies.

I'm cleaning up after our baking extravaganza when I feel a tug on the back on my shirt.

"Want to sneak out of here for a little while?"

It's Ethan, wearing a devilish smile, and one I won't even try to resist. Glancing around the kitchen, I know I should stay and finish the dishes, but I'm not losing this opportunity to be alone with him.

"Lead the way."

With my hand in his, we bolt from the camp and dash down the gravel road. Winding around a few of the other camps, we stop in front of a rather large one.

"Where are we going?" I ask.

"It's a surprise."

Not letting go of my hand, we make our way to the back of the house and up a set of stairs that leads to a balcony. I'm shocked when I make it to the top.

There's an old-timey black potbelly stove with a roaring fire inside next to a hammock loaded with pillows and blankets. It's colder here than I thought it would be, so the fire is a nice surprise.

I dive into the hammock without thinking twice and Ethan, after putting his jacket on the floor, isn't far behind me. It takes some moving around and a little readjusting before we're all cuddled up just right.

"How did you know this is exactly what I needed?" I say.

"Because this is what I needed, too."

And then he kisses me. We're close, very close, since our bodies have settled into the center. The blankets and fire have made it warm and toasty and the slight sway of the hammock mimics the rhythm of our bodies moving against each other.

His hands slip under the edge of my T-shirt and his calloused fingertips burn a trail up my back.

Ethan buries his head in the crook of my neck and mumbles something I can't understand, then he's back to kissing me in my favorite spot just behind my ear.

He moves over me until I'm pinned beneath him, his forearms framing my face and bracing his weight. The hammock closes in around us and it's like we're in our own safe little cocoon.

"I would give anything to stay just like this for the foreseeable future," he says with that dimpled grin.

"Me, too." I feel desperate. And anxious. But hopeful. And that is a new and wonderful feeling. "I think that's the best idea I've heard in a really long time."

We stay in the hammock for longer than we probably should and only move to get out when Ethan mentions he doesn't want our dads, armed with shotguns, to find us here like this.

We hold hands walking back to the cabin and I hate to think how miserable it would have been to leave Natchitoches without him.

"Well, there you are. I was about to send out a search party." Mrs. Landry gives Ethan an arched eyebrow and a look that means they will be discussing this later. "Don't forget why we're here."

I can feel the blush that races across my cheeks.

"We didn't leave the campground," Ethan answers back, his tone a little stronger than I've ever heard him use to his mother.

"Just the same. Don't leave without telling someone where you are going and taking some protection with you."

Oh God! My face is on fire.

Ethan pulls a handgun out of his coat pocket and drops it on the table. "I know better than to walk around without a gun."

Guns. She was talking about a gun . . . not the *other* kind of protection. I hope it isn't obvious my mind went straight to the gutter. It didn't occur to me to take a gun. Ethan is definitely more prepared for this than I am. And now that I think about it, even when the men chop wood, they're armed. And I've noticed that Dad and Mr. Landry took turns staying up last night. When Teeny started screaming in her sleep, Dad was in our room, armed and dressed, before I was fully awake. It's so quiet here, it's hard to remember that we may be in danger.

Mrs. Landry gives Ethan some chores and scoots him out of the kitchen. I turn to the sink and realize all the dishes are clean and drying on the rack. Guilt swallows me up instantly.

"It's okay. I knocked them out."

"I'm sorry, Mrs. Landry. We didn't want anyone to worry."

She puts an arm around me and pulls me in close. "I'd be worried about you even if you were sitting right in front of me and I had a shotgun pointed at the door. I just hate that this is happening to you. And Ethan." She moves a stray piece of hair out of my face. "I understand the need to spend some time alone. Just be smart about it, okay?"

I duck my head so she won't see the tears forming in my eyes. It's been so long since a mother figure has worried about me. Or hugged me so tight. Pearl's done a good job filling in the holes, but she likes to come off gruff. I miss my mother.

By morning of day three, Agent Williams calls the satellite phone with some great news. They've found Daniel Sanders and he's in custody. He warns us that we'll be here a little longer since they are hoping to catch Thomas before we come home.

We're so relieved by this news that another few days seems like no big deal.

Well, to everyone except Emma.

Mr. Landry and Dad both use the phone to check in back home. Dad asks for a little more time off of work and Mr. Landry talks to Will's dad, who is his partner in the farm. Luckily for him, this is the slow time of year; crops won't be planted for a few weeks so it's not a bad time for him to be gone. Ethan, Emma, Teeny, and I will have a ridiculous amount of schoolwork to make up, but if it means we get to stay in Natchitoches, it will be worth it.

Ethan is wrestling with the clothes in the laundry room when I poke my head back in.

"What are you doing?" I ask.

"Mom assigned me dirty clothes duty today." He holds up one of Emma's bras. "Sister or not, this is uncomfortable."

I can't help but laugh. "You want to do laundry or hang out with me?"

"Hmm . . . let me think. . . ." He's pulling me out of the laundry room before he even finishes. "You. Definitely want to be with you." He leans in close and whispers, "I've got an idea that can get us out of our chores."

We pass Mrs. Landry in the kitchen. Ethan says, "We're going for a walk. I've got a gun and we won't be long. I'm giving Anna another shooting lesson. Warn Dad and Mr. Boyd in case they hear us."

She nods, and replies, "Don't be too long. It'll be dark soon."

It's close to dusk when we plunge through the thick brush into the woods. It's hard to navigate with all the down trees and stumps, but each step we take away from the camp, the better I feel.

We get far enough from the camp to feel alone but not so far that I can't find my way back. It's quiet except for the few birds we spook as we crunch along the ground. Ethan finally stops, so I find a tree stump and sit down, pulling my knees up.

When Ethan drops down in front of me, he's holding the same small gun I fired at the farm in one hand and several bullets in the other.

"Do you remember how to load this?"

I'm nervous and excited looking down at it. A group of birds takes off from the ground a few feet behind me, startling me, and I almost fall off the stump.

"Maybe you're not ready for this again. I should have asked you first. We can go back to the camp."

He gets up and I pull him back down. "Wait. I want to try it again. Just give me a minute."

Ethan places the gun in my outstretched hand. I feel sweaty even though it's cold outside. The gun is heavy and all I can think about is how loud and scary it is when fired.

We sit in silence for a few minutes. All of those awful images of Brandon and his dad threaten to return, but I control my breathing and force them away.

"Just sit there a minute. I'm going to find a stick or something we can use as a target." He stands, and searches the ground.

I flex my fingers over the gun, trying to get used to the feel of it.

"This'll work," he says and lifts a small piece of wood in the air. He takes a step toward me then grabs his left shoulder with his right hand. He stands there a moment, a dazed look on his face, before he crumples to the ground, hitting it with a thud.

I race to where he is. "Ethan! Ethan!"

Shaking him does nothing. He's out. Completely unconscious.

Oh my God!

Did he hit his head? I feel around but nothing, no blood, no bumps. I gauge the distance back to the camp and decide to run for help. It's close to dark and if I wait much longer, it will be too hard to find him here on the ground.

I jump up and slam into something hard but warm. Hands form steel bands around my upper arms and the face I hoped and prayed never to see again comes into focus in front of my eyes.

Thomas.

Chapter 9

NEW RULE BY ANNA BOYD:
Paranoia isn't enough.

I throw up on his shoes. Not a lot but enough that he pushes me down to the ground and shakes the chunks off into the dead leaves.

"If you scream, I'll kill him," Thomas says in a controlled voice.

Ethan is still knocked out a few feet away. "What did you do to him?" I ask.

The gun in my hand is useless without the bullets. I search the ground to see if I can find where they fell out of his hand.

Thomas uses a stick to scrap off the last bit of puke from his running shoes. "Tranquilizer dart. He'll be unconscious for a few hours."

He uses a hard, clipped tone that's different from the one that reeled me in when I thought he was a federal agent. And his movements are different. Everything about him is.

"Why are you here?"

He snatches Ethan's gun out of my hand and puts it in his pocket. "You involved the U.S. Marshals Service when you shouldn't have."

"Me! You sent the flowers. And brought the journal back. It's your fault they're involved, not mine."

He crouches down in front of me, his face just inches from mine. "Keep your voice down."

My mouth snaps closed. Despite the heavy coat, a chill races through my body. I look at Ethan and watch the slow rise and fall of his chest. Thank God he's breathing.

"Are you . . . you going to . . . to . . . to kill me?" I stutter out.

"Not if you do exactly as I say." Thomas stalks toward Ethan and kneels beside him, while I scramble to throw myself across his body.

"Don't hurt him!" I scream.

Thomas grabs my face, squeezing my cheeks until tears form in my eyes. He pushes me off Ethan and I fall back on the ground.

Flipping Ethan over, he pulls a zip tie from his coat pocket and binds Ethan's wrists. Tears stream down my face. My heart races and I feel clammy. My mind is churning—*what do I do . . . what do I do. . . .* I've never been so scared in all my life.

Thomas finishes with Ethan and turns back to me. "Stand up."

"Not until you tell me what you're planning to do."

Thomas crouches down and leans in closer until our noses are inches apart. I'm instantly more uncomfortable than I ever thought possible. The differences in him are alarming. His eyes are ice cold, and every move he makes is calculated. His gaze stays on me like he's absorbing everything I'm thinking. It's hard to believe he's the same person who tried to befriend me just a few short weeks ago. I realize now just how naive I've been. No matter how many times I tried to convince myself that I'd rather face Thomas than run—that was a lie. This is so much worse than I ever thought it would be.

"The very nasty people who pay me to do very nasty things were not pleased when I allowed you to live. It was the first time I did not fulfill a contract. I assured them you would not cause a problem, but you have proven me wrong." He runs a finger down the side of my face. I try to back away from him but he grabs the front of my shirt and hauls me back in.

I slap my hand over my mouth, praying I won't throw up again. He doesn't blink. Or move. His eyes bore into me and I know I'm looking at a monster. He flings me back and I land hard on the ground for a second time.

Thomas stands quickly and whistles. Within seconds another person emerges from the woods. The light is fading and I can't tell until he gets closer that he's wearing a black ski mask. I can barely make out his eyes from the tiny openings. He's wearing all black clothes and black combat boots. I can't quit staring at him. Is he one of the suits who Agent Williams thinks is the mole—Agent X?

He looks nervous, eyes darting back and forth between me and Thomas.

"Pick him up," Thomas says to the masked man.

"No." I stumble forward, trying to get to Ethan before the other man does. I can't even think about what Thomas has planned for him. My fingers dig into the rough ground as I claw my way back to him. Ethan's warm breath hits the cool night air and I take comfort in the fact he is still breathing. I cover Ethan's body with mine, offering him any protection I can. I'm praying one of the dads will appear, shotgun in hand, but so far it's just us out here. Even if our families hear something, they probably won't come looking since they think Ethan is teaching me how to shoot a gun.

The masked man stands over us but doesn't move toward Ethan. He looks back at Thomas as if asking how he's supposed to pick Ethan up since I'm draped over his chest.

Thomas pulls me off of Ethan, restraining my arms. As much as I struggle, I can't move an inch. "If you continue to fight me, your boyfriend will pay the consequence," he growls.

I stop moving instantly.

The masked man struggles lifting Ethan until he finally gets him over his shoulder.

"You don't need him! Take me! Leave him here!" I shout.

Thomas squeezes my arms so tight behind me I think they're going to pop out of the sockets.

"Be quiet. This isn't just about you anymore," he whispers in my ear.

Thomas pushes me in the back and we follow Ethan and the masked man into the darkening forest.

"Where are you taking us?"

"Those nasty bosses of mine . . . they've hired my replacement to finish the job," Thomas sneers.

I suck in a deep breath and stumble over a small log.

He steadies me before pushing me again to keep me moving.

"What does that mean?" As afraid as I am for him to answer this question, I have to know what we're up against.

"That means," he grits out in a harsh tone, "not only are there contracts out for you and your boyfriend, but for my friend and me as well. My boss decided the best way to clean up this entire mess is to get rid of all of us."

I crumple to the ground. Oh. My. God.

Thomas jerks me back up and pushes me forward.

"But I don't understand. Why are you here? Are you turning us over to them?" My mind is racing and I can't seem to get a grip on what's happening.

He ignores my questions completely.

It only takes a few more minutes until we reach an all-terrain vehicle similar to what Ethan uses on the farm.

"Where did you get that?"

"We borrowed it from one of the camps last night."

Last night? How did they get here? Or know we were here to begin with?

Masked man dumps Ethan in the cargo area, but Ethan doesn't even flinch. There's no telling how sore and banged up he's going to be when he finally comes around.

With gloved hands, Thomas grabs a small black object from the front seat of the vehicle.

It's a video camera.

"You will say exactly what I want you to say and nothing more. Do you understand?"

My body is shaking so hard, it's tough to nod.

"You will tell them I have taken you from this island. You will tell them they have my word I will not kill you unless my orders are disobeyed. Your father and the Landrys are not to leave the island.

They are not to contact anyone in any way. If they do not follow my orders, then I will break my word."

He presses a button and a little red light blinks on, then a bright light beams from the top of the camera, chasing away the impending darkness. I'm staring at the lens and everything he just told me to say jumbles in my brain.

"Umm . . . Thomas wants me to tell you he is taking us off the island." My voice sounds rough . . . unfamiliar and I have to brush away a stray tear that slips out of the corner of my eye. "He said . . ."

Oh God, I'm drawing a blank!

I look at Thomas and he is mouthing the words he wants me to say.

"Um . . . he said you have his word he won't . . . kill . . . us if you follow his rules."

I swallow the lump and try to remember exactly how he worded the next part.

Thomas moves the camera in closer and the bright light blinds me for a second. He's moving his finger in a circular motion, wanting me to get on with it.

"Rule number one: You are not allowed to leave the island. Rule number two: You are not allowed to contact anyone."

I take a deep breath before I finish the last part. "If you break his rules, he will break his word and kill us."

And then he ends the video, flips the screen, and reviews what he filmed. I can't see it, but I can hear my shaky voice and can only imagine how awful it will be when Dad and the Landrys watch this.

"Get her the paper and bring me the box," he says to the masked man, then turns to me. "Write: *Push play* on that paper."

I do as I'm told and he takes the paper and the camera and puts it in a large white box.

Handing it to the masked man, he says, "Leave this closer to the camp. Be fast, we need to get moving."

Masked man runs back the way we came, the box in his hands so white it's glowing in the darkness. There's no way our parents won't find it when they start looking for us.

I'm so mesmerized by the box, I don't realize Thomas has zip-tied my hands behind my back until it's too late.

The masked man returns and sits in the driver's seat, then Thomas throws me inside the vehicle—I'm sandwiched between him and the masked man on the small bench seat. Masked man's breathing is heavy, probably from carrying Ethan and running through the woods, and a scary image of Darth Vader pops in my head. Soon I can't think of anything else when I see him. There's no space separating any of us, and it makes my skin crawl. Vader cranks the vehicle but doesn't turn on the headlights.

"Sissy?"

I freeze. Spinning around, I see Teeny step out from behind a tree. Oh. My. God. She must have followed Vader back after he delivered the box.

"RUN, TEENY!" I scream.

Thomas mutters something under his breath then bolts out of the vehicle, pulling his gun out of his waistband.

Teeny panics. Doesn't move a muscle. Before I can make it off the bench seat, Vader throws an arm around my chest and pins me to his side.

"Da—" His other hand slaps over my mouth before I get the rest of the word *Dad* out.

Thomas raises his arm and fires. Teeny drops to the ground. I let out a muffled scream. Thomas walks back to the vehicle and aims the gun at me.

Everything goes dark.

Chapter 10

NEW RULE BY ANNA BOYD:
You can't always know what you're getting into, but you can sure as hell find
out as much as you can once you're there.

"ANNA."

I hear my name but I can't lift my head. There's no feeling in my
arms—the only thing I'm sure of is they're stuck behind my back.

The ground bounces. My face slams down hard and my cheek
explodes in agony.

"Anna, open your eyes," a voice whispers.

I can't. They're so heavy. My tongue sticks to the roof of my
mouth and it's hard to swallow.

"Anna."

My face hurts. I try to open my mouth and pain slices through
my cheek. Something taps my knee. It won't stop.

Tap. Tap. Tap.

I shake it off but it just comes right back.

Tap. Tap. Tap.

I peel one eye open. It's dark.

Slam. My head hits the ground again. I moan but I'm not sure
if the sound actually leaves my lips.

The tapping turns into a kick.

"Anna." The whispering gets louder. Ethan. A wave crashes over me—scenes of Ethan and Teeny dropping to the ground surge through my brain. Oh God. And Thomas.

He's back.

I try to roll over but my arms are dead behind me. Twitching my head, the damp hair covering my face falls to the side, and I try to focus on where I am. I'm inside the back of a truck or van. My clothes are wet and I'm cold. Really cold.

Slam. Again my head nails the floor. Tears burn my eyes and I'm afraid my cheekbone may be broken.

"Anna."

I tilt my head up and find Ethan's face a few feet from mine. He's stuck in the same position—he's on his stomach, hands bound behind his back.

"Are you okay?"

I pry my tongue loose and croak out, "No. I hurt."

I run through a mental inventory of my body. Not only is the pain in my cheek excruciating, but it surges through my shoulders, hip bones, and knees as well. Every time this truck hits a bump or hole in the road, my entire body slams down on the metal surface.

Teeny! Where is Teeny? I rotate my head around until I get a glimpse of the top of her head. She's on my other side, but I can't make out if she's tied up or not.

I swivel back around to Ethan.

"Where . . ." It hurts so bad to talk.

Ethan inches toward me; it takes forever, but finally he gets close enough that our foreheads barely touch. The contact with him overwhelms me and I start to cry.

"What happened? And Teeny . . . ?" he asks.

I swallow the dry lump in my throat. I mouth the word *Thomas*. This is bad. Oh. My. God. This is so friggin' bad.

"I figured." Ethan propels himself another few inches closer until his mouth is near my ear. "Do you know where we're going?"

I shake my head just enough to answer. Every movement sends waves of pain through my entire body.

"There's some other person back here," he whispers. "Besides the two people up front. I don't know who it is, but he's passed out in the front corner."

I lift my shoulders to see who it could be and wince from the pain. There're a hundred things I want to say to Ethan right now, but my body won't cooperate. My eyelids droop. They're too heavy to remain open for even a second longer.

Slam! My head smashes the floor again, and once again the blackness washes over me.

The fog clouding my brain seems a little thinner when I finally open my eyes again. It's still dark. I'm still tied up. And my entire body still hurts.

The hollow sound inside the moving vehicle roars through my ears. I lift my head, slowly, testing to make sure the entire van doesn't start spinning, and check on Teeny. She's still knocked out behind me.

And then I hear Ethan. He's whispering but it's loud enough that I recognize his voice. The lower half of his body is still close enough to me that I can feel him, but his head and torso are bent away.

He's talking to the other person who's in the back of the van with us.

I nudge Ethan's leg and he slowly twists around to me. "Anna, you're up. You'll never believe who's back here with us. . . . Agent Parker."

What? Agent Parker. What is happening?

"She's beat up pretty bad," he says.

"I want to talk to her." I start moving in her direction and it's tough. When I get close enough to see her, I'm shocked by her appearance. One eye is almost swollen shut and her lip is busted. Her clothes are torn and the closer I get, the more I can smell her, and it's really not good. Seeing her here like this devastates me.

"Agent Parker, what's happening?"

"Thomas," she says then stops to use her shoulder to wipe a trail of saliva that escaped along the corner of her mouth. "I was instructed to stay in Natchitoches while Agent Williams went after Daniel Sanders." It's hard for her to talk, her top lip is so swollen it barely moves. "Your father gave us permission to use your home as a base. One minute I'm going over your case file at your kitchen table and the next I'm in the back of this van."

She's whispering although the road noise makes it near impossible to hear her. "He made me give up your location." She breaks down and cries, "I'm so sorry, Anna."

"Where's Agent Williams?" I ask.

"I don't know." The van hits a bump and we're all bounced against the metal floor. Agent Parker lets out a moan while tears spring to my eyes. We all need this van to stop moving. "The last time I spoke to him was yesterday morning."

Ethan rolls around until he gets a little closer to Agent Parker and asks, "Who is the other guy? Is it the mole?"

She shrugs and I can tell even that small movement is excruciating. "He hasn't taken the mask off." Her eyes move to mine and she says, "I'm so sorry."

Another bump makes us shuffle around the space.

Neither of us asks her anything else, mainly because it looks so painful for Agent Parker to move her jaw when she talks.

The van slows and then swerves off the road before coming to a stop.

There are a few tense seconds before the back doors open, then I'm being dragged out. My arms burn as hands yank me out of the van by my underarms and the pain radiates all the way to my fingers.

"You're hurting her," Ethan yells.

The hands let go and I flop outside the van onto the hard concrete road. It's cold and my partially wet clothes are not helping.

And I've got to pee. Bad.

Ethan is pulled out after me, then dumped on the ground a few feet away from the van. His expression is hard to read as his eyes move between Thomas and Agent Parker, who is still inside the van. I can't see her but I hear her moaning. Teeny hasn't moved.

"Why isn't she awake yet?" My throat burns. Did they shoot her with the tranq gun, too, or a regular gun? What if they gave her too much?

Thomas pulls a knife from his back pocket, flipping it open in front of me. Before the fear in my brain can travel to the rest of my body, he tosses me over and cuts the zip ties loose.

Blood rushes through my limbs and I fall over from the burn of it, hitting the already abused side of my face. After a minute or so, the scorching in my arms lessens to pins and needles. I try to lift myself back up but my arms give way every time I put any pressure on them. Thomas grabs me, hoisting me to a standing position.

He hands me a bottle of water and I drink so fast water dribbles out of the side of my mouth. I drain half the bottle then limp to Ethan, holding it up for him to have the rest. Once the bottle is empty, Thomas pulls me away from him.

It looks like we've made a pit stop on some deserted section of road in the middle of nowhere.

"I assume you need to take care of some personal matters?"

I guess this is Thomas's way of asking me if I have to pee.

I nod and he drags me away from the van. My feet stumble around, trying to keep up. We get several yards away from the road until we're just inside the tree line. Ethan is still on the ground, watching us.

I need to get him talking. Find out whatever I can. "What's your real name? I know it's not Thomas."

"Thomas is the only name you need to know. You have three minutes. And this will be the one and only bathroom break."

"I don't understand any of this," I croak out. "Where are we going?"

"No more questions." He starts walking away.

"You won't get away with this," I say quietly. They have Daniel Sanders in custody and hopefully it won't be long before they identify who Thomas really is.

He stops and pivots around, his hands behind his back. He's taller than I remember and much more intimidating. His eyes and hair seem darker against his black clothing. He watches me a moment and it's hard to hold his gaze with that intense look in his eye.

"How long did you wonder why I let you live in Scottsdale?" He closes in and begins circling around me, whispering in my ear. His breath puffs out in small clouds and the dead leaves and brittle sticks break at every step. "How many nights did you lie in your bed and worry I was outside the window?" He moves around until we're face-to-face again. "How many times did your father or sister leave the house and you had a sinking feeling that they wouldn't return alive?"

I hug myself hard, trying to get my shivering body under control. My teeth chatter and I'm hoping that he doesn't actually require an answer because there is no way I could form a single word and expel it from my mouth. A thousand times in the last week I thought those things. It's like he opened my head and pulled every fear I had right out. On the outside I was a girl embracing her new life and her new freedom, but on the inside I was preparing myself for the day something bad would happen to my family.

"I plucked you right off of that little island and no one even saw me coming. I'm sure your father is still scratching his head, trying to understand what just happened."

It's more like Dad is probably going nuts right now. The Landrys, too.

"You better hope I get away with this, since I am the only chance you have in surviving this. I have worked for the Vega family all my life. Señor Vega does not tolerate mistakes and this new turn . . . with the journal proves to him that it was a mistake that I didn't kill you in Arizona."

None of this makes sense. Why did he give the journal back if he knew it would cause so much trouble? There's something missing. . . .

Thomas circles me again. "But now Señor Vega is the one who made a mistake—turning against me after so many years of faithful service. There is also the added insult of sending an amateur after me—and you—an assassin named Mateo. He is trying desperately to make a name for himself, so you will find him quite eager to finish this job."

"B-b-b-but I don't understand. He'll come after you no matter what happens to us? Why would you risk coming for me and Ethan? And why bring my sister?" My voice cracks at the mention of her.

He takes a small step closer. "I'm going to let you in on a little secret. The only reason I didn't kill you in Arizona is because I gave my word to someone that you would not die by my hand."

What? "Who?" I ask. My mind races trying to figure out who in the world he could be talking about.

"And the only thing keeping you and your boyfriend alive right now is the fact I don't want the person who replaced me on this job to fulfill any part of the contract. It's my pride that saves you now.

So make sure you understand your place. This is not about you, or really ever has been. You just found yourself in the middle of a very dangerous power struggle. Mateo wants you, but he'll have to get through me first. You and Ethan are going to help me lure a killer."

He backs up and slowly picks a stray dead leaf from his sleeve. "Teeny . . . that's what you call her, isn't it? Teeny turned out to be a nice surprise. I may need a little extra incentive for you and Ethan to cooperate." He crushes the dead leaf as his gaze zeros in on me. It's as if the temperature drops the closer he gets to me.

"Were you the one who left the journal in my pocket?" *SHUT UP, ANNA!* my mind screams, but I can't stand not knowing what is really going on. Now that I see what he really is, I don't think it could have been him—but who else could it have been?

A strange look comes across his face. "Don't mention the flowers or the journal again." Then he turns to walk away.

"I have one last question." I know I'm pushing my luck but I can't stop. "What will stop Señor Vega from sending someone else after us?"

"Once I put a bullet through his head, it will be difficult for him to give any more orders."

Oh. My. God.

Thomas moves away and I quickly undo my jeans to take care of business. I can see Thomas haul Ethan off the ground and lead him in the opposite direction. I want to believe he won't hurt us, but everything Thomas has ever told me has been a lie. Why should I trust what he says now? I race back to the van, trip on a tree root, and go flying, landing head first in the dirt. My face will not survive this.

"Are you okay?" Vader calls out to me. It's the first time I've heard his voice and it's not what I expect. Deep, but not too deep—and somewhat familiar.

Yes, asshole, I'm just great. I brace my hands on the ground, ready to heave myself up, when my palm scrapes over something hard. I pull it back and a small trickle of blood runs down the inside of my hand. On the ground is a thick wedge of green glass with a little piece of label on it. Maybe it's a broken beer bottle. The edges are pretty dull, but it's better than nothing. I quickly scan the ground around me to see if there is anything else I can maybe use as a weapon.

"Do you need help getting up?" Vader asks as he moves toward me. His tone is nice, not like the mechanical sounds that come from Thomas. Then he seems to check himself before continuing in a harsh voice, "Get up and get back to the van."

"I'm trying."

There's nothing else, so I grab the green piece of glass and shove it in my pocket as I rise from the ground. I try not to cry out as it digs into the tender part of my hip.

Ethan and Thomas are back by the time I make it to the van.

I step toward Ethan. I'm scared and all I can think of is being near him, but Vader stops me by grabbing my arm.

"Let her go!" Ethan yells, trying to shake free from Thomas's grasp.

Thomas hits him on the back of his head and Ethan falls to his knees. "Remove the agent."

Again, Vader hesitates a moment before finally doing what he's told. Agent Parker kicks his hands away, knocking him back.

He climbs in and struggles to get her to the edge, but she fights him. Thomas, who looks frustrated, knocks Vader out of the way, then pulls her out himself. Agent Parker, either from fear or pain, screams the entire way out.

She's like a wild animal, fighting with him, even with her hands tied.

Thomas knocks her to the ground and she crumples in a heap. I try to crawl to her but Vader steps in front of me, blocking my way.

Thomas heaves her over his shoulder, calling back to Vader, "Get them back in the van." Then walks toward the wooded area.

"Put your hands back behind your back," says Vader.

"No!" I hold my hands out in front. "Please don't tie us back up that way. My arms hurt so bad."

He's silent a few seconds then pushes Ethan back into the van, climbing in behind him. He binds his hands together in front of him, then secures his wrists to a strap anchored high on the inside wall of the vehicle.

I'm not sure this will be better.

I crawl in and go to Teeny. I run my hands through her hair and down the side of her cheek. She looks so peaceful, sleeping curled up in a little ball. At least her hands are tied in front of her.

I nudge her softly. "Teeny." Nothing. Then I shake her a little more. "Teeny. Wake up."

She mumbles and rolls around a little but doesn't open her eyes.

"What if she doesn't wake up? How much tranquilizer did you use on her? She's just a little girl!"

Vader grabs my hands together, securing them the same way he did Ethan's, and doesn't answer any of my questions.

Just as Vader turns to crawl out, Thomas appears outside the back of the van, the long blade in his hand. He runs it across the leg of his pants, leaving behind a dark red trail of blood. My thoughts fly back to the man in Arizona who got his neck slit open from one side to the other, and I wonder if this is the same knife.

"Where is Agent Parker?" Ethan says, just as I yell: "What'd you do to Agent Parker?"

He ignores us, instead speaking to Vader, "Notify Hammond it's done. We're far enough away that no one should stumble on that island."

Hammond. One of the agents Agent Williams mentioned.

Vader nods then slams the back doors.

Tears racing down my face, I crumble to the floor as much as my pinned arms will allow. Ethan's body does the same. Agent Parker is gone, along with any hope that we will get out of this alive.

Chapter 11

RULES FOR DISAPPEARING
BY WITNESS PROTECTION PRISONER #18A7RO4M:

~~Always act like you know what you're doing. Even if you have no idea what you're doing.~~

NEW RULE BY ANNA BOYD:
Sometimes freaking out is okay.

ETHAN and I suck at lip reading. Twenty minutes later I'm still trying to mouth that I have a dull, broken piece of glass in a pocket I can't reach. He's repeating a sentence over and over to me, too, but all I'm getting is something about a cup and a banana. I'm sure I'm getting it wrong.

This position is really no better than when my hands were behind my back. Now my hands are eye level and the zip tie is really tight so they're numb again. All the blood has drained from my arms.

I struggle to a kneeling position despite the van pitching me around. Ethan mouths, "What are you doing?" Ironically I can read that and nothing else, but I shake my head. There's no way to explain. It takes some maneuvering but finally I'm half-standing and some of the blood rushes back to my fingers.

Glancing to the front of the van, I hope to see Vader without the mask on. Since Thomas told him to notify Agent Hammond, I know he's not the mole. Unless there is more than one mole.

But no luck; he's sitting low in the seat and I can't make out anything about him. My eyes move across the front of the van until they collide with Thomas's in the rearview mirror.

"What are you trying to do?" Thomas yells from the front. Even when he raises his voice, it sounds controlled.

"I couldn't feel my hands," I yell back, even though I know I probably shouldn't talk to him like this.

The van swerves off the edge of the road before coming to a swift stop. Ethan and I fly around like rag dolls even though we're anchored near the van's ceiling. Teeny whimpers but doesn't wake up.

The back door opens and Thomas climbs in the van again, the knife at his side. He cuts me down, but keeps my hands bound together. There's a faint red streak of blood still on the blade.

He cuts Ethan down then looks around the interior of the van. He must be searching for another spot to attach us. The back of the van is sparse—no seats, nothing soft—just metal from top to bottom. There doesn't seem to be anywhere else to tie us.

He brings our faces close to his and says, "Understand that I will not stand for any foolishness." He looks directly at me and says, "Remember what I told you."

And my heart sinks. He'll use Teeny to keep me in line.

He shoves our heads down and we fall back to the floor of the van. Thomas hops out of the van and back in the driver's seat.

Like magnets, we're side by side before the van gets moving. I burrow into Ethan. He can't put his arms around me since his hands are joined together in front of us, so he throws one leg over mine and pulls my lower body in close.

Ethan whispers, "What was he talking about?"

I tell Ethan everything I know, including Thomas using Teeny as extra incentive for my cooperation.

He tries to pull me in closer and whispers in my ear, "We'll figure some way out of this. Plus, our parents have to know we're gone by now. Agent Williams probably has people out looking for us."

I shake my head. "No. They can't call him. And they can't leave the island." I tell him about the video and the white box. "He killed Agent Parker. He's going to use us, and then we're dead. No way he's letting us live when this is all over. And that's assuming Mateo doesn't get to us first."

I think about my dad stuck on that island and my mom stuck in the treatment facility and I physically ache to see them both. Especially my mom. It sickens me to think the last time I may ever see her was the night she was taken away. I'm scared and hurt and I know Dad's probably going out of his mind right now. And the poor Landrys, too. They sure didn't ask for this, and now their only son is tied up in the back of a van driven by a madman.

They probably started looking for us shortly after Thomas took us off the island. Did they find the white box immediately?

Ethan brings his hands up and traces the side of my face with one finger. "How bad is your cheek?"

"It's got to be cracked. Or broken. My whole head hurts. I probably look like you did the first time I saw you." An image of the ugly brownish yellow bruise that stained Ethan's cheek for weeks after his fight with Ben, Emma's boyfriend, fills my head.

He chuckles softly. "Yeah, I forgot about that."

We're both silent for a while. Teeny continues to moan and

mumble, but I can't see her. She's behind me, toward my feet. Ethan lifts his head every few minutes to look at her.

"I know you want her to wake up, but I hope she stays knocked out until we get to where we're going. We can't do anything for her back here like this," he says.

I dig in deeper at his side. "We're going to die," I whisper.

"Shhh . . . don't say that."

I pull back and look at him. "I love you. More than anything. I'm sorry I didn't say it earlier."

"I love you, too, but don't you dare say your good-byes and give up on me. We're not going out like this," Ethan says, kissing the temple that's not hurt. We ride in silence for a while. I have no sense of time or direction and it's confusing. My head spins with desperate plans to save us, but the pain radiating from the side of my face makes it hard to hold a thought for long.

I blink wildly at the bright lights that spill in from the front windows and realize I must have dozed off.

"I think we're pulling into a gas station," Ethan says in my ear.

The van stops and I hear a door open and close. I try to twist around to see if Teeny is all right, but my body has stopped cooperating. Every inch of me hurts.

"She's still out, but I don't think it'll be long before she's up. She's been mumbling a lot."

I nod and get as close to him as I can, putting my mouth right next to his ear. "I have a piece of broken glass in my pocket." My words come out in a soft whisper since I'm assuming Vader is still in the van.

He shifts his head so his mouth is near my ear. "Which pocket?"

"Left."

His hands move toward my left side. The way our hands are bound makes doing anything awkward, so I just try to relax. Ethan slowly rolls his hands around and then whispers, "Raise your left hip up a little." Struggling, I manage to lift up just enough so he is able to get two fingers in my front pocket. I feel it when they wrap around the glass. Ethan slowly pulls it out and it scrapes along my hip every inch of the way. I bite my lip, trying not to think about how much it hurts.

Again, his mouth comes to my ear. "Do you want to try something?"

I shake my head and shift back to his ear. "No. I'm not sure I could even walk right now and Teeny's not even awake yet. I just want you to have it in case something comes up." I'm not sure I can physically lift my arms, much less do any good with a dull piece of glass.

We move around again, trying to get the glass into his front pocket. I glance at Vader and he seems oblivious to what's going on back here. Ethan finally shoves the glass into his jeans.

"Do you know who the other guy is?" Ethan asks.

"No. I don't think he's Agent X since Thomas told him to call Hammond. Maybe there's more than one mole. I keep thinking he looks like Darth Vader in all that black."

"Do you recognize him?"

I shake my head. "No. And Thomas is freaking me out. He's a total psychopath. I can't believe how different he was in Natchitoches."

The van door opens and the engine roars to life. Once we're

moving, Teeny starts moaning again. I hope she doesn't hurt as bad as I do. The sounds from Teeny are the only noises that fill the van. Thinking back, I can't remember a single exchange between Thomas and Vader since I got hit with that tranquilizer gun. When we were outside the van, he wasn't very tall, maybe the same size as Ethan. I tick through my memories of all the different agents and it's hard to remember details like their height. Looking through those slits in the mask, I couldn't make out any of his features. But it's his voice—I can't shake the feeling that he's familiar in some way.

A few miles down the road, Teeny's moans turn into crying, soft sobs that hit you right in the gut.

The sound of that pitiful weeping washes over me and I feel even more broken. Why is this happening to us?

"We should have left her behind," Vader says from the front seat.

Thomas answers him in rapid Spanish, his tone harsh.

Vader answers Thomas equally as fast. The two go back and forth in Spanish and the only thing I can make out is Teeny's name, Vader saying it several times.

Why do they keep saying her name? Is Vader trying to talk him into getting rid of her? Will Thomas use the knife on her like he has so many others?

Images of the blood he wiped across his pants leg fill my head and my body starts shaking. Every inch of it. I try to relax so it will stop, but it only gets worse.

"Whoa, what's happening?" Ethan asks. He pulls me in a little closer but it doesn't stop my trembling. In fact, my body is shaking so hard it makes Ethan's body shake.

I can't form an answer so I just shrug.

Ethan holds me tight, trying to get me to stop shuddering but it doesn't work. His face comes close and his cold cheek brushes up next to mine.

I can't breathe . . . I can't breathe . . . I can't breathe . . .

"Anna, you're sweating," he whispers. His voice sounds panicked.

He buries his head into my neck, right near my pulse. He pulls back and yells to Thomas, "Hey! Pull over. Something's wrong with Anna."

No response.

"Pull over! She's shaking and sweating and her pulse is going crazy."

Thomas swerves to the side of the road but doesn't get out of the van. "If this is some stupid trick . . ."

The interior light flips on and Vader says, "I don't think he's making this up. She looks terrible."

Thomas and Vader both bolt out of the van and the back doors fly open within minutes.

Thomas cuts my hands loose with a few swipes of his knife.

"Make sure he stays in the van," Thomas shouts to Vader.

I hear Ethan and Vader yelling at each other but it sounds like I'm underwater.

Thomas pulls me out and the cold night air washes over my sweat-streaked face. I try to stand but fall to the ground. The total blackness of the empty back road surrounds me, strangles me. I've got to get out of here. The desire to run is overwhelming. Thomas pulls me back up, sitting me on the rear bumper, and then pushes my head between my knees. Tremors rush through my body.

Thomas jumps back inside and I can hear sounds of Ethan struggling. I'm so dizzy I can't lift my head to see if they're hurting him. The clawing fear squeezes my neck. I try to suck in air but nothing happens. The fighting in the van seems to have stopped, but I'm frozen. Thomas jumps out of the van, dropping next to me on the ground.

My mouth is open but nothing goes in or out.

"Calm down," he says. "Deep breaths, in and out." His voice sounds weird, like he's trying to be nice but it's a completely foreign concept.

I try. I lower my head and for the first time, I'm able to draw in a deep breath.

"Relax."

I throw my head up, head-butting Thomas by accident.

"Relax?" I manage to scream out between labored breaths.

He pushes my head back down then moves away, and I risk raising it slightly so I can see if Ethan is okay. Glancing inside the back of the van, I see Ethan pinned to the ground with Vader sitting on top of him, Ethan's hands tied behind his back. A stream of blood oozes from his mouth. The broken piece of bottle is a few inches away. Teeny is curled into a ball and whimpering softly. I'm not sure if she is awake or still unconscious.

My throat feels like it wants to close up again, so I pull myself together and try to get my breathing under control.

In and out.

I clasp my hands together, trying to stop the shudders racking my body. I can't think about where we are or what's going to happen to us.

So I think about Ethan. I picture us on a blanket near Cane River in Natchitoches. Our favorite spot.

Deep breaths. Eyes closed.

Teeny's there. She's flying a kite down the bank, running around and laughing.

Air in through my nose. Air out through my mouth.

Ethan takes my hands, pulls me in, and kisses me. Soft lips, just enough pressure. It makes me feel warm. And safe.

I'm not sure how much time passes, but my body eventually stops shaking. My breathing returns to normal, and I don't have that clammy, about-to-throw-up feeling.

I hold on to the mental image a little longer, pulling every piece of strength I can from it. We're still on that blanket, sitting cross-legged, facing each other. My hands in his. Our faces close.

We are strong together. We are smart together. Ethan will protect me and I will protect him. We will both protect Teeny.

Opening my eyes, Thomas is in front of me, watching. Staring. The one thing I know about him is he always has a plan. Agent Parker died because she wasn't useful any more. Right now he needs us alive. And as long as he needs us, we're not in immediate danger.

But now he is. And not just from the unknown assassin out to get us all. If hurting Thomas saves us, I will not hesitate a second.

Chapter 12

NEW RULE BY ANNA BOYD:
Sometimes it's all you can do to stop yourself from falling behind.

THE rest of the ride is excruciating. Ethan's hands and feet are bound together in one clump, or as they would say on the farm: hog-tied. He struggles for a while but I have to turn away, it's too hard to watch.

Not long after we're back on the road, Teeny wakes up and crawls to me. Thomas only tied one of my hands to the wall of the van, so luckily I can curl the other one around her when she gets to me.

She burrows in close and asks in a surprisingly clear voice, "Is Thomas going to kill us?"

I tell her no.

I'm not sure she believes me.

I'm so relieved she never knew Agent Parker was here or what happened to her in the woods. I promised never to lie to another member of my family again, but now is not the time to tell Teeny just how much danger we're in.

Teeny and I lay together inside the van for a long time. She doesn't ask anything, not how we got here or where we're going. Doesn't ask for Dad. Or Mom. Doesn't cry. Nothing. Her level of calm is scary. And wrong.

Just as dawn breaks through the front van windows, Thomas pulls inside some structure—whether a garage or warehouse, I don't know. It's pitch-black and strangely quiet.

As soon as the van stops, both men jump from the vehicle and are gone.

There is no sound except the occasional ping from the cooling engine.

"Are y'all okay?" Ethan asks.

"I guess. Are you okay?"

Ethan grunts and struggles to free himself again.

"Do you know where we are?" Teeny asks.

"No," I whisper.

Ethan struggles to raise his head off the van floor. "Look, I'm not sure what's about to happen but we have to be smart about this. Anna, try to get him talking. He wants to lure in the Mateo guy— we need to find out how he plans on doing that. Information is vital—the more of it we have, the better chance we have to figure a way out of this. And look for a weapon. But don't use it unless it becomes absolutely necessary. There may be a time where we need to be able to protect ourselves. Do not blindly do what he asks. Make him explain why he wants you to do it. Hound the shit out of him. And Teeny, stay strong. You're a brave girl and I know we *will* get through this."

"You're talking like you won't be with us!" I say, panicked.

"I don't know what he's going to do, but I won't be surprised if he separates us. It will be the best way to keep us all in line."

Teeny buries her head in my chest and lets out a muffled cry.

I look over her head to Ethan and mouth the words *I love you.* He sends a tiny smile back my way and says, "Me, too. More than you know."

Ethan finally goes limp. Teeny is quiet. We're all waiting for what's next.

Shocked is the only thought that comes to mind when light finally floods the interior of the van. It's Thomas . . . dressed as a priest. He's wearing long black robes, a funny little hat, and that white collar thing.

What the hell?

He pushes a large hotel-style laundry cart to the back of the van.

"Anna, you and your sister go first. My associate will stay with Ethan. Once we've quietly gotten to our destination, we'll bring him up. Do you understand?"

I squeeze Teeny tight and nod.

Thomas pulls out the familiar knife and removes the zip tie from around my wrist, leaving a ring of red skin. After removing Teeny's bindings, he motions for her to climb inside the cart. She hesitates for just a second or two before jumping in.

Ethan looks defeated and I try to not let that scare me to death. He was right, we're being separated. I give him a small smile before climbing into the cart. Vader moves closer to the cart and I can see through the hole in the mask that he wants to say something.

Thomas puts a hand on his arm and squeezes, silencing anything he might have said. I may have just found the weak spot of this situation.

Thomas covers us with several layers of sheets and I say a little prayer that this isn't the last time I'll see Ethan's face.

The trip is bumpy and includes what feels like a short elevator ride. The second the sheet covering us is yanked away, a gross smell fills my nose.

Old. And mildewy.

Peeking over the rim of the cart, I take in my surroundings. The ceiling of the small room is short with rough wooden beams running like stripes from one side to the other, and the faded plaster walls are missing big chunks. The floors are old, scuffed wood, a minefield of splinters, and coated in dust. The only furniture in the room is a bare mattress and the only source of light is an old sconce with one of those little pull cords. A few stray rays of light make their way through the closed wood shutters covering the only window and making it too dark to see what's on the other side of the interior door.

Thomas pulls Teeny out of the laundry cart and she sprints to the other side of the room, as far as she can get from him, the second her feet touch the ground. He tries to help me out but I knock his hands away.

It takes me a few minutes to get out of the cart on my own. My body is battered and exhausted and not cooperating at all. Thomas doesn't offer to help me again.

I nearly collapse when I finally make it out of the cart. Thomas takes the sheets we hid under and throws them on the mattress.

"There is a bathroom through that door," Thomas says as he points to the small opening.

He steps out of the room long enough to retrieve a small ice chest and a brown paper bag.

"This should be enough for now."

Finally, he shuts the door and we hear the turn of the lock.

Teeny goes straight for the food while I throw the sheet over the old mattress and eye the room. Door: locked. Shutters: locked. Ethan's instructions play on repeat through my head. I'm looking for something, anything that I can use against Thomas. The room is bare.

Teeny pulls out a long, skinny loaf of bread and a package of lunch meat.

"I guess we can make a sandwich with this." She turns toward me and asks, "You want one?"

"Sure."

I don't know if I could actually eat right now but I'm happy for anything that will keep her busy. Truthfully, I'm waiting for her meltdown. I know there's one brewing.

I get the bed made, as much as you can with just a couple of sheets, and crawl toward the food. Teeny breaks the bread in half and then pries it open. Since there's no knife, the bread is pretty butchered by the time she piles the meat inside.

I hug my knees to my chest and try to process what's happened. This feels wrong on so many levels. Why the priest costume? Does he pull that off as well as he did the U.S. Marshals act?

"Maybe let's not use all the turkey. We don't know how often he'll feed us," I say. I don't trust him, no matter what. We've got to be smart about this—just like Ethan said.

Teeny looks at her sandwich, then removes half of the meat, returning it to the container. I do the same with my half and open the ice chest. It's full of bottled water and I want to cry at the sight of it.

We both grab a bottle and drain them in seconds. Opening and closing my jaw to eat sends waves of pain through my face, so I give up and crawl to the mattress.

Teeny finishes and follows me to the bed.

We lay there for a while.

At some point, Thomas opens the door and says, "Ethan's in the room next door. I don't trust you together. Everyone will be fine as long as you don't do anything stupid."

The door shuts and locks again.

My confidence shakes but it doesn't shatter. Ethan warned me this might happen, and even if I hate that we're not together, it doesn't mean Thomas wins in the end.

Be smart.

Get him talking.

Find a weapon.

I repeat this simple list to myself over and over, hoping it will help me find the strength to handle what's next.

Chapter 13

NEW RULE BY ANNA BOYD:
Random people may not be so random after all.

I feel like I've been asleep for days. I have vague memories of downing more water and crawling to the bathroom, but that's it. My body is disgusting, my hair greasy, my breath foul, and every move I make hurts like hell. Teeny's twisted up at my side, but springs to life after I stretch around.

She sits up quickly and asks, "Are you awake now?" Her voice sounds panicked.

"I think so. How long have I been out?"

"A whole day, I think. I only know that the room got really dark and then not so dark. We got more food. I ate without you." Her head hangs.

I pull her in close. "I'm glad you did."

She buries her face into my shoulder. "I didn't think you were ever gonna wake up."

"I'm better now." A small lie. I feel like I could sleep for a week more. But I'm starving too and that right now is overriding the urge to crawl back underneath the sheet. And Teeny's pitiful face.

"What's there to eat?" I ask.

Teeny pops up and runs across the room. There is now a small card table full of snacks, fruit, bread, and soft drinks. It's almost a ridiculous amount of food for just Teeny and me.

The small ice chest is tucked underneath the table. Teeny fixes me a plate with a banana, a honey bun, and a handful of grapes. "Did Thomas or the guy in the mask bring all this food in?" I ask with a mouth full of grapes.

"The guy in the mask. And he brought me some books."

This is freaking me out. Who in the hell is the dude in the mask and why is he going out of his way to be so accommodating?

Teeny sinks back down on the mattress with a sudoku book while I check out the shuttered window where a draft of cool air blows in from the outside. It's an odd shape, arched on top, and no glass—just the old wood shutter tucked back in the wall. The space is small; I can barely fit in front of it. The latch is locked with a small brass padlock.

Squinting through the crack I see another building. We're only about three or four stories up and the building across from the window is yellow. Bright yellow. But the position of the window doesn't allow me to see what's below it.

The sound of a lock turning makes us both jump.

Vader sticks his black ski-masked face inside. "You're awake."

No kidding.

Neither of us says anything to him. He steps inside and glances toward the food.

"Do you need anything?" It's a nice enough question but delivered in the same sharp tone he used earlier.

I'm listening to his voice and again there is a pang of recognition. I scroll through the countless suits who rolled through our placements in my mind. A sea of ordinary men parade through my memory. I'm sure I've met him before.

"We could use a shower. The bathroom only has a toilet and sink," I say.

"And a toothbrush and toothpaste," Teeny adds.

"Um . . . yes. Can I see Ethan?" I ask. "I just want to make sure he's okay."

"No. He should be the least of your worries."

"I won't try anything, I promise. It would make me feel better just to see him. Please."

This seems to piss him off.

"You know, it would make me feel better if there wasn't an assassin out there trying to end my life. I couldn't care less if you want to check on your boyfriend. He's lucky to even be here."

It's the way he says lucky that makes the hair on the back of my neck stand up.

He turns and leaves the room, locking us back in.

I drop to the floor and think about Ethan. Vader's entire demeanor instantly changed the second I mentioned him. Oh God . . . what if they did something to him? Thomas could have lied to me when he said Ethan was next door. My head pops up—next door. I run to the side of the room opposite the bathroom and knock on the wall.

"Ethan."

Knock, knock.

"Ethan."

Knock, knock.

Nothing.

Teeny watches me from the mattress but doesn't say anything.

I run to the small bathroom. There is barely any space but I knock on the wall behind the toilet.

"Ethan."

I repeat this over and over, back and forth, from one wall to the next.

Nothing.

I crumple to the floor near the toilet. Teeny comes in and hunches down next to me.

"Maybe he's sleeping. Or the walls are too thick," she says.

Or maybe Thomas was lying to me.

I run from the bathroom to the locked door and use both fists to pound on the wood, screaming Thomas's name. Horrible thoughts are flying through my head and visions of Brandon's dead body and my blood-covered hands flood my brain. I hate getting sucked back into the horrible memories I kept buried for so long, but I feel the same now that I did in that room. Helpless. Scared. Almost a year later, I'm still suffering the consequences of witnessing their murders. I don't know that I will ever get to a point where that night doesn't haunt me.

I have a sinking fear that Ethan's gone. Really gone, like Brandon. I need to see him and there's only one person who can make that happen.

Little bits of plaster fly off the wall and little puffs of fine dust float through the room. The beams in the ceiling vibrate. I bang and scream until my voice is hoarse.

My hands throb, but I beat on that door for what feels like forever. A huge piece of plaster separates from the wall in a sheet and crashes to the floor. A cloud of dust forms and threatens to overtake the room, so I grab the sheet off the bed and throw it over the food.

All I've managed to do is make our conditions worse.

The door flies open. Vader is back.

"What in the hell are you doing?"

I launch myself at him, hitting him in the head, the stomach, and pretty much any other spot I can. I hate him—both of them for doing this to us. For killing Agent Parker. I want to hurt Thomas, too, but Vader's the only one in front of me right now.

He pins my arms and holds me tight. Teeny rushes to my side and starts kicking him and yelling, "Don't touch her! Leave her alone!"

Vader pushes Teeny away and she falls back on the mattress. "Stop fighting me or someone could get hurt. I won't hit a girl but I will go rough your boyfriend up instead. Maybe that will make you think twice before you attack me," he says.

I stop fighting him immediately.

His grip on my arms remains strong. His face is close. I search through the opening of the mask around the eyes and mouth. I know this person. I've met him before.

"Who are you?" I ask.

He shoves me back and I land next to Teeny.

"If you know what's good for you, you'll stop banging on these walls. I may not be the one to come check what's going on next time." He turns away and pulls the door shut.

"Teeny, did you recognize that guy's voice? Do you think he's one of the suits?"

Thomas told him to call Hammond so I know it's not him. For the second time, I wonder if there could be more than one mole.

Teeny pulls her knees in close and props her chin on top of them. "Maybe. He scares me with that mask on."

I nudge her arm and say, "He didn't seem to scare you too bad. You were pretty awesome with those kicks."

She smiles and I feel a little lighter inside. I throw an arm around her shoulder and pull her in close. "I shouldn't have attacked him. I'm just really worried about Ethan."

"Well, Ethan said to be smart about this and I don't think that was very smart." She's got a little bit of the bratty tone to her voice and I love hearing it. It's normal Teeny—not scary calm Teeny.

"I know. We both need to be careful and use our heads." I pause a moment then ask, "Do you want to know what Thomas told me? About why we're here?"

She picks at her thumbnail and creases race across her forehead as she studies her cuticle. "Ummm . . . I guess."

I repeat what I told Ethan, leaving out what Thomas said about her, as simply as I can.

"So there's another assassin looking for us. Because that's what Thomas is, right? An assassin."

"Yes, I think that's what he is."

"And this other assassin is trying to take Thomas's place. And to do that he has to kill you and Ethan and Thomas and the guy in the mask?"

"Vader."

She looks at me for the first time since we started talking, letting out a small laugh. "Yeah, I guess he looks a little bit like Darth Vader."

"Well, I figured he needed a name. Thomas isn't Thomas's real name but we have to call him something, so why not give masked man a name, too?"

"Who do you think is going to win? Thomas or the other guy?"

I don't want to say that I think whoever wins probably won't let us live in the end, so I say, "I'm betting on us. I think in the end, we'll win and go back home."

She smiles again and I shake the sheets out, remaking the bed.

"What's that?" Teeny asks.

She's pointing to the ceiling where rough boards are now visible.

"Just some old boards that are behind the walls," I answer.

"No, what's that between those two boards?"

I stop making the bed and look up to where she's pointing. There is something wedged in there.

I kneel down. "Here, get on my shoulders and see if you can grab it."

Once she's sitting on top of me, she can reach it but just barely. Tugging away a few random pieces of plaster, she manages to pull it out.

"It's a box!" Teeny sounds like she's won a prize.

Teeny hops down so fast we both almost fall over and my sore muscles scream. It is a box. A very small box. And it's old and covered in dust.

Teeny cracks open the lid. There are a few envelopes bound by a faded, yellow ribbon, an old pocket watch–type thing, a piece of fabric, and a small framed picture. Teeny goes for the envelopes while I pick up the frame. It's tarnished but you can still see the intricate scrollwork that surrounds the image. I flip the small latch on the back and pry the door open, pulling the picture out. It's faded. It looks like a boy but it's too damaged to make out any details. On the other side is a single word: Henry.

I glance at Teeny, who is trying very carefully to separate the envelopes. She's gotten the ribbon off but every time she tugs at a piece of the paper it rips apart.

"I don't think I can open these without ruining them," she says.

I hold my hand out and she gently lays the stack of envelopes inside. The front is yellowed with age and the writing is smeared like maybe it's gotten wet.

The name and address on the top envelope are barely legible. In fancy cursive is the name Henry, but all you can tell from the last name is that it starts with S-t-a. Underneath there is only one word you can read: Rye.

"What does Rye mean?" Teeny asks.

"I'm not sure. It's probably just some street name or name of a town. No telling how long this has been up there."

"What kind of weirdo is Henry that he's got a frame with his own picture in it?"

I giggle and say, "I don't think this box is Henry's. It's got to be a girl's box of things. Maybe she never got around to mailing the letters."

Teeny rummages through the rest of the box. The pocket watch stopped working at 6:17—but who knows how many years ago—and the fabric is blue and thick with a raised pattern on it.

"Can I keep this stuff?" she asks.

"I don't see why not." I put the photograph back in the frame and close the back. It's small, barely fitting in my palm, so I take the yellow ribbon and thread it through the scrollwork on the top of the frame.

"Turn around," I tell her, and then drape it around her neck, tying the ribbon in a knot. "Now it's a necklace."

She lies back on the mattress and stares at it in her hand. While Teeny's interests are with what's in the box, mine are more on where the box came from.

The boards near the ceiling are old and half rotten. Maybe if I could pry one out, it could be useful. Like beat-Vader-until-he's-unconscious useful. But how do I get up there?

The card table!

Once everything on the card table is on the floor, I gingerly climb on top of it. It's wobbly but if I space my feet just right, the table holds still. The ceiling is low enough that I can reach the wood with no problem.

"What are you doing?" Teeny asks.

"Looking for a weapon."

I can get my hands around one of the boards but when I pull, nothing happens except that I feel like I'm about to fly off this table. I glance around the floor searching for anything that may help.

There's nothing.

And then I hear it. It's faint, but there . . . a scratching noise.

I run to the wall next to the mattress, pressing my ear against it.

"What are you doing now?" Teeny asks.

"Do you hear it? That noise?"

She gets up from the bed and squats down next to me on the floor.

We both hear the noise this time and Teeny's eyes get wide.

"Is it like a mouse or something?"

I shake my head. "I don't know. Maybe. Maybe not."

Knocking on the wall, I shout Ethan's name again. Just a few scraping noises answer me back.

Teeny gets bored quickly and moves back to the mattress. Using my fingers, I dig into the plaster wall. It feels good doing something. As much as I hate not having Ethan here with me, I'm so glad he gave me something to do. I work until my nails are broken and my fingers are on the verge of bleeding, yet I've only removed about a square inch of wall. How can an entire piece fall by banging on a door but still be strong enough to withstand direct force?

Scratch, scratch, scratch.

There it is again.

And then I hear something . . . a muffled sound. Words, but I can't make them out.

"What was that?" Teeny asks.

I shrug and then lie on my back with my feet against the wall. I line both feet up where I've made the small dent. Using all my strength, I pound both feet against the wall one good time. Vibrations run up my legs and the wall shakes but nothing else happens. I brace myself and kick again. The plaster caves in a bit and a layer of dust floats over me.

Moving in front of it to hide the damage, I wait to see if I've alerted Vader again. Teeny looks from me to the door and back again a dozen times. Not sure how much time goes by but I feel like if he's coming, he'd have gotten here by now.

"Sissy, what if there's a mouse in there and you let it out? What if it comes in here?" Teeny asks in a panicked voice. How can she be cool with being a hostage, but the idea of a mouse getting in here makes her nervous?

"I don't think it's a mouse. I'm hoping it's Ethan on the other side of this wall."

I chip away at the wall until I finally break through the plaster and even a small piece of the wood. It's not a big hole, but it is a hole.

The opening is triangular, and when I pull a loose piece of plaster out of the way, I can just make out one eye, part of a cheek, and half of a nose.

It's not a face I recognize.

"Is it a mouse?" Teeny asks.

"No. It's a person."

Teeny springs up from the bed and squeezes her head next to mine so she can see.

"Is it Ethan?" Teeny whispers.

I shake my head. "Hello?" I call through the wall. "Can you hear me?"

"Yes." The voice answers back. It's a young boy. "Who's there?"

"My name is Anna. I'm here with my sister, Elena. Who are you?"

Part of me is devastated it's not Ethan, but hopefully this person will know where we are.

"Noah. Noah Barnes."

He's trying to get a better look inside our room. I stare at him, but it's hard to get a good idea of what he looks like when you can only see bits and pieces at a time.

"What happened to your face?" Noah asks.

My hand flies to my cheek and I realize I still haven't seen how bad the damage is. There's no mirror in our small bathroom.

"It's fine. Are you okay?"

"I'm fine," he answers.

He doesn't sound fine. He sounds scared. I can't see anything wrong with him, but my view only shows about ten percent of his face at a time.

"Do you have food?" Teeny asks.

"Yeah, some water and bread. A little turkey."

I'm guessing he doesn't have the same little buffet we've got. I turn to Teeny and say, "Find some food small enough to fit through the hole."

She scurries over to the card table and grabs a banana and a honey bun. It takes us a few minutes but we finally get the food through to the other side.

It really makes me nervous there's another kid here. There is obviously way more going on than Thomas is saying.

While he eats, I ask, "What are you doing here?"

His eye fills the hole again and his eyebrow scrunches up. "I don't know. That guy won't tell me anything no matter how many times I ask."

"What's the guy look like?"

"I don't know. He's always wearing a ski mask."

I take a deep breath and try to force down the rising anxiety.

"You haven't seen the tall, dark-haired guy? He may have been dressed like a priest."

"You two are the only other people I've seen since I've been here." Noah backs away from the hole. He's gone for a while and I have a crazy fear he won't come back. Finally, his brown eye fills the space again.

What the hell is going on? Who is this boy and what does he have to do with any of this?

"Have you ever heard of a guy named Daniel Sanders?" I ask.

He's quiet a moment while he thinks. "No. That name's not familiar."

"Where are you from?" There has to be some sort of connection.

"El Paso, Texas."

Okay. We never had a placement in Texas, but Ethan and I did drive through there on our way to Scottsdale.

"How old are you?" I ask.

"Twelve."

Teeny's head pops up. He's only a year older than she is.

"Have you ever been to Natchitoches, Louisiana?"

"No. Is that close to New Orleans? The only place I've been to in Louisiana is New Orleans," he answers.

"No, it's like four or five hours away."

I tick through all of my identities from when we were in the program: Hillsboro, Springfield, Naples, Conway, Bardstown. Noah has never been to any of those places.

"Does your mom or dad work for the government? Maybe the U.S. Marshals Service?" I'm reaching now. Trying to find some sort of connection.

"No. But my granddad does."

Oh. Shit.

I'm almost afraid to ask the next question. There's only one agent I think of when the word grandfather comes to mind.

"Is his name Greg Williams?"

His brown eye gets big. "Yeah. How'd you know that?"

Chapter 14

NEW RULE BY ANNA BOYD:

Hell, no. If you love the life you have—fight for it.

I turn away from the hole in the wall. Noah calls for me, but I don't get up. Why in the world is Agent Williams's grandson being held captive in the next room?

My mind spins with accusations. Agent Parker told us she was the one who told Thomas where we were. How is Agent Williams involved with this?

The lock on the door turns and I sit up quickly. I whisper through the hole for Noah to be quiet and then lean against the wall, blocking the hole with my back.

The door opens slowly and Thomas sticks his head in.

He looks at Teeny on the mattress and then at me sitting on the floor. "I heard there's a problem in here."

Oh, crap. Vader told on me for banging on the walls. "No, everything's fine. It's fine."

Thomas stands straight, arms by his sides. "You didn't ask for a shower and toiletry items?"

I sit up straighter. "Oh . . . yes. Yes, we want a shower and to brush our teeth."

Thomas enters the room and walks to the card table. He's still dressed as a priest, his long black robes picking up the white powder that covers the floor. He runs his finger over the surface of the table, coating the tip in plaster, and holds it up to me.

"Will it become necessary for me to separate you to ensure good behavior?"

This is one of the strongest threats Thomas has against me right now. I'm worried about Ethan, but he is strong and resourceful. Teeny is another story. I can't imagine what it will be like for her if she's stuck in a room like this by herself. And as much as I hate to admit it, I don't want to be by myself either.

"No," I answer.

"Anna, I know how your mind works. There's nowhere to go."

I can almost hear Ethan's voice in my head—get him talking.

"Why would I believe anything you say? You're a murderer. And a kidnapper. And God knows what else."

I worry for a moment that maybe I took the wrong approach.

He doesn't move or answer me. Teeny pulls the sheet on top of her, trying to hide underneath it. I've scared her and regret that.

But I can't lose this opportunity.

"I know you have some plan that includes us. Please tell me what it is. We should all work together on this." I hate the begging tone that creeps in my voice.

Not even a flicker of emotion crosses his face. "Would you like to know about the man who has been hired to kill you?"

Um . . . hell no.

"I guess," I squeak out.

"I mentioned he's trying to take my place. And I've mentioned he's eager to make a name for himself. That's not all of it. He's brutal when he fulfills a contract." He pauses, then repeats, "Brutal."

I try to swallow the lump in my throat but it won't go down.

"Mateo likes to mark his victims to ensure that he gets credit for the kill. He burns a cross onto their chest until the skin all but melts around it. It's just a shame he does it while they're still alive." His left eyebrow arches slightly when he asks, "Would you like for me to tell you what he does just before he burns them?"

"No!" Teeny and I both yell at the same time.

"Does he know you have us?" I ask. I never thought I'd feel safe with Thomas, but he seems to be the better of two evils.

"I'm certain he knows by now."

Teeny's head pokes out of the sheet and she has tears in her eyes. "Why can't Ethan be with us right now?" she asks.

Thomas's expression doesn't change a fraction. "You are easier to control separated."

I want to ask how Noah fits in but I'm not ready to show all my cards right now.

"What's your exact plan?" I ask.

He shakes his head, but doesn't answer.

"You owe us that." I wait a moment, debating what to say next, then decide to push him, bringing up the one thing he told me not to mention. "We're only back in this because of those stupid flowers and my journal. And I don't think you're the one who sent them.

Who was it? The least you can do is tell me that. Is it that guy Daniel Sanders who Agent Williams caught?"

His left cheek twitches and I know I'm on to something.

"If you want a shower, I'll take you one at a time. I've no problem affording you the basic necessities. Who wants to go first?"

He's not biting. But at least I'm cracking that shell.

Teeny shakes her head. It might be better for me to go first so I can at least tell her what to expect.

But how do I move away from the wall without him seeing the hole? I don't want him to know that I know about Noah.

By the way Teeny's looking between me and the wall, I can tell she's worried about the same thing.

She hops away from me to the other side of the room. Thomas follows her with his eyes and I stand slowly, keeping my legs together to hide the damage.

"Do you promise she'll be okay?" Teeny asks.

He stares at her. "If she doesn't do anything stupid, she will be fine."

I move to the door and turn to Teeny just before I step out of the room. "I won't be gone long."

We're in a narrow hall with a row of closed doors on each side.

"Can I see Ethan just so I know he's okay?" I ask.

"No."

Following Thomas, it takes everything in me not to knock him in the head or kick him in the butt. I want to hurt him. But that would be stupid and Ethan told me to be smart. I can't do anything until I have some sort of plan. And know where we are. Or exactly what we're up against. I can't forget he's a cold-blooded killer.

We turn into the last door on the left. It's another small room, very similar to ours, but this room is furnished: a real bed, nightstand, and a small desk cluttered with papers.

Thomas points to another door inside the room. "There is a full bath in there. Towels are under the sink. You have ten minutes."

I sprint to the door, not wanting to waste a second. Sure enough, the bathroom looks just like the one in our room, but this one has a small shower stall. And a mirror.

I look like crap. My cheek is dark purple rimmed in a really gross brown. My blond hair looks brown from the amount of grease in it. And I'm pale. Too pale.

On the edge of the sink, there are a couple of toothbrushes still in the package and a brand-new tube of toothpaste. I've never been so happy to see toiletry items in my entire life. I waste no time cranking up the hot water and jumping inside.

Nothing can make you feel human again like a hot shower and clean teeth. I hate having to put on the same clothes again, but they're my only option.

Thomas leads me back to our room and I quickly glance at the hole in the wall. It doesn't look as noticeable as I thought it would. With the big piece of plaster missing above it, the hole seems rather insignificant.

It takes a few minutes to convince Teeny that it'll be okay to go with Thomas, and promises of clean teeth and non-greasy hair seem to do the trick.

Once Thomas is gone, I scurry to the hole in the wall.

"Noah."

Nothing.

I peek into the hole but can't really see anything.

"Noah," I say a little louder.

A big brown eye appears in the opening.

"You're back. That other girl wouldn't come to the wall."

That doesn't surprise me. She's chewed her fingernails down to the quick and now she's doing that thing where she ties a small section of her hair in a knot then unties it . . . over and over. Teeny looks fine on the outside, but I know she's hanging on by a thread.

"Look, I've got some questions. Did the guy in the ski mask ask about your grandfather or anything about his work?"

He shakes his head. "No. He barely talks to me. He only comes in once a day to bring me more food and change out the bucket."

"Bucket?"

His eye wanders off to the side. "Yeah, you know. The bucket you use the bathroom in."

Oh, man. That's disgusting.

"We have a bathroom in here. You don't?"

"No! I've been going in that bucket for days," he says. "You have a regular toilet? This sucks." I feel the vibration when he hits his side of the wall and a small amount of plaster dust falls on my newly clean hair.

"How long have you been here?" I ask.

As his head drops down out of sight, Noah mumbles something.

"You have to talk through the hole or I can't hear you."

His head pops back up. "I'm not sure. I think four days."

I'm pretty sure this is our second day. If he's been here for four days, then Thomas got him about a day or so before he came for us.

"Do you remember the ride here? Or how long it took you?"

Maybe if it didn't take long, that means we're in Texas somewhere.

"No, I was knocked out. I barely remember leaving my house. It was late and I was coming home from a friend's house. I felt something prick me, like a shot, then I woke up here."

There's no way for me to know how long Ethan and I were out, but we still spent a lot of time awake in that van. If Noah was knocked out for his entire ride, then we have to be closer to El Paso than Arkansas.

Oh God, what if we're in Mexico? That would make escaping that much harder.

"Noah, do you have any idea where we are?"

"No."

Noah and I talk a little longer. He asks about us, but I keep him in the dark about who Thomas is and how I know him. There's no reason to scare him any more than necessary.

The lock turns again and a squeaky-clean Teeny bursts into the room. Thomas doesn't come in, just closes and locks the door again.

"That was the best shower I've ever had," Teeny says as she drops back down on the mattress.

Noah wants to keep talking—I'm sure he's bored out of his mind—but I can't sit here and do nothing.

I walk to the shuttered window and pull on the padlock but it won't open. Maybe if I had something to beat it with, it might bust loose.

The sun is fading fast and the light from the sconce doesn't do much to chase the darkness from the room. Teeny's underneath the light, staring at the bundle of envelopes like she can pry them open with her mind alone.

"Where do you think we are, like a house or something?" Teeny asks.

"I don't think it's a house." Aside from the occasional scratching noises that scamper across the ceiling, it's way too quiet. The place feels big. And empty.

I run my hands along the dilapidated wall. There are bits of old wallpaper still attached in places that have yellowed with time and the old light fixture looks rusted in places. This room is really old . . . and forgotten. What is this place? Looking back at the shutters, they seem much newer than anything else in the room, especially with the shiny brass lock and hinges.

"Do you think this was that girl's room? Why would she hide her things in a box in the wall?"

I listen to her with half an ear. If I can pry off one of the hinges, I can probably get one of the shutters off and see outside.

"And that boy in the other room—does that mean Agent Williams ratted us out?" Teeny asks in a whisper, even though there's no way Noah can hear anything we say unless we talk directly through the hole.

"I don't know. If he did, wouldn't the kid be back with his family by now?"

Teeny's quiet for a few minutes then squeals, "I got the group of letters unstuck from each other without ripping them apart. There are five of them!"

"Can you make out the address on any of the others?"

"They all say the same thing except one. It has an X through Henry's name and then some fancy writing off to the side." Teeny leans in close, eyes squinting, and reads, "'Return to Francesca

DuBois, Ursuline'—and then two words I can't pronounce. V-i-e-u-x C-a-r-r-e and then there's that little mark on top of the last e."

I stop working on the shutters and turn to Teeny. "Vieux Carré?"

Teeny shrugs. "Yeah, I guess. Do you know what that is?"

I sink to the floor. "Yes. It's what they used to call New Orleans when it was first settled. The French Quarter actually. It's written on all that touristy stuff back in Natchitoches and I asked Ethan one day what it meant." I glance around the room. "Teeny, we're only about an hour from where Mom is."

Teeny's head pops up. "How far are we from Dad?"

"Well, I'm not exactly sure what part of Arkansas we were in, but it's at least five or six hours away."

Teeny goes back to the letters and I go back to the window. My mind spins, trying to absorb all of this. Even if we get out of here, what do we do about Mateo? I probably shouldn't have asked what he does to his victims because my mind has been running with horrible thoughts of burning flesh and melting skin ever since Thomas said the word *brutal*.

I work on the window until the room is almost dark, using a splintered piece of wood to pry at the hinges. Teeny has positioned herself underneath the small light and her fingers are delicately trying to pry one of the letters from the envelope. It's slow work for us both. If this was Francesca's room, I feel a little sorry for her, and I wonder if it felt like a prison for her as well.

Noah called for me a few times but I told him to get working on his window. It won't hurt to keep him busy either.

What may be the hardest thing about being stuck in this room is not knowing how much time has passed. Is it midnight yet? Or three in the morning? The time thing is really starting to mess with me.

Teeny finally falls asleep and I haven't heard from Noah in a while. I'm determined to get these shutters open and look outside. I get as far away from the window as I can, then barrel toward them.

A loud *thump* vibrates through the room the second I hit the shutters, then I fall back on my butt.

The shutters hold firm, but a searing pain radiates down my arm. I wait a moment to see if I've alerted anyone, but the room stays eerily quiet.

One more try. I massage my sore arm, wincing. If I'm going to do this, I have to ignore the pain. This time I crouch like a football player, turn to the side, and drop my shoulder.

I nail the shutters again, and again nothing but pain. Are there bars behind the shutter that I can't see?

"Ugh!"

I'm so tired, and pissed. And completely done with this. I stomp around the room, muttering to myself.

I kick the door and pound on the wall before collapsing on the floor, not caring if someone hears me or not.

Why does everything have to been so damn hard?

Noah's big brown eye peeks at me from the hole in the wall, and I crawl to where he is.

"Anna, are you okay?"

"Yeah. I'm just sick of being in this room," I answer.

"Tell me about it. Did you get the hinges off?"

"No, I need a tool or something. This room looks like it's going to fall apart around us, but that stupid shutter will still be in place."

His eye closes for a long minute. "Do you think he's gonna let us go?"

"Maybe. Maybe not."

Noah disappears from the hole, and I'm sorry I had to be so blunt, but I've learned that being prepared for the worst possible scenario is sometimes the best way to avoid the worst possible scenario.

Chapter 15

RULES FOR DISAPPEARING
BY WITNESS PROTECTION PRISONER #18A7R04M:

~~Be forgettable. No name brand clothes or anything remotely cute. . . .~~

NEW RULE BY ANNA BOYD:
Be unforgettable and high maintenance. It's surprising how well this can work
for you if done in the right way.

THE door pops open and Vader sticks his masked head inside.
I've been waiting for this moment all morning.

"Do you need anything?" Vader asks.

"Yes. I need tampons. And Advil. And possibly a heating pad.
And a change of clothes and new underwear."

I may not know what he looks like but I know he's a guy and not
a very old one. If there's anything that freaks a guy out, it's talking
about your period and actually asking for them to buy supplies. A
girl's menstrual cycle is a guy's kryptonite.

Even with the mask, I can see the panic in his eyes.

"I'll probably need another shower, too."

My plan is to get out of this room again and I hope faking a
period will do it. I was so focused on taking a shower last time that
I completely forgot to scope out that other bathroom for something
that could help me. And what are all those papers on the desk?
Thomas's plans? I need to get back to that room.

He mumbles something I can't understand and quickly slams the door then turns the lock.

It doesn't take as long as I thought it would before Thomas sticks his head back in the room. It's the first time since we've been here that he's not dressed as a priest.

"I understand you have some feminine issues this morning."

Luckily, I was already in the fetal position on the mattress so I look the part. "I have really bad cramps. I'm going to need a change of clothes and some tampons."

"I don't believe you." This doesn't faze him like it did Vader.

Oh, crap. He's calling me on this.

"What do you hope to gain by this?" he asks.

Staring at him for a few seconds, I try to figure out how to handle this.

"Look, do you need to see proof?" I raise my eyebrows. "I'm not exactly thrilled about this either. Show me you're just a little bit human."

The door shuts and the lock turns.

"What are you doing now?" Teeny asks.

"I need to get back to that room with the shower. It's full of stuff. Maybe something we can use."

"I don't know if that's the way to get back in there. I think you pissed him off." She looks a little nervous. "I know what Ethan said, but I'm really worried about this Mateo guy. He wants to kill us. I know Thomas isn't saying he won't kill us later but he's not saying it right now and I think we stay with the guy who is not saying he will kill us."

I love Teeny's ability to whittle this down to the simplest issue, but she doesn't know about Agent Parker. And she also doesn't know he will most likely dispose of us just as easily. But I look at her face and that misleading calm still etched all over it and decide I can't shatter her completely right now.

"I know, Teeny. I'm more than willing to let Thomas take care of Mateo. But what happens after that? It won't hurt if we have some way to take care of ourselves, too. I won't do anything until we both agree to it." She doesn't look like she believes me. "Tell me the latest on Francesca. Did you get one of the letters out?" I need to distract her.

She picks up a single page. "I got the one that was returned to her out but it's hard to read. The writing is so small. I think it's written to the guy in the picture, Henry, although the name is smudged pretty bad at the top. And from what I can get it's really horrible. She's telling him what happened to her—why she disappeared. She got tricked into getting on the wrong ship in La Rochelle—*Les Deux Frères*—but she doesn't know who did it. And she says she's living in a convent right now. And she gets paraded around in front of these really gross old guys to see if any of them want to marry her. And the other girls are really mean to her. And she's scared. She's worried that by the time this letter gets to Henry and he comes to get her it will be weeks and weeks and probably too late."

"Weeks? Where does Henry live?"

She flips the page over. "She's from France. She got on a boat thinking she was going to England. But she came to the Vieux Carré instead. Maybe he lives in England and that's who she was going to see."

"You said she lived in a convent? If you think this is her room, does that mean we're in a convent?"

Teeny shrugs and I stare at the wood beams crossing the ceiling, thinking about Thomas in the priest outfit. For some reason, he's dressed like a religious person. That would make sense.

I read the letter for myself—the parts that are legible—and Teeny's right. It is pretty horrible. When Thomas opens the door, I slide the paper back to Teeny. He's got a plain white plastic bag and motions for me to follow him. I'm hoping he lets me have the whole room to myself, not just the bathroom.

When we get to the room, I stop in the middle and hold my hand out for the bag. He passes it to me but doesn't move.

"Uh . . . I need some privacy."

He motions to the bathroom but doesn't say anything. I open the plastic bag, trying to stall for some time. There's a box of tampons, Advil, a black pair of exercise pants, and a three-pack of panties. Even though I asked for the panties, I'm a little grossed out that Thomas or Vader picked underwear out for me.

"This is the last *errand* we'll be running for you."

Great. I'll have to make the most of my time in this room since I might not make it back in here. With my head turned down like I'm looking in the bag, I eye the room for anything that could be of help.

The bed . . . nothing.

The nightstand . . . small lamp, book, newspaper. It's folded and too far away to read what it says.

The desk . . . laptop, lots of papers, pens, books, more papers . . . that's it.

Thomas clears his throat, loudly, and I move to the bathroom.

There's no doubt he's waiting on the other side for me to finish.

Glancing around the bathroom, there's just the usual stuff. Nothing that could be a weapon or a tool. I start the water and undress. No sense in wasting this opportunity.

It was probably overkill asking for all this stuff, but he got everything on my list. Maybe I shouldn't have used my only *favor* on this. I wad some wrapper paper from a tampon in the trash can just in case, and then I see it. It's a wooden handled plunger tucked behind the toilet. Once I pull the rubber part off, I've got a pretty thick solid piece of wood, almost like one of the clubs cops use.

I roll it up in my dirty jeans and smile to myself—I now have a weapon.

Chapter 16

RULES FOR ~~DISAPPEARING~~
BY ~~WITNESS PROTECTION PRISONER #18A7R04M:~~

~~Don't be afraid to get down and dirty.~~

NEW RULE BY ANNA BOYD:
Maybe you should be just a little afraid of this.

$\mathbf{I}$ decide it's best not to tell Teeny about the plunger just yet. She's been so weird since all this started—barely upset, hardly any tears. I plan on using it to bash the padlock on the shutter door until the damn thing comes off, but I'm going to wait until nighttime. I made a lot of noise last night and no one checked it out, so I'm assuming they can't hear what's going on in here from that far down the hall. If I do manage to get out of this building, I don't want to run into Thomas right outside. I haven't seen Vader all day, maybe because he's scared of what I'll ask for next, or what other female problems I might drop on him.

I'm so worried about Ethan. Every time my mind drifts to him, my confidence shakes, but then I remember his instructions. Be smart. Get him talking. Find a weapon. God, if I could just talk to him once—see if he's made any progress.

Noah is driving me crazy. I really feel bad for him, but I can't sit at that wall and small talk with him all day. I finally convince Teeny to talk to him; he's closer to her age anyway. She's sitting on the floor, telling him all about Francesca and the letters. She's completely obsessed with her and has invented this whole star-crossed-lovers thing between Francesca and Henry. I think she has lost herself in their world so she doesn't have to think about ours. I can't hear Noah's side of the conversation but I'm sure he'll listen to Teeny talk about a girl who's been dead for a couple of hundred years all day just to have something to do.

God, I wish I could talk to Ethan.

Teeny finally falls asleep not long after the room gets dark, so I dig the plunger out of my jeans. There is a small gap between the shutters and the padlock, just enough to get a small slice of view, but not wide enough to get the thick wooden part in there.

I stare at the shutters a while. I need to get it open, but it can't be obvious to Vader and Thomas what I'm doing.

I whack the lock a few times, but all I manage to accomplish is a lot of noise. Louder than the night before. It's a miracle I haven't woken Teeny, but she's sleeping like the dead right now. I can't risk them hearing me, so I change tactics. Positioning the stick above the small padlock, I push down with all my weight. The wood creaks, and that's all I need to keep going. It takes several tries, but the latch from one of the shutter doors finally pops off.

I want to scream with joy. Instead I do a silent victory dance around the room. I push the small shutters apart and the night opens up in front of me. It's dark and really quiet. The window is small but there's a good view of the grounds in front of the building we're in as well as the buildings across the street.

There's some sort of courtyard below my window with maze-like shrubbery. From what I can see in the darkness, it looks beautiful. And far away. We're at least three stories up and the roof tiles look slick. I debate climbing out of the window. I'm not sure there's any way down, but maybe I can get to the next window over. If Noah is on one side, Ethan has to be on the other. Unless Thomas lied—which is totally possible.

I stick a leg out and test the tiles. Smooth. I glance back at Teeny and she's fast asleep. I have to try this. Once both feet are out of the window, I stick my head out so I'm sitting on the ledge. It is a long. Way. Down.

I stand but hold on to the window frame with a death grip. I feel like I could slide down the roof and off the edge any second. Looking around, it doesn't look like the roof connects with another building or any other structure, so this is a dead end as far as exits go. But I do get a bird's-eye view of the street.

If every movie and picture I've seen of the French Quarter is right, we're definitely in New Orleans. It's hard to make out many of the details since it's so dark out, but it's hard to miss the narrow streets and different-color buildings, the iron balconies and old lampposts. Instantly I miss Front Street in Natchitoches, which so resembles this area.

I hear the clip-clop of hooves and see a horse-drawn carriage heading away from us down a side street. This section of the Quarter is quiet, but I can make out lights and hear the faint sounds of music a few streets over.

Looking down, I see that this building and a few others near it seem to take up most of the block. The courtyard creates a nice distance between this building and the street. I can see the outline of what looks like a church next door once I'm on my tiptoes. Several statues on the ground below look religious, like angels and other . . . religious-y things. I'm starting to think maybe this really was Francesca's room and we actually may be in some sort of convent.

I glance toward the window where I think Ethan is. These windows jut out from the roof a little, but there are still quite a few feet between them. I step away from my window but each movement feels uncertain. I get far enough that I'm only holding on to the shutter by one hand and I'm still not anywhere close to Ethan's window. And I'm too chicken to let go. Retracing my steps, I crawl back inside. Defeated, I inch into the bed next to Teeny and pray sleep finds me.

Early the next morning, Vader pops his head in but won't look at me. He's got a bag, probably with more food, and a few more books for Teeny.

I feel around for the stick I've hidden in the sheets and think really hard about beating him with it then making a run for it. The only thing that stops me is, what then? I don't know where Ethan is for sure or if I can even get to him. I don't trust the suits since Agent Williams's grandson is next door. I don't trust the local police against Mateo. We're pretty much screwed.

"Do you need anything else?" Vader asks, still looking at the floor.

That voice. I look at the food he set on the card table and realize it's full of Teeny's favorites: double-stuffed Oreos, sour-cream-and-onion chips, and dry-roasted peanuts.

A sick sensation forms in the pit of my stomach. He knows us well.

I hop up from the mattress and stop about a foot from him. His eyes dart to mine, almost challenging me.

"Why do you wear the mask? I know you, don't I?" I step in just a bit closer.

Vader tries to leave, but I run to the door and slam it closed, leaning my back against it.

"Move out of the way. I will hurt you if I have to." He grabs for my arms but I push him away.

"No, tell me who you are." I shove at him again.

Teeny scoots to the edge of the mattress and says with her voice full of warning, "Sissy."

Vader stands up straighter and throws his shoulders back. His voice gets deep and firm, sounding older than it usually does, and he says, "You're about to screw up. Move out of the way."

He reaches for me again and I throw myself at him. He's trying to push me away from the door and I'm doing everything in my power to hold my ground. It doesn't help when Teeny starts pulling on me, too.

"Sissy, stop. Please, stop," she whines.

The closer I get to Vader, the more I know he's no stranger to us. Teeny's scared but I can't let go of him. He jerks me hard and I fall to the ground, but I hold my grip and he tumbles to the floor with me. Teeny is sobbing loudly.

Vader gets up on one knee and drags me from the door. He

ducks his head down and he's close enough that I'm able to grab the back of the mask with one hand. He freezes and I yank.

The mask comes off.

I stare at his face and fall back to the ground. Teeny's cries stop as we both try to process what we're seeing.

"Oh. My. God. What are you doing here?"

Chapter 17

RULES FOR DISAPPEARING
BY WITNESS PROTECTION PRISONER #18A7R04M:

~~Never, under any circumstances, try to re-enter your old life in any way.~~ . . .

NEW RULE BY ANNA BOYD:

Sometimes your old life sucks you back in. Reacting to what you're feeling
does not lead to smart decisions. Even if you feel like bashing someone's head
in and throwing him out of the window. It may make you feel better, but it won't
help your situation.

HE backs away until he hits the door and stares at me with
hard eyes.

The urge to slap his face conflicts with the urge to throw my
arms around him. This internal power struggle makes me want to
vomit.

My stomach is in knots as my brain races to comprehend this.
All that time I worried about him. Worried what he thought when he
showed up at my door and we were gone. How horrible for him that
there wasn't a trace left of us and how long he must have wondered
about what happened to me. All that friggin' time and here he is—
in a ski mask helping Thomas hold us hostage. Tyler Collins—the
first boy I trusted once I was in the Witness Protection Program.
The first boy I allowed myself to have feelings for even though I
knew I'd have to leave him behind one day. The boy who made it
so hard to open up to Ethan—because I didn't want to lose anyone
else—has been right in front of me for three days.

There are no words. Questions and accusations race through my head but I can't force any of them from my mouth.

"Good; you obviously didn't forget about me completely," Tyler says.

Tyler looks the exact same as he did when we lived in Florida except for the row of fresh stiches across his cheek.

Teeny starts sobbing again and races to my side. "I don't understand," she says through hiccups. "Why are you here? Why are you working with *him*?"

I try to comfort her but some unknown sensation has settled in my chest and frozen everything inside.

Tyler's here.

He's here and he's helping Thomas.

As I stare at his face, my mind flashes between his unapologetic expression and his sun-kissed face the last time I saw him in Florida. It was the afternoon just before we were yanked out of that placement and we were playing in the waves . . . jumping in them and splashing around. A big one had knocked us both under, and the current pushed me headfirst into the sandy bottom. But Tyler was there to pull me back up. We stood in the water, body to body, while he dusted away the wet sand that stuck to my cheek. It was the first time since we'd gotten into the program that I felt truly happy. Teeny called from the shore that I had to come home. Tyler kissed me lightly on the lips and said he would pick me up at seven for our date. That was the last time I saw him.

Until today.

I feel paralyzed by that memory.

Teeny pulls her head away from where she's buried it in my side and yells at him, "You're a big liar! I hate you!"

The fire Teeny feels slowly breaks through the cold panic I'm in. I stroke her head and ask him, "Is Tyler even your real name?" My teeth grind through every word.

He nods. "Yes. My real name is Tyler."

I take a deep breath in and try to control the burst of anger rushing through me. Teeny blubbers against my shoulder and it sounds like she's finally letting go. I'm so mad I can't think. I hope like hell the disgust shows on my face when I say, "Get out of my sight."

He waits a moment then stands quickly, leaving the room without looking back. He doesn't forget to lock the door, though.

Teeny cries and cries until I don't think there's any more water left in her body, then her sobs turn to sniffles. We're both in such shock that we remain on the hard, wood floor instead of crawling the few inches it would take to get on the mattress.

"Sissy, why is he here, doing this to us? I'm so confused."

"I don't know." How in the world is he involved with this? Sweet Tyler, who played Frisbee on the beach with us and showed Teeny how to catch sand crabs.

I think hard about each moment we were together, dissecting them so I can make sense of him being here.

Like the afternoon we were hanging out at our apartment and he wanted to watch the Arizona Cardinals game. Said he had always been a big fan of theirs. Kept asking me if I liked them. I thought it was fate at the time. How awesome that his favorite team was from my home state. Of course, I played dumb, I wasn't supposed to be from Arizona, but it was something that drew me closer to him.

Was he playing me? Trying to get me to slip up?

Teeny leans back and pulls the top sheet from the mattress so she can mop up her face. "Do you think he knew Thomas back in Florida?"

I shrug. "I don't know."

Now that I've had time to think, I'm mad at myself for not demanding some sort of explanation when Tyler was here.

Florida.

It was the last somewhat happy placement.

Agent Hammond was the one to relocate us to Florida.

Everything started falling apart once we left Florida.

"Teeny, can I borrow one of the puzzle books?"

She picks the one off the top and hands it to me. I always do better with a list, so it's time to figure this out.

I scratch out the things I know for sure on the back inside cover:

1. *An assassin named Mateo is after all of us.*
2. *Tyler is a piece-of-shit fraud.*
3. *Agent Williams's grandson is being held hostage, too.*
4. *I don't know where Ethan is or if he's okay.*
5. *We're in New Orleans but don't know who to trust if we make it out of this building.*
6. *Agent Hammond is the mole.*
7. *My only weapon is a plunger.*

That's it. I stare at it for a long time but can't add anything else to it. The light fades from the room and Teeny falls asleep much earlier than usual, probably exhausted from all the crying.

The lock turns, the door slowly opening, and I gear up for a confrontation with Tyler. I need to keep my cool and try to get some answers. But it's not Tyler. It's Thomas and he's not in the priest clothes this time. He's dressed as a cop: badge, gun, and all.

Oh, crap. If I ever thought the local cops could help—I don't now. Does he know Tyler's been outed?

"Get up."

I scoot back. "Why?"

"You want to see your boyfriend?"

I jump up from the mattress and race to the door. "Yes." I glance back at Teeny. She's still asleep.

"I know you better than you think. You're doing any and every little thing you can to find a way out of here. So let me give you a little reality check. If you find a way to contact the police, I will know. If you find a way to contact your father, I will know. Do not underestimate my power. I am everywhere, even the places you would never think to look."

My hands form fists the moment he mentions Dad. Is he that powerful or just a full-blown egomaniac?

Get him talking. Do not blindly do what he asks.

"How do I know you're not bluffing?"

His cold facade breaks and he looks pissed. For a second, I'm afraid he's going to hit me or something by the look on his face.

But instead he whispers, "Currently, your father and the

Landrys are still in Arkansas and are debating whether or not to defy me and leave the island. Mrs. Landry hasn't stopped crying since the three of you left."

I can't speak. And I can't imagine what it's like for Dad and the Landrys.

"I can tell by your expression that you believe me now."

Thomas steps aside so I can pass through the door before he shuts and locks it again. I say a quick prayer Teeny won't wake while I'm gone. I'm surprised when we head to a door across the hall rather than down it. Ethan's window isn't as close as I thought it was.

Thomas pulls a set of keys from his pocket and I stare at the patches on the uniform. City of New Orleans. The key ring is full, maybe thirty keys in all, but it takes him no time to find the right one.

The door opens and Ethan is tied to a chair in the center of the room.

I run to him, throwing my arms around him. He can't move but he burrows his head into my neck.

"Are you and Teeny okay?" He whispers in my ear.

I nod, unable to talk.

Ethan pulls back to look at me. "Your cheek looks terrible."

I let out a desperate laugh. "You don't look that much better. Weren't you the one who said to stay out of trouble?" He's got a black eye and a busted lip.

"Yeah, I'm having a little trouble taking my own advice."

His room is similar to ours—single mattress on the floor with the same white sheets. No card table of snacks though, just a small ice chest and the same little light fixture on the wall. And a bucket. He does have the same shuttered window with the same little brass padlock, but his room would look out to the back of the building.

"Why is he tied up like this?" I scream at Thomas.

He ignores my question. "Anna, kneel down beside him so your face is close to his."

This is such an odd request, I drop to my knees without thinking what he's asking. Ethan looks nervous and begins to fidget in his bindings.

Tyler steps in the room—mask back on—and hands Thomas a rolled-up newspaper and a camera.

Thomas says something to him in Spanish, then Tyler turns to leave the room without looking at me once.

Thomas hands me the paper and says, "Hold this in front of you."

I look down and it's the front page of the *Times-Picayune* with what I'm assuming is today's date. I hold it up and look at Ethan. I don't like the expression on his face.

"Anna, don't do it. Move away from me right now."

I don't understand. I scoot back, mainly because of the crazed look on Ethan's face, but Thomas stops me when he says, "Don't make me involve Elena in this."

I move back in and hold the paper up, just as he requested.

"Look right here."

I turn toward Thomas and blink at the flash from the camera.

"You son of a bitch, you're sending evidence you have us and telling them where we are," Ethan yells, then tries to get out of the chair but all he does is fall over sideways.

Oh my God, oh my God, Oh my God . . .

"Señor Vega required proof and I'm happy to oblige."

I try to pick Ethan up or untie him or something. This shouldn't be a shock—Thomas said he was using us as bait—but this makes it so real. Mateo will know where we are. He will come to New Orleans to kill us.

Thomas grabs my arm and starts pulling while I hold on to Ethan for dear life.

I whisper in his ear, "We're across the hall. Masked guy is someone I knew from Florida." I turn to Thomas and beg, "Please let him stay with Teeny and me. I swear we won't cause any trouble."

"No," he answers.

I kick Thomas away, hitting him on the side of the knee and he goes down. I dig in closer to Ethan again and whisper, "I got to the roof, it's steep. Don't know what to do."

Thomas gets up, grabs me by the shoulders and I feel a sharp prick on my shoulder.

"Ow!"

I stop moving. Thomas lets go and moves toward Ethan. It looks like Ethan's still screaming but I can't hear him. I can't hear anything. Vader leans over Ethan but everything gets blurry. Stars dance in front of my eyes and my tongue gets thick.

And then it all fades away.

My eyes pop open and I'm back in my room, in the bed with Teeny, who's sleeping next to me.

Did I see Ethan? Or did I dream that? I don't remember leaving Ethan's room. Or getting in this bed. My hand goes to the back of my shoulder, finding the tender part immediately.

He drugged me again.

The room is dark but there is a soft pink light filtering in through the crack in the shutters. I can't figure how long I've been out this time. I want to wake Teeny up and ask her how much time has passed, but I don't. I'm scared to know. Crawling out of the bed, I start pacing the room. We have to get out of here. Out of New Orleans. That may not be the best solution, but it's better than staying here, a pawn in this sick game between two assassins.

I really hope I haven't lost too much time. I pinch off a chunk of bread from the loaf, praying it will settle my stomach. Whatever Thomas gave me has left me feeling hungover.

And then it dawns on me: I forgot to tell Ethan about Noah.

Teeny finally starts moving.

"Teeny, how long was I gone?"

"Huh? Gone? Where'd ya go?" she asks, and then stretches back, arching her back off the mattress.

She was asleep when I left to see Ethan. Does this mean I left and came back before she ever woke up?

I tell Teeny I saw Ethan but I don't mention the newspaper or the camera or blacking out. Mainly because I'm freaked out over the whole thing.

An entire day goes by without a visit from Thomas or Tyler. It's the longest day of my life.

When the light starts fading from the room, I wait patiently for Teeny to fall asleep. The second her breathing changes and I know she's out, I throw open the shutters. It's quiet again but there's traffic on the street. It's still early, darkness hasn't completely taken over yet. I hear the clip-clop of the horse hooves again, and this time the carriage is headed in my direction. It's a long carriage, holding maybe ten people. The driver is turned to the side and seems to be giving some sort of tour. The closer he gets, the easier it is to make out his words.

I need to time this perfectly. I have no doubt things will be bad for us on our own, but I feel certain that once Mateo gets to town, things will not end well for us.

And as sure as I am it will be bad for us to stay, I'm equally scared to death to leave. Even if we're rescued, there's still the contract on us. We'll be out in the open. Agent Williams's part in this will likely rip the entire program apart. There's still Agent Hammond to consider as well. I sink back in the window and fight down the bile that crawls up my throat. What would Ethan do? Yell at the top of his lungs for help? Figure something else out? I'm completely torn.

I hide out of sight, but keep the shutters open so I can hear when the guide gets close. I don't want to scream for help until I'm sure he can hear me. It would suck if I started yelling and Thomas heard me first.

The carriage driver stops right in front of our building and turns to his passengers. He's talking to them through a microphone attached to a speaker and his scratchy, amplified voice echoes through the street.

"And here we are at the Old Ursuline Convent. Today, it's a museum run by the priests over at the cathedral. It's the oldest building in the French Quarter, completed in 1750, and the only building left after the great fire."

I have to try something or I may regret losing the only opportunity I get to save us. Hanging the top half of my body out of the window, I wave my arms back and forth. The driver has his back to me and the people in the carriage don't seem to notice my movements.

The driver keeps talking, his booming voice filling the empty night air. "After the fire, the Spanish ruled this area for a short time and rebuilt everything in the Spanish style, which is why Ursuline is the only building in the French Quarter with French architecture. But it was the residents of Ursuline who are the most interesting thing about this convent—and I'm not talking about the nuns. I'm talking about the Casket Girls."

I can hear some faint mumblings of the passengers but for the most part, he's got their full attention.

Just as he's about to explain what or who the "Casket Girls" are, another carriage turns onto the street from the opposite direction. But this carriage is partying. It's as full as the other one, but the riders seem young, college age or just older, and they are having a *very* good time. Instead of the driver giving a tour, he's playing music over his speaker, a loud, thumping mix. The carriage shakes as the girls dance in their seats and one even uses the pole that holds up the canopy as a . . . pole to dance on. It's amazing the whole thing hasn't tipped over.

I just need one person to see me.

Camera flashes pop and I'm still waving my hands around like a lunatic. The talking tour guide starts yelling at the music tour guide. They pass each other almost right in front of my window.

Nothing.

No one sees me.

Dumb tourists.

The room gets darker and the quiet cool night air fills our room as I settle in for the next carriage to come our way.

Chapter 18

NEW RULE BY ANNA BOYD:

Keeping secrets usually makes everything worse—not better.

I dreamed about Tyler last night. I was back in Florida with my long blond hair and still somewhat carefree attitude. Like Witness Protection wouldn't last forever and somehow I'd have my perfect life back. It was really more like a memory than a dream. We were on the beach, hanging out with a few friends and it was nice.

There was a street fair going on and he pulled me in the photo booth that was set up on the sidewalk. We smiled at the camera and then he kissed me for the first time.

Later that day he was teasing me, asking me about old boy-friends . . . wanted to know if there was any boy back home that I still had a crush on . . . now that I was his girl. And I got so nervous when I thought about Brandon. Now I understand why.

The truth about his murder was locked in the deep recesses of my brain, but I still wasn't ready to let it free.

And again, I think Tyler was trying to get something out of me and I was totally blind.

My stomach is in knots trying to understand how the guy I knew then could be wrapped up in something as sick as this. Was he in it from the beginning? Or was he brought in after the fact? The first time I ever saw Tyler was just after we moved to Naples and I was still beating myself up over screwing up our last placement with my drunken escapade on Facebook.

Mom was still under control and Teeny hadn't completely closed off. Looking back, we were in that sweet spot right before the storm. We had hope. After leaving Florida, it was a disaster. But there, with our apartment a mere two blocks from the beach, life wasn't completely horrible.

Tyler was on the beach, just sitting in the sand. He asked if I wanted to throw a Frisbee around, said he'd been ditched by his friends. He was so cute, I couldn't resist. And for the next several nights, he was just sort of there. It wasn't long before the two of us were making plans and spending a lot of time together.

Until we got hauled out of that placement.

My last day in Naples was the best and worst. The best because I felt like Tyler and I had really connected in the sweeping warm waters of the Gulf and the worst because it's the day it was all ripped away. The suits busted through our apartment door, and within twenty minutes there was no sign that we had ever lived there. I left that placement dressed like Sandy from *Grease*—supertight black pants and all—waiting for Tyler, who was supposed to be dressed as Danny, to pick me up for a Halloween costume party.

I spent the next two placements, short as they were, being a total bitch to any boy who approached me. It wasn't worth the feelings of guilt that swamped you after deserting someone who cared about you.

And then I met Ethan. And he got under my skin in a way that no one else ever had, including Tyler. And as much as I tried, I couldn't scare him off. He called bullshit on my bullshit. And now he's in this mess because of me and for whatever reason, Tyler has something to do with that.

"Sissy, do you think Francesca and Henry finally found each other?" She doesn't wait for me to answer, just keeps talking. "I think they did. Maybe he found out she got on the wrong boat and he came here to get her. How cool would it be if he just showed up here one day and rescued her!"

I start to worry that maybe the letters are becoming too important to her. But then if she's going to obsess over something, I'd rather it be them than Thomas and Tyler.

"Francesca says it was miserable being here during the summer. Like it was really hot and there were huge bugs and people got sick all the time just from their bites." Teeny scans the newest letter she was able to free from the envelope. "I guess they didn't have any air-conditioning back then."

I crawl across the room, exhausted, since I fell asleep leaning against the wall, waiting for another carriage to come by.

"What's it say?" I ask.

Teeny hands me the yellowed paper and my eyes try to focus on the tiny script. God, how did she write this small and neat?

And sure enough, she goes into great detail about the summer heat and how other girls who had come from France with her weren't handling the conditions here well and were getting very ill. I drop the letter and look to the ceiling. There wasn't air-conditioning back then, but there is now. So there has to be a vent, right? Maybe that's how we can get out of this room!

But all I see are rough wooden beams and plaster.

Running to our small bathroom, I flip the light and see a small grate in the corner, painted the same color as the ceiling. It's not very big but I might be able to squeeze through it. I never noticed it there. Judging by the walls, the bathroom was a later addition to this room and this space was probably part of the bigger room at one point. I can barely reach the grate.

Teeny follows me back into the bathroom once I've gotten the wooden plunger and watches from the opposite corner.

"Where'd you get that?" she asks.

"From the other bathroom with the shower."

I jab the grate until one corner pops out. Continuing around the edges, the entire thing breaks free. One more jab and the grate falls to the floor.

I'm so excited it's hard to breathe. "I'm going up."

"What?" Teeny squeals.

I put one foot on the sink and use it to push myself in the air, grabbing the edges of the opening. There's a white air duct fitted to the hole, but when I touch it it feels like fabric, and I unhook it from the opening, pushing it aside.

"Teeny, push my feet up."

With the extra help, I'm able to pull myself inside the hole and get my elbows braced inside. It's dark up here and bigger than I thought it would be. I heave myself all the way in then turn and look down at Teeny. She's got her arms raised like she wants me to pull her up.

"You stay. I won't be long—just taking a look around."

She nods and I move away before that disappointed face makes me change my mind about leaving her.

The area is big enough for me to stand and only duck my head a little bit. It's dark and the only thing I can really see is the maze of white ducts worming their way through the space. I head directly across from my room, hoping to find Ethan. It's super dusty up here and I'm terrified about the little creatures that call this space home.

At the spot where the air duct dives into the floor, I move it to the side and peer in. Pure relief. There he is.

But something is wrong with him. He's lying on his side, curled in a ball. His shirt has inched up and his side is black and blue.

Oh God! What happened to him?

"Ethan," I whisper. I pull on the grate, trying to get it open but it won't budge.

He doesn't move.

"Ethan," I say a little louder.

His head lifts off the mattress and he looks around the room.

"Up here. In the ceiling."

He turns over, letting out an awful moan. It must be so painful to move. "Anna?"

"Yes. Up here. Look for a painted grate." I'm still pulling and pushing on it but it's stuck. I've never felt so desperate to touch him . . . to be near him.

By the time he's standing underneath me, I want to cry. Pain is etched across his face.

159

"What happened to you?"

He holds his side when he tries to reach the grate. He's not even close. He jumps up once and comes back down, collapsing on the mattress.

It takes a moment before he answers me. "That asshole in the mask. After Thomas drugged you, he turned on me and started kicking me. I was tied to that chair and couldn't even defend myself."

We have to get out of here. I scan the room and there's nothing for him to stand on.

"How'd you get up there?"

"Mine was in our bathroom. I stood on the sink and pushed myself up."

"How'd you get yours open?"

"I have a wooden plunger that I poked it with until it popped off."

Ethan eyes the grate from the mattress. "I'm not sure I'd fit through there even if it was open and I could get to it."

"How long did they keep you tied up?"

"I woke up untied. Thomas drugged me once the other dude finished beating the shit out of me. I don't think I've been awake long. Everything is sort of running together."

Things are so much worse for Ethan and I'm sure Tyler is the reason.

"The roof is really steep. I got outside but couldn't get anywhere. We're in the French Quarter and I think this building is an old convent that's now a museum. I saw two different carriages full of tourists last night. I waved at them but they didn't see me. We're pretty far from the street."

"Well, at least we're not too far from home. That sucks no one saw you."

"Yeah, but if it's a regular tour, they'll be back tonight. I'm really torn about taking a chance on our own or trusting Thomas not to kill us. But after seeing you like this, we can't stay here."

He runs his hands across his face. "I've been thinking the same thing. We've got to figure out where we go if we get out of here. Who do we trust?"

I shrug. "I don't know. Thomas told me yesterday that if we called the cops he would know and if we called our dads he would know. Told me my dad and your family is debating whether or not to defy him and leave the island. Do you think we'd be better off staying here?"

Ethan closes his eyes and it's so hard to see him like this. "I don't know, Anna. I might have said yes until he killed Agent Parker. My gut says to scream until you're hoarse at anything and everything that passes by your window. Don't even wait for it to be dark. But the thought of someone out there hunting you down makes me want to kill someone. Maybe if we could get out of here and get in touch with Agent Williams . . ."

"Oh my God, I totally forgot to tell you! Agent Williams's grandson is in the room next to us."

"What?" Ethan sits up quickly then groans, grabbing his side again. "What the hell is going on? Do you think he was blackmailed into giving us up? Does the grandson know anything about any of this?" Ethan asks.

"His name is Noah, and, no, he doesn't. He's young, just a year older than Teeny, and pretty terrified. He got here about two days before us. And if it was blackmail, why's he still here?"

Ethan moves slowly to the edge of the mattress and rolls to a sitting position. "So who's the guy with Thomas? You said it was someone you knew from Florida. What's he got to do with this?"

Ethan doesn't know about Tyler. I just didn't see the point in talking about him. Now, it seems like a pretty bad idea to tell him he's an old boyfriend, especially since he seems to be taking out his hurt feelings on Ethan.

"Just a guy I knew. I haven't talked to him since I yanked that mask off, so I don't know why he's here."

He has a funny grin. "You yanked his mask off?"

"Yeah. I couldn't quit thinking his voice was familiar and it was making me nuts. So I grabbed it when he got close enough."

"How old is he? He doesn't seem that old."

I shrug, then realize he probably can't see that. "Not sure. Not much older than us."

"Did he go to your school?"

Ethan knows I'm hiding something, and I swore I'd never lie to him again. But I can hear that tone in his voice. It won't help if he knows we used to date. No telling what Ethan will say to him. Thomas doesn't need a reason to decide Ethan is too much trouble to keep around, and he can't handle another beating.

"No, just someone who hung out at the beach near our apartment."

He picks up an empty water bottle and throws it across the room. "I knew he knew you. He's baiting me. Drops little comments about you every time he walks in the room. And then when he was kicking me, it felt personal." He looks up at the grate. "Be careful around him. I think he's got a thing for you. He's psycho."

Yeah, I definitely don't need to tell him we dated.

"Ethan, don't fight with him and give Thomas a reason to get rid of you. He's not worth it."

Ethan stares at the ground for a few minutes before looking back up. "How's Teeny?"

"She's okay. She broke down yesterday but I think that's good. She doesn't need to hold it all in."

Ethan nods and asks, "How about you? You okay?"

My throat gets tight and it takes a few seconds to answer. "Yeah. Definitely better than you." My voice sounds all funny.

"I'll survive." And then he smiles. "I was thinking about that hammock and how I wish more than anything we were back there. I miss kissing you."

I get warm all over and that desperate, crazy feeling rushes through me.

"Me, too. Maybe we can go back there when this is all over. Just the two of us."

"It's a date."

I hate having to talk to him like this. If I could be near him or touch him, I would feel so much better, but I'm stuck in the ceiling and he's stuck in his room.

"You've figured out where we are and who the masked guy is, opened your shutters, discovered Agent Williams's grandson next door, and found out how to escape your room. I'm just lying around over here."

A giggle escapes and it feels good to have something to laugh at. "I took what you said to heart. It's the only thing keeping me going," I finish in a whisper. "I've had some help. We found some girl's letters from like two hundred years ago. She helped us figure out where we are and about this attic space up here."

Ethan falls back on the mattress again. "Anna, I don't want you to stay up there too long. You never know when they're gonna pop in the room. If you can, come back tonight and bring the plunger."

"I will." I hesitate before crawling away, but he's right. I reattach the air duct and move away from his room. On my way back, I can't help but check out a few more grates.

What's in the room next to Ethan? It takes a few minutes before I can remove the air duct since I'm trying so hard to be quiet. It's darker in this room but all I can make out are filing cabinets. Lots of them.

I follow the big white worm to the next room. My clothes are completely covered in filth and dirt at this point, but I'll worry about that later. Muffled voices filter through the white fabric so I remove just one corner of the duct. It's the room with the shower. And there is Thomas, sitting at the desk shuffling through some papers. He's dressed as a priest again and has an open bottle of bourbon next to him. He doesn't bother with a glass, just takes a shot straight from the bottle.

I watch for a few minutes. He shuffles papers and curses, over and over.

Things don't seem to be working out for Father Thomas.

Glancing around the room, I spot Tyler kicked back on the bed, looking at a device, maybe a phone. He seems completely at ease with Thomas, and my blood boils.

"Is Hammond in town yet?" Tyler asks in English. Do they only speak Spanish in front of us because they know we won't understand them?

"No," Thomas answers. "But I don't need him here until tomorrow." He stops shuffling papers and turns to look at Tyler.

"I'll be at the other location tonight so you'll need to handle things around here."

Other location?

Thomas turns away from Tyler just as Tyler whispers, "I think Anna is on to me."

Tyler stops digging through the papers and looks back at Tyler. "And why would you think that?"

Tyler shrugs. Obviously I'm more than a little on to him. He must be feeling Thomas out to see how bad it will be if he finds out that I know who he is. I definitely have a little something to hold over him now.

"Does she seem like she's up to something?" Thomas asks. "I mean, other than that ridiculous banging around she's doing?"

He knows. And he doesn't care?

Tyler moves to the desk, perching on the corner and plays with a small figurine. "I haven't been in there today."

Thomas leans back in his chair. "Well, maybe you should go check."

Oh, no!

I scramble back to my hole. Tyler will beat me there if he leaves Thomas's room immediately and I look like I've been rolling around in the dirt.

Shit. Shit. Shit.

I stick my head in the hole and Teeny's sitting on the bathroom floor, tears streaked down her face.

"You're back!"

She jumps up and holds her arms out like she's going to catch me.

"Teeny, Tyler's about to open our door. Go out there and stall him. I have to clean up before he sees me."

She shakes her head, fast. "I don't want to see him."

I drop my legs through the hole, holding myself up on my elbows. "You have to. I'll be just a minute or two behind you. And shut the door. Tell him I'm using the bathroom."

Teeny backs out of the room and pulls the door shut. I drop down and cringe when the vibrations shoot up my legs. There's no way to get the grate back up there or the air duct attached, so I just hope they don't come in the bathroom and look up.

At the sink, I scrub my hands, arms, and face. My T-shirt is a wreck. I pull it off and turn it inside out. The dirt blends into the black yoga pants so I'm okay there.

I leave the bathroom and Tyler's near the door, the mask back on.

"What's in your hair?" he asks.

My hands fly to my head and a layer of dust drizzles down around me. Not good.

"Nothing. We need to talk."

The door is still open and Tyler peeks down the hall.

He seems torn. His attitude toward me has been hostile, which I don't get. What did I do to him to make him so resentful?

I've got to try to understand what's going on and what part he's playing in this. And as Pearl always says, you get more bees with honey than you do with vinegar.

"Tyler, please talk to me."

He turns back to me, pulling the mask off, and shuts the door.

Teeny folds her arms in front of her and stands firmly in front of him. I love that even though she's scared right now, you wouldn't know it by looking at her.

"I don't think there's anything to say."

"Please tell me what's going on?" I ask.

He shakes his head and presses his lips together.

"Can you tell me why you have stitches?"

His fingertips go to the side of his face. "That's compliments of your boyfriend and a jagged piece of glass in the back of the van. He cut me through the mask."

And now he's taking his revenge on Ethan.

"Did you have to go to the hospital?" Teeny asks. She's terrified of needles and doctors and hospitals.

"No, Thomas stitched me up."

My jaw drops. "Thomas?"

"He's not all bad. There are some very good things about him."

"Can you tell me how you got mixed up with this?"

"No."

I inch toward him and I feel Teeny try to pull me back. "How about I tell him I know who you are. Will he like that?"

Tyler's eyes get big and he takes a deep breath. I've made him mad. "You have no idea who you're dealing with or what he's risking by saving you like this."

I'm momentarily speechless. What he's risking . . . this is the last thing I thought he would say. "What are you talking about? He's a killer! And a kidnapper! And you're helping him."

Tyler looks straight at me. "I will not talk about him with you."

"Okay, did you know who I really was when we were in Florida?"

A short pause, then he answers, "Yes."

That answer is like a knife to the gut.

"Were you supposed to hang out with me? Was it like your job?"

Tyler's head tilts to the side and I can tell he doesn't want to answer me.

I can't stop now that I've started. "So everything between us was fake. You acted like you cared about me, but you were just doing a job. For a killer."

His expression hardens. "It wasn't like that. I was glad we met. I was glad we were together. It meant something to me. Obviously more than it did to you."

I feel myself getting angry but I hold it in. I need answers, and kicking him in the balls won't get them for me.

"Were you supposed to be nice to me, too?" Teeny asks.

The lines from Tyler's forehead loosen and he actually smiles at Teeny. "I wanted to be nice to you. You're a cool kid."

Teeny rolls her eyes and mutters "Whatever" under her breath.

"Did you know I'd be leaving Naples that night of the party?" I ask.

"Yes. That was part of the plan."

I blink a few times. Plan? Whose plan . . . Thomas's? "Finish. Tell me what plan."

"No."

I clench my jaw and try very hard to keep my cool.

"If you don't tell me, not only will I tell Thomas I know who you are, but that you told me everything."

Tyler throws the mask on the floor, frustrated. "Thomas didn't believe you lost your memory that night Price and his son were killed. And Sanchez told him you said you knew where the ledgers were. He thought the memory thing was just a hoax. He needed the ledgers and you were the only person who knew where they were. He thought if you met someone—someone you cared about—that you'd confide in them."

Just a mention of that night starts to throw me into a panic, but I push it back. I can't fall apart right now.

"And you were supposed to be that person?" My voice is controlled. I'm hanging on to my anger by a very thin string right now.

He ignores my question. "But you weren't talking."

I throw my hands up and pace around the small room, Teeny following my every step. "Because the memory loss was real, you asshole."

He won't look at me but at least he keeps talking. "He decided on a different tactic. You and I were getting close." Tyler looks up, his expression pained. "My feelings for you were real."

He waits for me to say something, anything, but I don't trust myself to speak.

"If he forced a relocation, we thought you'd confide in me. Refuse to leave and tell me what was happening to your family. Tell me what you knew."

I drop down to the mattress. "This is why you kept telling me that day you'd be at that restaurant, HB's, right until you picked me up for our date. You wanted me to be able to find you."

"But you never came." He won't look at me, but keeps going, "Even after you left, I thought the plan would still work." He pulls a cell phone out of his pocket and holds it up. "I still have the same number. Just in case you decided to call."

My mouth drops open. "Why on earth would you think that plan would work? This doesn't even make sense."

His head cocks to the side, pissed. "You did exactly what Thomas wanted you to do, Anna. I just wasn't the guy you trusted."

Chapter 19

NEW RULE BY ANNA BOYD:

Conflict can't always be avoided, so be prepared for the worst. Or as Pearl likes to say, "If you're up shit creek without a paddle—don't think your hands ain't gonna get dirty."

THE room is silent. Even Teeny seems frozen beside me. Part of me is furious with him. Really, beyond furious, but then there is a small, very small, part of me that feels like I'm supposed to apologize to him for not liking him as much as I like Ethan. Because he's right. I told Ethan everything and even fled town looking for a way out of this rather than leave him behind.

So this is why he's so angry and taking shots at Ethan. He's jealous I picked Ethan.

And then I remember a conversation Thomas and I had in the laundry room back in Natchitoches. It was just after my memory returned and I had called him to talk about my options. He asked me if this sudden change in my behavior had anything to do with a boy.

I haven't given Thomas nearly enough credit.

Tyler stands up quickly and pulls the mask back on. "That's all I can tell you. He'd kill me if he knew I'd told you this much."

Somehow I don't think Tyler's "kill me" is as big of a threat as the "kill me" vibe I get from Thomas.

He leaves the room, locking it behind him.

I drop back against the mattress and stare at the ceiling, trying to work everything out in my mind.

Teeny's at the wall talking to Noah and I jump when she's starts yelling.

"Stop!" Teeny screams. "Where are you taking him?"

I rush to the wall and look through the hole—Thomas is pulling Noah out of the room.

Oh no, oh no, oh no . . .

"What's happening?" I ask Teeny.

"I don't know! I was talking to Noah and the next thing I know, Noah's face is gone and Thomas's fills the hole. Then Thomas started dragging Noah out of the room," she finishes in a cry.

They're already gone by the time I look through the hole again. Teeny hugs me and I hug her back just as tight.

"Wha . . . wha . . . what does that mean? Do you think he will . . . will . . . hurt him?" Teeny stutters out.

My stomach drops. "I hope not, Teeny."

"I want to go home. I want to see Dad. And Mom. And even Ethan's parents. Mrs. Landry's probably going nuts." Teeny moves away from me and hits the mattress, soft at first and then much harder. "I hate Thomas. And Tyler. And can you believe Tyler was lying to you back then? I mean, everything he said about who he was—it was fake. I really liked him. If Thomas forced us to move from Florida, did he force us to move all those other times?" She falls back on the mattress. "We were like puppets."

I have no answers for her and hearing Teeny voice all the same concerns I have is my undoing. I've tried to shut out thoughts of my parents, and Ethan's parents, knowing they're going out of their minds with worry. But I can't anymore. And now this news from Tyler. We're still puppets.

The people around me are dropping like flies—first, Agent Parker killed and now Noah taken away. There will be no way for the carriage full of people to miss me tonight. Thomas said he was going to be gone tonight when I was eavesdropping in the grate, and even though I think Tyler is nuts, I don't think he'll hurt me.

Once it's dark, I'm going to throw that window open and yell at any person I see. I don't trust the police but I don't think they will do anything bad to me on the spot. I'm also worried about Dad and the Landrys, but I know they would want us to escape if we had a chance. If I can get us out of this building, then maybe we can sneak away. It's a risk, but I don't have any other options.

When I inch open the shutter, I'm shocked. There are three carriages, all full of people, parked on the street in front of the convent. And probably another ten people milling around on the sidewalk. It's not a huge crowd but definitely more than I've seen the past few nights. In unison, every person picks up a camera and flashes pop like I'm the Duchess of Cambridge.

The door bursts open and Tyler, unmasked, fills the doorway. "What the hell did you do?"

I slam the shutter closed.

"What?" I go for the really confused, innocent face.

He stomps to the window and examines the shutters.

"You've screwed up so bad. I have to fix this. He'll flip out when he gets back and sees what's outside!"

I'm not sure he's actually talking to me, more muttering to himself, but he's scared. His eyes dart around the room and he's rocking back and forth. I've never seen him like this and it's freaking me out.

"You just had to stay here, tucked away until it was all over. That was it. That was the plan. This is bad. So bad."

He pulls a cell phone from his back pocket and shows me the screen. It's a dark, grainy picture.

"What is that?"

"It's this building. And that," he points to a whitish blob in the top of the image, "is you."

There is no way anyone could make out the details of my face because it's dark and too far away. Hell, you can barely tell there's a person in that picture.

"You can't tell that's me! That could be anyone!"

"But the crowd is here because of that picture. You can't stay here now. He's here." He taps the screen of his phone a few times before continuing, "Mateo is here."

What! "I don't understand? Why would Mateo be here?"

Tyler looks away from his phone. "Because Thomas was reeling him in slowly. We sent another message yesterday that brought him to the Quarter and the Quarter isn't that big. He's been wandering around the area all day. I don't know if he's just hanging around to see what the crowd is doing or if he thinks this has something to do with us. Either way, he's right outside and you just stuck your head out of the damn window."

My mouth is dry and it's hard to squeak my question out. "But why is everyone here? I don't understand."

"The crazies saw that picture and now they want more. They think this place is haunted, like the stupid tour guides say." He paces around the room and yells, "Son of a bitch!" And then his eyes fly to mine. "I can't get Thomas on the phone. You can't stay here. I can't handle it if Mateo finds a way inside." He grabs the phone and the keys and stops before he leaves the room. "Grab your stuff! We're leaving."

Teeny and I scramble around the room, grabbing not only our shoes but our jackets and other belongings we've accumulated. This is not our first grab and go. I'm not sure if I'm scared because Mateo is outside or because Tyler is freaking out.

We get to the door and I sneak a peek down the hall. I expect to find the assassin creeping toward us, but all I see is Tyler running down the hall.

"Wait! What about Ethan?"

He stops. He's obviously fine with leaving him behind but I'm not.

"I won't leave without him," I say.

Tyler comes back and begrudgingly opens Ethan's door.

Ethan's on the mattress, right where I left him earlier, but gets up as quickly as he can when he sees Teeny and me.

I run in his room and resist tackle-hugging him. "Hurry, Ethan. We've gotta get out of here!"

When I turn around, Tyler has a knife to Teeny's neck. "Don't try anything. We're just going a couple of blocks to another location."

Ethan moves closer to Tyler. Tyler's eyes get big and I tug on Ethan's arm until he's back by my side. I would bet everything I had that Tyler wouldn't harm Teeny, but that's still not enough to take the risk.

"Let her go," Ethan growls. "Now."

Teeny's eyes are frantic as they dart between me and Ethan.

"It's okay, Teeny. Just stand really still," I say to her in a low voice.

"Mateo's here. He's outside," Tyler says.

With my hand still on Ethan's arm, I can feel how tense he is. "I don't believe you."

"He's out there. Standing with the crowd looking at the building. Mateo is here." It's obvious Tyler is legit scared out of his mind right now.

I feel like my knees are going to give out.

Ethan asks, "What does he look like?"

Tyler pulls Teeny back into the hall. "We're not opening that window again. You can see if he's still there when we get outside. He's in black pants and a jacket. Hands in his pocket. Black hat." Tyler swallows deep and continues, "Cross tattoos in a line around his neck. That's how I know it's him. He gets a new tattoo after every hit."

Thomas said Mateo burns a cross into his victims' chests. A cross for both of them.

"We've got to go!" Tyler yells and begins dragging Teeny down the hall.

It only takes a few seconds to get to the end.

We race down the stairs, and I stumble most of the way down. I'm terrified to find out what's waiting for us outside.

"What's happening?" Ethan asks as he grabs my arm to steady me. He's wincing with every step, yet still trying to hold me up.

"I don't know! There was a crowd outside my window tonight, but I have no idea why."

"Keep moving," Tyler says and we follow him down the hall on the first floor. The entire bottom floor looks like any other museum. Statues of religious people and paintings and even jewelry with the tiny little plaque next to it describing the who, what, when, and where litter every possible space.

We pass through a second set of doors and find ourselves in the middle of a very small but ornate church.

Tyler seems to have forgotten that he's supposed to be holding us captive. The knife is down by his side and he's racing ahead of us, dragging Teeny, not even looking back to see if we are following. I wonder, not for the first time, how he got involved with Thomas. He is completely inept at this and Thomas seems like someone who doesn't tolerate mistakes.

"This way," he calls over his shoulder.

He pushes the side door open, slowly. After he's satisfied Mateo isn't lurking outside the door, we follow him through. We empty out into a deserted side street and run in the opposite direction of the crowd. After zigzagging through some side streets, we all stop to catch our breath.

Tyler remembers a moment too late that he's dropped his guard.

"I don't think you know how to use that knife," Ethan says to

Tyler. He pulls Teeny away from him, then pins Tyler against an old brick wall behind a Dumpster. "You better start talking or I will kill you." And he is dead serious. In this moment, I think Ethan would do it.

And Tyler must think that too, because he wastes no time. He gives Ethan the quick and dirty version: he was set up to be my boyfriend in the hope I would confide in him what I knew.

"He pretended to be my friend, too," Teeny says.

Ethan throws me a glance over his shoulder. I feel the accusation there. I had a chance to tell him about Tyler—what he was to me, what we were to each other—and I lied. And it was the one thing I swore I'd never do again, especially to Ethan.

"Who is Daniel Sanders? His prints were on her journal."

Ethan has to loosen the grip on Tyler's neck before he can answer. He looks at me when he says, "I'm Daniel Sanders. I sent the flowers."

I gasp and even Ethan seems taken aback.

"And I tracked you down at that party so I could return your journal."

"I . . . don't . . . understand. . . . I asked you if Tyler was your real name!"

"My name is Daniel Tyler Sanders. Tyler is my real name and what my mom called me. I didn't lie to you," he answers.

"And the 'T' was for Tyler, and we all assumed it was for Thomas. You're the reason we're here!"

Ethan punches him in the face before I can process what's happening. And he keeps hitting him.

Blood squirts from Tyler's nose and he goes down into a

crouched position to protect his face and body. Ethan grabs him by the throat and lifts him up against the wall. "I ought to kill you."

I've never seen Ethan so angry.

Grabbing Ethan's arm, I try to pull him away from Tyler, but he won't budge.

"Don't do this, Ethan. Think about this. We need answers. Let's hear what else he has to say."

Finally, I break through the rage he's in and he lets go of Tyler, who slides down the wall. He's moaning and bleeding and I try to find an ounce of sympathy for him, but I can't.

Ethan squats down, getting in Tyler's face. "Tell me his plan or I will beat you until you're unconscious."

Tyler spits out a mouthful of blood on the ground next to me. "Just like what he said. Mateo is after us. He's using you as bait. He plans on killing him. He's going to kill the head of the cartel who ordered the hit, Vega. He's going to take over. I'll tell you everything you want to know. Just let me catch my breath."

"How does he plan on doing that?" I ask.

Tyler shrugs. "I don't know. He doesn't tell me everything."

Ethan, Teeny, and I stand there forever, all of us trying to absorb what Tyler said. And then I remember what Thomas said to me in the woods, *This is not about you, or really ever has been. You just found yourself in the middle of a very dangerous power struggle.*

Ethan moves back and Tyler inches back up until he's standing.

"Keep talking," Ethan says.

Tyler looks at me when he finally speaks. "I didn't know what was going on when he asked me to get close to you in Florida. I didn't know anything . . . about his profession. Once I figured it out,

I made him promise not to fulfill the contract. I never ask him for anything, but I asked for this."

I move in closer to Ethan. The night air is cool but I'm freezing inside. I keep thinking this is a horrible dream and I will soon wake up.

And then it dawns on me. Tyler is the person who made Thomas promise not to kill us. Tyler is the reason I'm alive right now.

"When he got back from Arizona, he gave me your journal. Said you obviously liked me more than we both thought you did based on what you'd written about me. He thought I would want to keep it, but I really wanted you to have it back. I could tell how important it was to you."

I feel sick.

"So I went to Natchitoches and followed you and waited for the right moment to give it back. But I didn't think it through. I didn't think you would tell the feds. When Thomas found out through his sources that they had the journal and were going to test it for prints, he knew they would find mine and he wanted to get the journal back before that. That's why he broke into your house. Finding me would lead to him."

"This is so screwed up," Teeny says and for a second I want to laugh. This *is* so screwed up.

Ethan still doesn't look convinced. "But how did his boss find out about all of this?"

"That agent put it through the system that there was an informant ready to flip and tell everything about Thomas. You don't get to be in Vega's position without having your own sources. He heard this and cut Thomas loose immediately and found a replacement. There is a line of guys waiting to take his spot."

"What are you doing with him to begin with? Why does he trust you?" I ask Tyler.

Tyler is quiet a moment before whispering, "I'm his brother."

Holy shit.

"Why did he bring us here, to New Orleans?" Ethan asks after he somewhat recovers.

"He keeps places all along the southern U.S. border. Gives him somewhere to regroup when he comes in and out of the country. This one just happened to be the closest one we could get to. It was the perfect hiding place," Tyler says. "In a quiet part of the Quarter. No one messed with it."

And this reminds me of the crowd outside. "Why are all these people here?" I ask.

Tyler lets out a nervous laugh. "They're here for you." Maybe he's just glad there's something wrong that he didn't cause.

"Me? All I did was open my window. I don't know why those people started taking pictures of me."

"All those carriages are from the same tour company. I checked their site when I saw people out there. Some woman on a haunted tour last night took a picture of Ursuline. After looking back at her pictures this afternoon, she noticed one of the images had a girl hanging out of a top-floor window of Ursuline, waving her arms around. She sent her picture and story to the haunted tour company and they posted the story and picture on their site. Told everyone to come back at dusk to see if there would be another 'sighting.'"

"And those people are here to see a girl hang her head out of a window?" Ethan asks.

Tyler rolls his eyes and says, "She stuck her head out and stirred up the rumor. Every other building in this area is supposedly haunted or has some dark rumor attached to it, but no one ever sees anything weird on those tours—until last night. There will be two beliefs floating around with the locals about that picture—it's fake or it's part of the three-hundred-year-old rumor associated with Ursuline."

"What rumor?" Ethan and I ask at the same time.

"The Casket Girls," Tyler answers. "For the last couple hundred years, one of the biggest superstitions in the Quarter is that the third floor of the Ursuline Convent is where the vampires live, and that tour company is going crazy with what they call 'proof.'"

"What?" we all ask at the same time.

Tyler shakes his head, "Not here. It's a long story and it's not safe standing around here with Mateo so close. Come with me. I can take you somewhere safe."

"We're leaving, just the three of us. You can sit here and piss yourself for all I care."

"You have no idea what you're up against," Tyler says.

"You're probably right, but at least we'll be in control of what happens to us." Ethan says. Then he knocks him out cold.

Chapter 20

NEW RULE BY ANNA BOYD:
Forget the backup plan—just make sure you have *a* plan. Even if it sucks.

THERE are people everywhere. By the time we stop running, we're several blocks away from the alley where we left Tyler hidden behind one of the Dumpsters. As much as I hate him right now, I don't want Mateo to find him. I take a quick look at the street sign—Toulouse and Dauphine—although that means absolutely nothing to me. We stand in the middle of the sidewalk and try to take it all in.

Ethan is still furious—with Tyler, with Thomas, and probably with me for not telling him the truth when I could have. And he's favoring his left side, so I'm guessing he's in a lot of pain, too.

Another wave of guilt washes over me for getting him involved with this.

"We need to keep moving," he bites out.

There is a huge group of girls heading toward us and they seem to be holding up this one girl in the middle. She's hammered drunk, stumbling with each step, and wearing a strapless black minidress and a wedding veil. And it's no regular veil—this one has condoms attached to it. Lots and lots of condoms.

"What kind of necklace is that girl wearing?" Teeny asks.

The group gets a little closer and I can make out a replica of a guy's private parts.

We push Teeny along and I walk behind her, trying to block her view of the roving bachelorette party behind us and totally ignore her question.

By the time we hit Bourbon Street, there's no hiding the craziness of the French Quarter from Teeny. Every other business is a strip club and some of the girls who work there, wearing very little, call to customers from open doorways. And if that wasn't enough, most of the windows to these businesses are papered with pictures of what goes on inside.

But the music is incredible. Every door has a different sound pouring out: jazz, rock, country, and blues. It's hard not to stop and stare and try to take it all in.

I hear little gasps from Teeny as her eyes soak up every single thing on this street—good and bad. We've slowed down to try to blend in with the crowd as they flow down the street.

So this is Bourbon Street.

"Ethan, what's the plan? Where're we going?"

"I don't know," he grits out through clenched teeth. "I'm looking for somewhere we can sit and figure this out."

The next block still has an abundance of strip clubs, but there are a few more bars and restaurants. Ethan ducks into an open doorway, Teeny and I right behind him. It's a small restaurant, really just a wide hallway with a bar on one side and a row of booths on the other.

The place looks like a dive but the smells are incredible. We pass trays of boiled crawfish with corn and potatoes and it's like swimming through a sea of seasonings.

We slide into the only empty booth in the back.

"What are we gonna do?" I ask. "We don't have any money."

Ethan looks at me for the first time and it breaks my heart. I can see the disappointment in his eyes. "I know. I know. I just need to sit for a minute and think," he answers back.

"Can we call Dad?" Teeny asks.

I take a deep breath and tell her about the video Thomas left behind.

Her eyes well up with tears but they don't spill over. I couldn't be more proud of how she's handling all of this.

An older woman walks up to the table and just looks at us, no greeting, nothing.

"We're waiting on some people. Can you give us a minute?" Ethan asks.

She glances at the bar. "A few minutes then you gotta order or get lost."

Teeny tugs on my sleeve and whispers, "Do you think they'll give us some water for free?"

"Can my little sister have a glass of water while we wait?" I ask the waitress.

Her mouth puckers and a million little lines form around her lips. "Y'all in trouble?"

We all shake our heads, probably a little too enthusiastically.

"No, trouble. We just need a minute and a glass of water. Please." Charm oozes from Ethan and just like that, the waitress is gone. Seconds later, she's balancing a tray with three waters and a basket with a hot loaf of buttered bread. I hope the drool running from my mouth isn't obvious.

"Thank you so much," Teeny says as she breaks off a huge chunk and shoves it in her mouth.

"That's on the house. But you got about five minutes before Sam notices you ain't ordered nothing. Better get moving 'fore then."

The bread is gone within seconds and the hunger I was only vaguely aware of earlier is screaming its presence now. Even with that huge amount of food in our room, I had no appetite while we were there.

"Do we have anything we can hock? We need money. We've got to get off the street," Ethan says.

I look at my hands; no watch, no rings, nothing.

Teeny's head drops a little as she digs something out of her front pocket. She opens her hand to show what's inside.

The pocket watch from the box in the wall.

I put my arm around her. "Will you be okay giving up the watch? Hopefully we can get enough for a room somewhere for tonight. Otherwise, we've got nowhere to go."

Teeny hands it to me and nods. "Yeah, it's fine. It doesn't work anyway."

From across the table, Ethan lifts it out of my hand to get a better look at it. "What's it made out of?"

I shrug. "Not sure. It's pretty tarnished. Probably silver."

"What the hell are we going to do?" Ethan asks, rubbing a hand over his face.

I shrug, feeling hopeless. "Thomas warned me if we called the cops, he would know. He was wearing that police uniform and I really believe him even though I'd love nothing more than to dial 911 right now."

"I don't think we can trust Agent Williams, either," Ethan says. "We still don't know exactly what reason Thomas had Noah."

Ethan's right. I've never felt so powerless.

I look at Ethan and say, "Maybe we can figure out somewhere to take Teeny. To get her away from this."

Teeny's head pops up. "If I can't be with Dad, I'm staying with you. I don't trust anybody else. And don't talk about me like I'm not sitting right here."

Ethan looks at me a moment, his expression weird. "Tell me everything you know about the brother."

"I met him when I was Avery Preston in Florida. We started hanging out, a little at first then more regularly."

"Is that a different way to say y'all were dating?" he asks.

"Are you mad?" I ask back.

He drops back against the booth hard enough to make the table vibrate. He's shaking his head before he starts talking. "Why would I be mad that you had a boyfriend *before* I ever met you? I'm mad you weren't straight with me the minute you found out he was under that mask. Why did you make it out like he was just some random guy you knew? It's not like this isn't a big deal, Anna."

He's right and I feel terrible. Worse than terrible.

"You were so hurt and frustrated when I got to your room. And look at how you reacted when you found out that we had dated! You nearly beat him to death. I didn't want to give Thomas any reason to get rid of you. I thought I was doing the right thing."

He spins his empty water glass on the table. "And to think it's his fault we're here. He was there, at the party. He knocked into our chair so hard you almost fell out." He looks up at me and asks, "You didn't see him there?"

I hold my hands up in front of me and say, "No! I swear. I didn't see him." I scoot out of the booth and then back in on his side. I move as close as I can to him and I'm relieved when he doesn't back away. My arms go around him but he doesn't hold me back.

I turn my head toward his ear and whisper, "And the reason I never mentioned him to you before is because he never entered my mind. I liked Tyler. At the time, it was nice to try to be a normal girl with a normal boyfriend. But I never loved him like I love you."

Ethan closes his eyes, tightly and says, "I just thought we were done with the lies. I understand you couldn't tell me everything while y'all were in the program, but we're past that now. We will not get through this if we can't trust each other."

"You can trust me." I can't lose him over this.

"We'll talk about this later. We need to find a place to stay for tonight."

On the way out, Ethan pulls the waitress aside and talks to her quickly, then he ushers us out of the restaurant.

"She said there's a pawnshop not far from here. Let's go."

We walk back the way we came, getting off Bourbon and heading down Orleans Street. It's still crowded but significantly less so.

Ethan pulls Teeny close. "Scan the crowd. Mateo won't stand

around Ursuline long. Look for the cross tattoos on his neck."

Ethan starts for a side street but Teeny grabs his arm, pulling him back. "Look what that guy's handing out!"

Both Ethan and I look in the direction she's pointing. There's a guy wearing a T-shirt with the same logo that was on the side of the carriage.

Teeny runs toward him before we can stop her.

She takes a flyer from a guy named Jimbo, according to his name tag, and it's the same picture Tyler showed me on his phone.

"Tours every hour. Ten bucks a head," Jimbo says.

"What is a Casket Girl?" Teeny asks.

We don't have time for this. I try to pull Teeny away but she won't budge.

Ethan leans in close and whispers to me, "If we're going to try to sell that watch, we should at least know something about it."

Jimbo's face lights up since it sounds like we may be interested in the tour. "They were orphan girls from France. Early on, this place was crawling with men. Not many girls, or at least the ones you'd want to take for a wife. Those girls got here and they had all their stuff in these little casket-shaped trunks. The nuns over at Ursuline locked 'em up tight, ya know, to preserve their virginal qualities."

He grins big. Obviously he enjoys retelling this story. "Pretty bad times for those poor girls. Most of them got sick on the way here—skin and bones they were, white as damn ghosts. Some even had a raging case of tuberculosis. Rumors started flying 'round pretty quick. It was the coughin' up blood that made people think they were vampires. Said they smuggled vampires into the Quarter in those trunks of theirs. Most of 'em died. It's said that the nuns locked those casket-shaped trunks in the third-floor attic and the upstairs windows were nailed shut with eight thousand screws blessed by the pope himself."

Then Jimbo laughs and leans in close. "And if you go on one of our tours, there's a real good chance you'll see one of them leaving through an open window."

Teeny is fully engrossed with his story and it's hard to pull her away. Jimbo calls after us, dropping the price of the tour but we ignore him.

The flashing pawnshop sign is half a block ahead and we pick up the pace. My mind races as my eyes dart from person to person. Every time I see a tattoo, my heart drops, but thankfully none of them are what Tyler described. We have wasted too much time out on the street.

Ethan walks inside and it's empty. It's not a big area, just a square-shaped space big enough for a handful of people and a counter on the back wall protected by iron bars and thick Plexiglas.

We walk to the small opening at the counter and Ethan presses the call button. A loud buzzer echoes through the room and a really short man appears on the other side of the bars. His head barely makes it over the counter and he's got one of those awful greasy comb-overs. And his teeth are disgusting, yellowed and broken around the edges. I feel dirty just looking at him.

"Whatcha got?"

Teeny takes forever but finally turns the pocket watch over to me. She may understand that she needs to give up the watch, but she really doesn't want to. I slide it through the metal tray to the other side.

He holds it up and inspects it closely then opens the latch and studies the inside.

"What's the story on this?" he asks. "Looks like crap, but it's old." He spins the knob on top. "It got a story?"

"It belonged to one of the Casket Girls," Ethan says.

He looks down at the watch again, like he's seeing it for the first time. "No shit. Can you prove it? If you can, it's worth a lot. If not, I'll give you ten bucks."

"Ten bucks," Ethan spits out. "Ten bucks?"

We have no proof of where we got it. And ten bucks isn't going to do anything for us.

"Have you seen any pictures of a girl hanging out of the third-floor window of Ursuline?" I ask.

"You mean that tour company that's saying they have proof of a sighting and flashing pictures around to anybody walking around the Quarter?"

"That's me! I'm the one in the picture!"

The man says, "Girlie, I don't think that picture is real. That's somebody getting a little crazy with the Photoshop. If that's all you got, my offer is ten bucks."

"Wait," Teeny says. She lifts up the edge of her sweatshirt and I see the packet of letters hidden there. Francesca's letters. "If we have proof of where it came from, how much can we get?"

The pawnbroker steps up onto something because he's grown at least a foot and leans toward the plastic barrier. "Whatcha got there?"

Teeny holds them up but away from the metal tray. "Letters between Francesca DuBois and a boy named Henry. The same

Henry written on the back of this picture." Teeny unties the ribbon from around her neck and holds it and the envelopes up in front of the thick window. "Francesca was a girl from France who lived on the third floor of Ursuline and she writes all about it here."

His eyes get huge. "Let me see 'em," he says.

Teeny shakes her head. "No. That girl in the picture is my sister. We have been in a room on the third floor of Ursuline for several days. You make me a deal first then you get them. You're not the only one who will give us money for this."

I'm in awe of her right now. Ethan is, too. I know how much she treasures that picture and the letters. The distraction of reading them is probably the only thing that got her through our captivity.

Teeny and the pawnbroker haggle back and forth, but he finally gives in to Teeny's demands. When a small stack of hundred dollar bills slide through the tray, I want to cry.

The pawnbroker scurries to some hidden back room with his newly acquired treasures before we finish pulling the bills from the tray.

We step out of the shop and I pull Teeny in close. "I'm sorry you had to give it all up. I know how much it meant to you."

She shrugs and says, "Francesca was trapped. She wouldn't have wanted us to be trapped, too. Do you think she died of that sickness he was talking about?

I hug her tighter. "No, I think Henry showed up and took her back to England. And they had ten kids and lived to be ninety-two."

She giggles.

Ethan shoves the money in his pocket and we're on the move again. "Okay, this is what we'll do. We'll grab a cheap room for the night where we can shower, sleep, and decide what to do next. At least we'll get off the street."

"Food. Let's get food, too," Teeny adds.

"Anything you want, since you saved the day."

Twenty minutes later, we've got a piping hot pizza, a bag full of touristy T-shirts and sweatpants, and we're making our way to our room.

Chapter 21

NEW RULE BY ANNA BOYD:

Make as many friends as you can. If you get in a bind and need help, at least
there will be someone willing to come when you call.

TEENY shuts the bathroom door and starts the water for a
shower. Ethan and I look anywhere but at each other. It's awkward.
And totally awful.

"Do you want to talk about it?" I ask.

He's pacing the room, taking bites of pizza. We let him shower
first since it would be his first since the island, and now he's pad-
ding around in a Saints T-shirt and sweatpants, with fat wet curls.
He looks adorable.

"I'm not sure I'm ready to talk about it. I'm still so pissed at
Tyler. And Thomas. It's making me insane." He throws me a look I
can't read. "Let's figure out what we're going to do and we'll figure
out the other . . . part later."

I swallow hard and try not to cry. "Okay, who do we call? No
police. No parents. What are you thinking?"

"I don't know. . . ."

"Do you think Thomas has someone in Arkansas, watching

them? How would he know what they're doing?" I ask as I use my fingers to brush through the tangles from my wet hair. "Definitely no local police. What do you think about calling the police from a different city? What about Sheriff Pippin?"

"I thought about him, but I'm afraid to call him. He's pretty tight with Agent Williams—what if he calls him even if we tell him not to? He would automatically believe that Agent Williams is a good guy and I'm not sure that's true."

I think about Agent Williams and his part in this. "I don't think he's a bad guy. I think whatever he did, if he did anything, was because Thomas had Noah."

"Still doesn't mean we want Sheriff Pippin calling him and telling him where we are."

I pull the comforter off the bed and throw it on the floor. Teeny and I saw a show on TV once that did a story on really disgusting things found on hotel bedding and I can't look at that faded paisley blanket without imagining what it looks like under one of those creepy lights. I climb on the bed and sit cross-legged on the scratchy sheets, but don't feel like these are any cleaner.

Ethan throws the pizza crust in the trash and continues the pacing. "What part do we think Agent Williams played in this? You said Thomas took Noah away; where do you think he took him? I don't think Agent Williams is on our side until he has his grandson back."

"Me, either."

"Are we sure Agent Hammond is the mole?"

"When I was crawling around the ceiling, I looked down into Thomas's room right after I left yours. Tyler was in there, too. Tyler asked Thomas if Hammond was down here yet and Thomas said no, but it was okay because he didn't need him until tomorrow."

Ethan comes and sits on the edge of the bed, far enough away from me as he could get and still be on the bed. "We need to get out of New Orleans. Quick. We can figure out what to do later, but I think the most important thing is to get as far away from here as possible."

"So how do we do that? And where do we go?"

And he's back up, wearing a path across the thin brown carpet from one wall to the other. "We can't go back to Natchitoches right now. We could go to Pearl's camp, but the suits know about that place. I could call Will. Or Ben. I doubt Thomas is watching them. I get that he's connected, but he can't have an unlimited supply of people helping him. They could come get us and I could get word to Fred about our parents stuck on that island. Ben's got family in Texas, an aunt I met a few years ago."

Fred is Ethan's aunt Pearl's boyfriend she doesn't think anyone knows about. And Will would come in a heartbeat, but the thought of Mateo harming him or Ben, just because of us, is frightening.

"You don't think someone will be watching them?" I ask. I mean, where does it end? Are they watching Catherine, too?

Ethan leans against the window, resting his forehead against the glass. "I have no idea, Anna." He sounds defeated.

I get off the bed and walk to where he is. I stand behind him, trying to decide if I'm brave enough to touch him. I hesitate a moment more then wrap my arms around him.

He tenses but doesn't pull away.

"Let's call Will. I hate this, too, but we're in over our heads. At least it will get us out of town and maybe we can go to the police in another town. Tell them everything."

"And then what? We'll still have that contract on us."

"We'll figure it out as we go." Resting my chin on his shoulder, I turn to kiss the side of his neck. "And I'm so sorry, Ethan. I really am. I should have told you everything I knew the second I had the chance."

He leans back against me and hope soars through my body. "I'm just so angry about all of this, Anna. And I hated that I found out what your relationship was from *him*. And I didn't understand why you would hide that from me. It just caught me so off guard. I really think I would have killed him if you didn't stop me."

Ethan slowly turns me around and backs me against the wall. He pins me there with his hips against mine and our hands locked together above my head. I can feel him pressed against me from my toes to my shoulders and up my arms.

"I was so jealous. The thought of that son of a bitch touching you makes me want to rip his head off. I'm sorry I was such an ass."

He leans his head in and we're kissing. The kind of kissing that we haven't done since that day in the hammock. His hands let go of mine and sift through my hair. I move against him, snaking my hands under his shirt, and wish we were anywhere but here.

His mouth moves to my neck and then to my ear where he whispers, "The water's stopped."

"Huh?" I answer between kisses.

"Teeny. She'll be out any minute."

I know this looks bad but I don't want to stop. It isn't until we hear the doorknob turn that Ethan backs away, and I almost fall to the ground.

"I'm done," Teeny says, looking between the two of us. "Were y'all making out?"

Oh, good Lord.

"I think I'll take another shower," Ethan says as he all but sprints to the bathroom.

"But you already took one," Teeny says just as he closes the door. "He must feel really dirty."

I crawl back on the bed and try not to let Teeny see me blush.

Morning comes after a restless night. There is only one bed in the room, a double, so Teeny started out between us, but ended upside down across us. I think she was the only one who got any sleep.

We've decided not to call from the room. If phones are being traced, whoever is looking knows where we are, but there's no need to lead them to our exact location.

The French Quarter is very different in the light of day. The streets are clean, mostly, and lots of shops and cafés are open for business. It's surprising to see so many art galleries sandwiched between touristy T-shirt shops. There was a huge discussion between the three of us before we left about whether leaving the room was stupid or not. But since we didn't want to call from the room, we didn't have much of a choice. We walk to the riverfront, passing by St. Louis Cathedral, in search of a public phone. We look for the man with the cross tattoos the entire time. After a few blocks, we find the first set of phone booths.

Ethan cashes in five dollars for quarters, drops a handful in the slot, then dials Will's number.

"Hey, it's me but don't say my name out loud. Are you alone?"

Teeny points to the building with a green-and-white–striped awning across the street where there are a line of people.

"Can we eat there? It looked good when we passed by."

"We'll see." I'm trying to hear what Ethan is saying and be on the lookout, but a group of street musicians crank up not ten feet from us. I can't even hear myself think.

Ethan gets off the phone and pulls us down the block.

"Will's coming. Leaving immediately and bringing some cash. He's stopping by Pearl's and telling her about what's happening in Arkansas. Fred is an ex-marine, so hopefully he can handle whatever is happening over there. We'll figure out where to go when Will gets here."

"I don't feel good," Teeny says.

"She's hungry. Let's walk over there." I point to the restaurant she showed me a few minutes ago and we get in line. Turning to Teeny, I say, "We'll get this to go and head back to the room. I don't like being out on the street."

The line moves slowly. It looks like they serve those same powdery fried donuts I've had in Natchitoches and my mouth starts watering.

The restaurant itself is open-air and packed. I can't help but laugh when I see the group of girls from last night. They're wearing the same clothes and look really hungover. The bride still has the veil on but all the condoms are gone.

"Did you tell Will where we're staying?"

"No, I want to be able to watch him when he gets here, make sure no one is following him. We came down here last fall for a Saints game and hung out in this bar on Bourbon. I told him to meet me there. I'll get there early while you and Teeny hang out in the room. When I know it's safe, we'll come pick y'all up."

I'm just about to argue with him that we shouldn't be separated when my eyes fall on someone familiar. Just a passing blur at first but when I spot him again, I know it's him the second I see his face. He's dressed like a tourist, shorts and a T-shirt, but that short haircut and perpetual scowl is unmistakable. It's Agent Hammond and he sees me, too.

Chapter 22

NEW RULE BY ANNA BOYD:

Forget the false trail—better to just run for your life if you get the chance.

"**GO.**" I turn around to Teeny and Ethan and start pushing them away from the man. "Go. It's Agent Hammond. He's here. Go!"

Ethan grabs Teeny's hand and we sprint from the restaurant. I know Ethan's side is still bruised and sore but thankfully it's not slowing him down.

"You're sure?" he calls back over his shoulder.

"Yes. And he recognized me, too."

We both look behind us and see him not far behind. He's not running full out but he's gaining on us.

"Is he going to kill us?" Teeny cries out.

"No." Ethan says then crosses the street and enters Jackson Square. As we get closer to the cathedral, there is a huge group of people on the front steps. It's a wedding party. They are parading out of the church following a jazz band, swinging white umbrellas and dancing to the music. We run through the crowd, then Ethan pivots so we're running toward the front of the parade.

He pulls us in close, and whispers, "Try to blend in."

The group following behind the bride and groom is large and it is easy to be absorbed inside. I keep Teeny close and in the center. We try to fake the enthusiasm shared by the crowd around us but it's hard. And I'm sure we look ridiculous.

Ethan stays to the edge, looking for Agent Hammond.

I catch sight of him in an alley on the side of the church. He busted through the crowd, same as us, but didn't stop. He's checking behind Dumpsters and coming up short. He glances back to the parade and Ethan pushes us deeper inside.

A large woman who seems plastered at nine in the morning hands me an umbrella and says, "Here! Shake whatcha mama gave you, honey. This is a celebration!"

I take the umbrella and hide us behind it. We stay with the parade for a couple of blocks. Ethan joins us under the umbrella and says, "He's making his way back toward the phones we were just using."

I let out a breath I didn't know I was holding. "Do you think he can figure out who we just called?"

"Hell, I don't know. We'll stay with this group until they get to where they're going then try to get back to our room. We need to get off the street."

The parade dances its way through the Quarter, ending in front of one of the fancier hotels. Once everyone starts heading into the lobby, Ethan, Teeny, and I break away from the group.

"Do you know where we are?" Teeny asks.

"Yeah, we're about eight blocks from our hotel." Ethan looks nervous.

"Should we take a cab? Would that be safer?" I ask.

"Yeah."

We walk down the block, looking for an empty cab, but they're all full.

"Let's head toward the hotel and hopefully we can catch a cab at the next block. Keep your eyes open, though."

I link my hand with Teeny's and we start walking. All three of us are breaking our necks as we scope out everything that happens in front of us, behind us, and to each side.

"There are some really weird people here," Teeny says.

"Yep," I answer her absently. Is Agent Hammond out hunting us down for Thomas? I could see the excitement in his eyes the moment he saw us.

"And stinky people, too. Did you smell that guy we just passed?"

Ethan runs a hand over her head, teasing her hair. "Teeny, you need to be on the lookout for Hammond. Or Thomas. Or Mateo."

Good grief, could the list get any bigger?

We go another block with no empty cab. We're walking at a good pace and may actually get to the hotel before we find a ride.

Until Teeny stops in her tracks. Ethan and I stop shortly after her and look back.

"What's wrong?" I ask. All the color drains from her face and her bottom lip quivers. I take the few steps back until I'm at her side, Ethan right next to me.

She pulls both of us inside a souvenir shop and all but hides in a rack of T-shirts.

"Teeny, what's wrong?" Ethan asks.

"There's a man out there. He's looking down at his phone and I saw a bunch of small crosses tattooed on his neck. Isn't that who Tyler said was after us?"

Ethan moves to the window in front of the store to look outside then ducks down just below the window.

I slip in next to Teeny and glance out the window. Stopped on the sidewalk is a man with long dark hair pulled back into a ponytail. And plain as day is a chain of crosses that almost circle his neck. They aren't big but there are a lot of them. This has to be Mateo.

He looks at his phone, then taps the screen. Waits. Then taps some more. He's communicating with someone.

While he waits, Mateo reaches in his coat pocket and pulls out a pack of cigarettes. Shaking the pack, he realizes he's out. And then he glances to the store where we're hiding.

Ethan, seeing the assassin walk toward the door of the store, pushes Teeny and me all the way behind the T-shirts but there's not enough room for all three of us. "Stay there," he mumbles and then moves to the rack across from us, diving behind a row of hoodies.

The bell on the door chimes as Mateo walks inside. He goes to the counter and asks for a pack of Marlboros.

I hold Teeny close and keep her head down.

From my view between the hangers, the clerk, Mateo, and we are the only people in the store.

He takes the cigarettes from the old woman behind the counter. She's looking around the store, though. She knows we're in here and seems suspicious now that we've disappeared.

Mateo turns to leave when the woman calls out, "Where you kids at? You better not be stealing my stuff."

He stops and looks back into the store. "Who are you looking for?" His accent has a thick twang to it. Maybe Texas?

She leans over the counter, trying to get a better look through the small store, and says, "Three kids. They ran in here a minute ago and now—poof—they gone."

He lets the door close and walks slowly back to the counter. "What did they look like?"

The woman swishes her hand in front of her face. "A mess. Street kids for sure. And one of the girls, so young."

Oh, no. She's caught his interest.

Mateo eyes the room, taking in every detail. "Do you have a back way out?" he asks.

"No. Just that door here."

Millimeter by millimeter, I slide lower behind the shirts. Teeny is shaking beside me and I grab her hands, hoping to keep her still. I can't see Ethan but I'm worried he'll do something stupid, just to distract Mateo.

His steps echo against the tile floor.

Closer.

My heart is beating so loud I'm sure he can hear it.

Closer.

He's standing in front of where we're hiding. All he has to do is move the T-shirts aside and we'll be in plain view.

His hand settles on the black T-shirt that hangs right in front of my face and he starts to drag it to the side, the hanger scraping the rod sends chills racing down my spine.

And then we're facing each other.

"Anna Boyd. I've been looking for you."

I'm frozen.

And then Teeny's gone—jumps out of the rack and head butts him right in the gut. They both fall back in a heap, probably because he wasn't expecting her to attack him and he was caught off guard, and before I can move an inch, Ethan kicks him in the head.

The woman screams at us, threatening to call the cops, and Ethan kicks Mateo one more time, then grabs Teeny.

"Anna, we gotta go!"

I still can't move, so Ethan grabs my hand and heaves me to my feet. Mateo starts to get on his feet just as we rush out of the store.

We run down the block and he's right behind us. There's no parade to blend in with this time, so we just start weaving through streets and alleyways. Teeny trips, splaying across the sidewalk, and Ethan scoops her up and keeps running.

We duck into an alley between a bar and another souvenir shop.

And it's a dead end.

Mateo runs in the alley and yells, "Stop!" And then a nearby bottle shatters, tiny shards of glass flying everywhere.

Is he shooting at us? I heard a loud pop but nothing like when Ethan shot that hog or when I shot the target at the farm.

We skid to a stop and Ethan throws both Teeny and me behind a large garbage bin and then runs back toward the assassin.

Before I can get up I hear another loud pop. I scream.

"Stay down, Teeny," I say, then peek around the bin, terrified of what I'm about to see.

Ethan is down on the ground, holding his arm. Mateo is standing over him, gun still out. There's already a pool of blood forming underneath Ethan. He pushes himself up on his good arm to a sitting position then scraps together a handful of loose rocks, flinging them at Mateo.

Mateo takes a running start then kicks Ethan in the head, knocking him back. "Doesn't feel so good, does it, you little shit."

Ethan doesn't move.

Oh my God . . . Oh my God . . . Oh my God . . .

"Come on out," he calls out to Teeny and me. "There's nowhere to hide. No matter where you go, I will find you."

We don't answer. Or move.

Glass and other debris crunch under his feet as he makes his way to where we're hiding.

I search the ground for anything I could use. And then I see it—an old beer bottle. I've got one chance to get this just right.

He comes around the corner, gun pointed at us.

I get up slowly, the bottle clutched in one hand behind my back, and push Teeny behind me with the other one.

"Let her go. You don't need her."

His smile makes me want to vomit. "I don't think so." He looks back toward the street. "You'll be coming with me now."

Oh shit. Images of burning flesh fill my head. We're not going anywhere with him.

He steps closer and it's so hard to wait for just the right moment.

I bend over just slightly like I'm going to cry or something and then with everything in me, I swing the bottle in a high arc and bust it against his head, right between the eyes.

The bottle shatters and Mateo goes down like a rock, his face covered in blood.

He doesn't move.

"Is he dead?" Teeny asks in a flat voice.

"I don't know." I grab his gun and point it at him. My hand curls around the handle and my finger rests on the trigger.

I could end this, right now.

No matter how hard I tense my arms, I can't make the gun stop shaking. I stand there for a full minute, wanting to pull the trigger, but I can't bring myself to kill him. Then a moan brings me out of my trance, and I shove the gun in the waist of my pants and race to Ethan, dropping down beside him.

"Oh my God, Ethan. Wake up!" I hook my arm around his non-injured side and pull him up. "Ethan, we've got to get you to a hospital. You're bleeding so bad!" I strip off my jacket and wrap it around his arm while he yells out in pain.

Ethan tries to stand, but he's wobbly.

"I'm calling an ambulance. Then the police. We can't handle this." I look around for someone to help, but the alley is empty.

"No! No cops. No ambulances. They'll find us. I can make it back to the room."

Ethan manages to make it out of the alley but there's no way he'll make it all the way to our hotel. I'm not even sure where we are. We pass people on the sidewalk and I want to beg them to help us, but I keep quiet. Teeny follows behind me, holding on to the bottom of my shirt. There's no telling what we look like, me with my still bruised cheek and Ethan with his busted face, walking like a drunk.

"I feel sick." And then he leans over and pukes all over the sidewalk.

A group of guys jump back from us and one says, "Whoa, dude. You're supposed to pace yourself."

"I need to sit down. I feel like I'm going to pass out."

We make it to an open doorway of an abandoned building and I help Ethan to a sitting position. He struggles to stay awake for a few seconds then he's out again.

We're only two blocks from the alley now and I don't like being this exposed. I'm pretty sure Ethan has a concussion on top of a gunshot wound, not to mention the other injuries.

Teeny sits down beside Ethan and holds his hand. "Is he going to be okay?" She's crying.

"I don't know."

He needs help, but the last thing he said to me was not to call the cops. And it will take Will at least four hours to get here.

What do I do . . . what do I do . . .

I check Ethan's arm. There's so much blood, I can't tell if the bullet came out of the other side or not.

People walking by are looking at us funny and it won't be long until someone calls the cops for us.

"Teeny, see if you can flag down a cab."

Maybe if I can get him to our room, I can wash his arm and see how bad it is.

She's at the curb, scanning the street, and then runs back to me. "Sissy, I don't see one. And I'm scared Mateo is going to come back. I don't like sitting here."

Mateo's words run through my brain—*There's nowhere to hide. No matter where you go, I will find you.*

I'm not prepared to outmaneuver Mateo, especially with Ethan injured. I can't even get us two blocks from where we were attacked. He may wake up any minute and he's going to be even more pissed off. If I call an ambulance and take Ethan to a hospital, what will stop Mateo from coming there?

I feel sick. I want to call Dad, but his cell doesn't work on that island and I don't know how to call that satellite phone.

I should have killed Mateo, because he won't hesitate to kill me.

Tyler's face with his fresh stitches pops into my head. Thomas stitched him up. And Thomas may be the only match for Mateo. Maybe he can fix Ethan's arm, too.

My mind spins as I consider our dwindling options . . . take my chances against an unknown assassin or trust the assassin I know?

"Wait here, Teeny. I'll be right back."

"Where are you going?" she yells at me as I'm almost across the street.

"I've got to make a call."

Tyler screeches to a stop on the street right in front of where Ethan is passed out in the doorway. It took him less than four minutes to get here, so that means they're still in the Quarter somewhere.

"I don't think this is a good idea," Teeny says for the fifteenth time. "He needs a doctor."

"Teeny, Mateo shot him right off a busy street. Do you really think he won't come for him in a hospital? At this point I'm just trying to keep us alive for the next couple of hours. I can't think past that right now."

Tyler goes straight for Ethan and manages to get him over his shoulder with little effort. This is the second time he's carried him in an unconscious state and chills race down my spine that I have made the worst decision ever. I didn't know who else to call, and then I remembered he told me at Ursuline that he kept his same number.

I follow Tyler to the car and help get Ethan in the backseat, while Teeny gets in on the other side next to him.

"I have to ask you to put your heads down before we can go." Tyler's face is black and blue but I don't feel sorry for him at all.

We both duck down and then we're racing through the Quarter and headed right back in the lion's den.

As Thomas helps Tyler get Ethan out of the car, I wait for the anger or frustration or something similar from Thomas. Surprisingly it doesn't come. I've decided Thomas is a sociopath without emotion.

We follow them through an iron gate, and it's not what I expect. It's like an oasis plopped down in the middle of this building and hidden away from the noise-filled streets of New Orleans. There's a small pool and several brick pathways that weave around over-flowing flower beds and overfilled pots leading to secluded seating areas. The inside walls are peppered with old French doors and gaslights and the hanging baskets attached to the second-story balcony drip with trailing plants. I have no idea if we're still in the French Quarter but wherever we are, it's beautiful.

They take Ethan up an outside set of stairs through one of the sets of French doors. It's a huge bedroom, probably twice the size of our hotel room, and has really expensive-looking antique furniture. They set Ethan down in the center of a queen-size bed.

Thomas stands over him but doesn't move to help him in any way. "What happened?"

I gently crawl on the bed and get as close to Ethan as I can. "Mateo found us. We ran from him but he cornered us in an alley. He shot Ethan, then kicked him in the head. Teeny and I got Ethan a few blocks away from the alley but then he threw up and passed out."

Thomas crosses his arms in front of him and continues to study Ethan.

"How did you get away from him?" He's showing more expression on his face than I've seen this entire time.

"I hit him in the head with a beer bottle and knocked him out."

A ridiculous grin spreads across his face.

"Tyler said you would help us," I say, feeling stupid the second the words are out of my mouth. Why did I think this was the answer? Why would I assume the person who once kept us bound and gagged would help save Ethan's life? I must be completely losing my mind.

He looks straight at me. "You want this over, you do what I say."

My only concern is keeping Ethan alive at this point and if I have to make a deal with the devil for that to happen, I will.

"Just me, not Ethan or Teeny. Just me," I say, holding his gaze.

Teeny gasps behind me but I don't turn to look at her.

"I'm not sure you're in a position to make demands." He's back to being cold.

"No, but I know it will be a lot easier for whatever you have planned if I cooperate. And if you help Ethan, I'll cooperate."

Thomas rolls up his sleeves and immediately starts unwrapping my jacket from around Ethan's arm.

"Ty, get my kit."

Ty. It's strange hearing him referred to by a nickname, especially from Thomas. Tyler sprints from the room. I hover over Ethan trying to get a better look at his arm.

"Move back; you're blocking the light."

I scoot back so quickly I almost fall off the bed.

Ethan's shirt is soaked with blood and Thomas tears it away to the shoulder. Tyler runs back in the room carrying a large black duffel bag.

"Hot water. And some towels."

And Tyler is gone again.

"How do you know what to do?" I ask.

He glances up at me, his face blank, then goes back to pulling out supplies from the bag. And all I can think is, how did he manage to come off so personable in Natchitoches? It's almost impossible to consider him being the least bit charming.

Once Tyler's back with the hot water, Thomas starts cleaning the blood away from the wound and Ethan comes alive. He sits up in the bed, a string of curses bouncing off the walls.

"Hold him down!" Thomas yells.

I grab his good side, throwing all my weight on him to get him back on the mattress while Tyler catches both legs. Thomas lays one arm across his chest while he digs in his bag with the other.

Ethan is looking at me with wild eyes, especially after seeing Thomas and Tyler. Not only is pain etched across his face, but confusion as well.

Ethan repeats, "What did you do?" over and over and I feel horrible.

Thomas pulls out a syringe and a small glass bottle. Once the syringe is full, he jabs it in Ethan's arm, right near the gunshot wound.

Ethan fights for another few seconds then his eyes roll back in his head and he falls against the mattress.

"Now, let's see just where this bullet went." And Thomas goes to work.

Chapter 23

NEW RULE BY ANNA BOYD:
And there's a time to stay and fight. . . .

IT'S dark out. Thomas and Tyler left the room hours ago. I don't think they locked the door behind them, but I haven't checked—they know I won't leave without Ethan.

Teeny's at the foot of the gigantic bed, asleep. And Ethan is still unconscious.

His last words to me repeat on an infinite loop in my head: *What did you do . . . what did you do . . .*

Thomas pulled the bullet out of the meaty part of Ethan's arm and stitched him back up. He said Ethan would be asleep for a while, but I think it's been too long. All I ever heard about concussions was to keep the person awake. But I don't think Thomas could have gotten the bullet out with Ethan conscious.

I hid the gun we took from Mateo the second Thomas left the room. It's a handgun, but I don't know what kind, and it has some sort of tube screwed to the end of it. A silencer, maybe? I guess that's why no one came running when he fired those two shots.

By now Will has gotten to town and he's waiting in some unknown club for Ethan to show.

This is so screwed up.

The door creaks open and Tyler's head pops in. "You have to be hungry. Come down and eat something."

I'm hesitant to leave Ethan and Teeny, but my stomach makes the most god-awful noise once he mentions food and I remember I haven't eaten today.

"Can I bring something up for them for when they wake up?"

He nods, and just like that, he's the friendly host.

I follow Tyler down a hall toward a set of steps. There are lots of doors, all shut, but once we get downstairs the whole room opens up. There is a living area with several different groupings of furniture, a long table and chairs, and then the kitchen. It's warm-feeling, which is not what I expected. I scan the room but don't see Thomas anywhere.

"Who's place is this?" I ask.

Tyler shakes his head and answers, "Please don't ask me too much." He's different and I wonder what brought on the change— Ethan beating the crap out of him or something else.

He gestures for me to sit at the bar while he moves around the kitchen. He pulls out long, slender white packages and small bags of chips from a white grocery bag.

"I got some roast beef po'boys. I think you'll like them."

I'm so hungry I could eat dirt, so I rip the package open the second he hands it to me and shove a huge amount of the sandwich in my mouth.

He brings over a small Styrofoam container and says, "It's better if you dip it in the gravy first."

I nod and try to choke down the food. It is a little dry and it's hard to force it down my throat.

"Can I have some water?"

Tyler brings two bottles and sits beside me.

We eat in silence and it's awkward. There are a million things I want to ask him but I don't know where I stand with him right now.

"Look, I'm sorry," he finally says. "If I had it to do over again in Florida, I would do things a lot differently."

I finish chewing and think about what to say to him. This is not what I expected. At all. I need to feel him out, see what's ticking in that brain of his.

"I thought after what Ethan did to you, you might not help him."

His left eye twitches before he says, "I would try to kill someone, too, if I thought they hurt you. He just doesn't understand what's going on here. I'm trying to save you. That's all I ever wanted to do. I would have never given you the journal back if I'd have known all this was going to happen. I swear. And I'm glad you trusted me enough to call when you needed help. Better late than never. No matter what I will always be here for you."

He's sick. Seriously sick in the head. Does he honestly think there's hope for us?

He reaches over and squeezes my hand. I hate him. The desire to hit him, like Ethan did, is so strong, but another idea pops in my head—what if I use this moment to my advantage? If I can make him believe I've forgiven him and there is the slightest chance for us, then maybe I can get us out of this mess alive. I just hope I can act nice without showing how I really feel about him.

I turn toward him, letting my knees bump his. Tucking a stray piece of hair behind my ear, I say, "This is all so hard to take in, but thank you for making sure Thomas didn't kill me or my family."

He blushes and plays with his food. "I wanted to tell you so many times who I really was." He looks around the room, making sure we're alone. Even though we're the only ones in here, he leans in close and whispers, "I'm so sorry about your mom. I really liked her. Is she getting better?"

Tears threaten to roll down my face. I do not want to talk about my mother with him.

"She is. I'm hoping she can come home soon. I'm hoping I can, too."

Tyler scans the room again. "It won't be long, I promise. Thomas plans on making his move soon. If it all goes as planned, you could be headed home in a couple of days."

"Do you really think he'll let us leave? You've been unmasked. And now we've seen this place." I gesture to the house around me. "How did you explain we got away?"

"Yes, I think you'll be going home soon," he answers with such conviction that I'm sure he believes it. "And I told him everything." The last part comes out in a whisper.

"Was he mad at you?"

"He wasn't happy."

"Will you please answer a few questions, just between you and me?" I move in a little bit closer, maintaining eye contact with him.

"This whole thing is making me crazy and I just don't know how you could be a part of it. Please help me understand."

His eyes lock on my mouth just like Ethan's do right before he comes in for a kiss. It takes everything in me not to back away. I've reeled him in; now I just need to keep him on the hook.

"What do you want to know?"

"If you're Daniel Sanders, who did Agent Williams have in custody?"

I'm starting out with something easy and nonthreatening, hoping to ease him into opening up.

He cracks a small smile and says, "Thomas had someone at my apartment pretending to be me."

And now I'm going to try to go a little deeper with him. "You and Thomas seem so close but so different, obviously. I don't understand that."

"Very different. We had the same mom but different dads. He had a . . . hard upbringing, living with his dad. I didn't meet him until I was ten. Mom died and I was just about to be put in the foster system when he showed up. I couldn't stay with him . . . since he, um, travels a lot, but he enrolled me in a really nice boarding school. Came to visit all the time. He was there for all the parent stuff. I don't know what would have happened to me if it wasn't for him."

Was not expecting that. It sounds more like the Thomas I knew in Natchitoches than what I see today.

"But how can you be okay with what he does? Why would you help him?"

Tyler looks uncomfortable now, and I'm regretting coming on too strong.

"I didn't know what he was until after you left Florida. Walked in . . . in on the middle of something. . . ." He gets up from the stool and takes our empty plates to the sink, rinses them, and loads them into the dishwasher. "You gotta understand, he was raised very different from me. He grew up in that environment. My mom got away, but she wasn't able to save him. He's all she used to talk about, and she constantly worried over what kind of person he would turn into . . . and what he saw. . . . He can't help what he is."

He doesn't continue and I don't push because I feel like he's seconds from closing off and there's still more I want to learn.

"What does Thomas do exactly? Is he just an assassin? Or does he do other . . . things?"

Tyler turns his back to me and I scoot off the stool, joining him in the kitchen. I turn him around and step in close. I don't feel bad playing him like this. At all. He's under some crazy delusions if he can make excuses for his brother murdering people for a living and for his part in this.

I put my hands in his and say, "Please help me understand."

I can see him cave before his mouth even opens. "He works for the Vega family. Always has. When he was younger, he did odd jobs and he worked his way up. Usually, the only people he . . . takes care of . . . are just as bad as the people he works for. His dad had the same job before he died."

"You realize he's sucking you into this same life. He convinced you to befriend a girl he was paid to kill, and you agreed to do it."

"No! It wasn't like that. I thought at first he just needed some information from you. When I found out about the contract, I made him swear, on our mother's grave, that he wouldn't harm you or your family. He gave me his word. We're the only family we've got. He wouldn't lie to me."

I drop his hands and turn away, too disgusted to keep up the pretense any longer. Grabbing the sack with the rest of the po'boys and a few bottles of water, I start to leave the kitchen but I can't help one last parting remark. "Tyler, just because we're still alive doesn't mean he didn't harm my family."

Chapter 24

NEW RULE BY ANNA BOYD:
You can't always be that picky. Sometimes you have to use any resource available.

ETHAN'S awake when I get back to the room. His face is pale and he looks pissed but I can't help but smile when I see his eyes are open.

"You're up!"

I rush to the bed and sit down a little too hard, his face scrunching up in pain the minute I make contact with the bed.

"Sorry. Sorry."

He struggles to a sitting position and a bead of sweat breaks out across his brow.

"Are you okay?"

He grunts and squirms, until he finally gets in a position where he's comfortable. "Why are we here, Anna?"

I was expecting the pissed tone but I cringe anyway.

"What else did you expect me to do? That man shot you. He told me that he could find us anywhere. That we would never be able to hide from him. You passed out blocks from the hotel. The last thing you said was don't call the police. Or an ambulance." I stand up and pace beside the bed. "We talked about this earlier and decided it wasn't safe to go to the cops. I didn't know what else to do. You needed stitches and I knew Thomas could do that. I also knew Thomas may be the only match for Mateo. I didn't know what to do and was just trying to keep us alive."

I get up from the bed and walk into the adjoining bathroom to wet a washcloth. Deep breaths, I think. Deep breaths.

I get back to the bed and kneel down beside it. "I can't handle any of this if we're fighting. I was so scared. I didn't know what to do. I don't trust Thomas—or Tyler—at all, but I can only deal with one threat at a time and Mateo seemed to be the biggest threat in that moment."

He reaches for my hand. "I don't want to fight either. My head and arm are killing me and Thomas's face is not one I liked waking up to." He pulls me closer with his good arm and kisses me gently. "I just hate that we're right back in this position." He tries to lift his left arm but it doesn't go higher than about an inch. "Especially with this useless arm."

"Just wait till you hear what she promised him," Teeny says from the foot of the bed. "Is there food? Because I smell something delicious and I'm about to starve to death."

Crap. I was hoping she would forget to mention that little bargain I made.

I move away from the bed and grab a po'boy out of the bag, unwrapping it on a side table in the little sitting area on the other side of the room. I need to get Teeny as far away from Ethan as possible. She finishes about half the sandwich before I get the top off the gravy container.

"What bargain?"

"Are you hungry?" I ask, completely ignoring his question.

"What bargain?" he asks again.

"I told Thomas I would go along with whatever he needed if he would help you. Here, take a bite, you need to eat."

He drops his head back and lets out a string of curses.

"She also promised that it would be just her helping, not us, too," Teeny calls from across the room.

Thanks, Teeny.

Ethan pushes the sandwich away but I bring it right back in.

"Look, if we're going to survive this, I can't have you weak from hunger. Eat."

Begrudgingly, he takes a few gravy-dipped bites then pushes the food away again. I hand him some water and he downs the bottle.

"You're not doing it," he says. "No matter what he wants, you're just not. I don't care what you promised him. And as soon as I can get out of this bed, we're gonna figure out how to get out of here. What time is it?"

"When I was in the kitchen, the clock on the oven said seven thirty."

"Shit. Will got here hours ago."

"Where is he? I never asked you that."

Ethan struggles with the blanket wrapped around him and pushes my hands away when I try to help.

"Remember that club last night, the one with the girls standing around outside?"

"Y'all went to Barely Legal? Those girls were disgusting."

He shakes his head, then drops it in his hands like that small movement hurt too much. "No, we went to the place next door. The Blues Club."

"You think he's still there?"

"Yeah, I'm sure he'll wait all night for us."

Teeny finishes the sandwich and stands at the end of the bed, licking her fingers. "She got the gun from that guy, so at least there's that."

This makes him perk up. "Where is it? Are there any bullets left?"

Teeny digs it out of the potted plant and hands it to Ethan.

"Whoa," he breathes out. "A Glock 26 9mm with a silencer." He empties the chamber and there're five bullets left. Studying one of the bullets, he lets out a soft whistle.

"What is it? Is there something weird about the bullets?"

"They're subsonic."

"What does that mean," Teeny asks before I have a chance.

"It means the bullet travels slower than the speed of sound. Most bullets travel faster than the speed of sound and that loud 'crack' you hear is when the bullet breaks the sound barrier. With these bullets and a silencer, this gun is very quiet."

"So that's why no one on the street heard him shooting at us," I add.

He looks at me and asks, "Yeah. How'd we get away from him? My brain is so fuzzy right now I can't remember."

"I knocked Mateo out with a beer bottle and when he fell, I picked up the gun and hid it in my jeans."

His mouth is wide-open—obviously impressed. "Damn."

For the first time today, a grin breaks out across my face.

He turns back to the gun and reloads it. He holds it out to me and I bury it back in the potted plant, then sit back near him on the bed.

"How do you know all that . . . about guns and bullets and the sound barrier?" Teeny asks.

Ethan shrugs then winces from the pain of the movement. "I've been around guns all my life. My grandpa loved collecting them."

"I found out a little more from Tyler," I say. "He and Thomas have the same mom but not the same dad. Tyler said he didn't meet Thomas until their mom died when he was ten. Thomas took care of him."

Ethan leans back against the bed and just watches me so I keep talking.

"Tyler said Thomas has worked for Vega since he was a kid. Worked his way up and does the same job his dad used to do."

I'm rambling but I can't help it. Ethan looks at me funny and it's making me nervous.

"But anyway, I didn't get specific plans. Just, you know, background kind of stuff."

"I hope you found out his favorite color and shoe size, too." The sarcasm is not lost on me.

"And you're pissed again. That's great."

"Yes, Anna, I'm pissed. I'm pissed that while I'm stuck in this bed, you're getting chummy with some stalker brother of a second-generation assassin."

"I'm doing everything I can to find out what's going on! That's it!"

After a few minutes, he's sitting on the side of the bed. "Where's the bathroom?"

I point to a door on the other side of the room as Ethan pushes off the bed.

"How do you feel?" I ask.

"Like I got shot and kicked in the head." And then the bathroom door slams shut.

Ethan is not up to handling whatever Thomas has planned. And I know him—he will push himself into a worse situation just to save me and Teeny. And no telling what will happen when he and Tyler are in the same room.

I have to get him out of here.

As soon as I hear the water running, I tell Teeny I'm taking the trash to the kitchen and sneak out of the room. I pad down the carpeted hall, quietly opening doors, but they're all empty.

I tiptoe down the steps and through the bottom floor. I finally find Tyler in a small sitting room off the kitchen, laid up on the couch watching a movie. Must be nice to be so relaxed.

He sits up quickly when I enter the room. "What's going on?"

"I want to talk to Thomas."

His eyes go big. "About what?"

"None of your business. Where is he?"

Tyler pulls out his phone from his back pocket. When Thomas answers, Tyler says, "Anna wants to talk to you."

A few seconds later, Tyler ends the call. "He'll be in here in a minute."

We wait. In silence.

Thomas finally shows through a door on the opposite side of the room.

"I don't like being summoned."

I take a deep breath and ask, "Will you still make Ethan go through whatever you originally had planned? He's injured and probably has a concussion. I can't imagine you . . . killing Vega if you're worried he may pass out at any moment."

He doesn't answer, just watches me closely.

I can't stand the silence so my mouth takes over just to fill it.

"And what about Teeny? She was never in the plan. No one was looking for her but here she is. She's just an innocent little girl. Are you leaving her behind? Is she coming with us?"

"Your sister will remain here as incentive for your good behavior. If Ethan is unable to join us, then he can wait here with her. Two reasons for you to cooperate."

This is what I was afraid of.

"I get this is bigger than me, but you need bait and here I am. I will help you, but only me."

Thomas chuckles softly. "You're not in any position to be making demands. You will help me willingly or your sister pays the consequence. It's really very simple."

I've been thinking about this all afternoon—if I'm brave enough to pull off this bluff.

"We called someone to come pick us up this morning. If we don't show—they will go to the local cops. You probably know people there since you were in that uniform the other day, but this person will be very loud and make a big scene. I can't imagine you want people looking for us. Or you."

Dead silence.

"Let Ethan and Teeny leave with them and I will stay and do whatever I need to do," I add.

Thomas studies me and I try not to squirm.

"I assumed you called someone," Thomas says. "So let me guess, one of your little high school friends borrowed some money from dear old dad and headed south. Do you really believe some kid is capable of whisking you away from all of this? Have you forgotten about the man in the alley who wants you dead?"

I cross my arms across my chest and match his gaze. "No matter what you say, you need me and I have to believe you would prefer my willing cooperation. And if you don't let them go, I will fight you the entire time. Ethan's injured and you don't need Teeny. Or maybe you never intended for us to survive this. If that's the case, I won't have anything to lose."

Tyler's head goes back and forth, like he's watching a tennis match.

Thomas rubs his hand across his jaw. I try not to panic. I'm showing all my cards and taking a huge gamble right now. "While I may be able to do what I need to do with just you, if I let your little sister and boyfriend go, what guarantees do I have that you will behave?"

"You don't have to keep them here for me to understand the threat against them. I'm well aware of your long reach."

He's quiet. I'm afraid I handled this completely wrong. I should have talked Tyler into sneaking us out.

Finally, he asks, "You're not worried about Mateo finding them once they leave?"

"Are you telling me you're not good enough to get them out of town safely?"

If there's one thing I know about him, it's that he's an egomaniac. I am worried about them leaving, but I think it's more dangerous if they stay.

He doesn't answer me.

"Mateo's in town. I know you plan to do something about him in the next few days. You plan on killing Vega, too. Let's just say I'm betting on you to win this game and neither of them will be in danger before long. Ethan and Teeny don't know much more than they did before you took us. They don't know where this house is. They know we were held at Ursuline but I have no doubt you've already removed every trace of us."

"Ahhh . . . but they know about Tyler now. His identity was to remain a secret."

I can see Tyler tense but I don't look at him.

"So do I. We won't say anything. I swear to you. We want nothing else to do with you. You will either let us live—like you promised Tyler—or you won't."

Tyler steps forward, like he's ready to jump into this conversation when Thomas puts a hand up, stopping him.

"I'm here. I will do whatever I need to do to make this end. Can you do what you want to do with just me?" I hate the pleading sound in my voice.

Another long, tense silence.

"The reason there is a contract on you and Ethan is because you both could identity me. If I'm arrested, Vega is afraid I will flip on him, and over the years I've seen enough that I could completely sink his ship. Vega is in New Orleans at my request. I've invited him here so we can kiss and make up. Or so I made him think. You are my peace offering—a sign of my good faith so that we can forgive and forget what has happened."

My stomach drops. "So you're giving me to him."

"He does not believe I am so good intentioned, but he will go along with the charade. And Mateo will be there with him, waiting to finish us off. He's agreed to come because he knows that they will never find me on their own. He thinks this will be the perfect time to kill me. I needed you both to get me through the door so I can get close enough to kill him first. It might work with just you."

Oh. Shit.

"So I would have to go there. Face him . . . and Mateo?" I ask.

"Yes, Anna. And now you have promised to walk in without complaint."

Tyler stands quickly and says, "I didn't know she would have to go near him. That wasn't part of the plan."

Thomas glares at him and he sits back down quickly. "Yes, that's always been part of the plan. Mateo is cocky but he won't know what hit him. And Vega won't have a chance once Mateo is dead."

Tyler steps between Thomas and me and says to him, "You made me a promise. She is not to be hurt. In any way. You swore on our mother's grave."

Thomas's eyes flash to me before settling back on Tyler. "I will not break my word to you. Anna will walk out of there, with me, and it will be over." He looks at me as he continues, "The journal has been destroyed along with any evidence there. Tyler and I will disappear and I assure you, no one will find a trace of us. You will be free to go back to your life. I made Ty a promise and I don't take that lightly. But if you, your sister, or your boyfriend mention him or his relationship to me to anyone, I will gladly kill you."

My knees go weak and I drop to a crouch. Tyler jumps up and moves toward me, but I hold up my hand for him to stop. I don't want him to touch me.

I never thought I would literally be right in the middle of this. But there's no way I can let Ethan be there, too. Or Teeny.

"I understand."

"Tyler, go get the car ready."

Tyler obviously doesn't want to leave the room with me still here, but eventually he does.

The second he's gone from the room, Thomas takes a step closer to me and squats down to where I'm hovering at the floor. "I don't trust you. At all. And just so we're on the same page, you will deliver Ethan and Elena to your friend and come right back. To the best of my abilities, I will see that they get out of town unharmed." He pulls a phone from his pocket and taps on the screen. "And just so we're clear with one another, please take a look at this."

He holds the phone in front of my face and I drop the rest of the way to the floor. It's a picture of my mother. She's sitting in a chair outside, head thrown back, soaking up the sun.

She looks beautiful.

I run my finger over the screen, "When was this taken?"

"Today. At the facility in Baton Rouge where she's recovering. If you try to run, I will not only retrieve you, Ethan, and Elena, I'll make a stop and pick your mother up as well. And I will make Mateo seem tender."

Ethan is out of the shower and finishing the rest of the po'boy when I get back to the room.

"Where have you been?" he says with a mouthful of sandwich.

"Working on a way to get us out of here. Tyler is sneaking us out; do you think you're up for that?" I hope they can't see the panic I'm feeling inside. I can't get the picture of Mom out of my head. She looks so good. And healthy. I'm sickened to think Thomas has someone there, watching her.

Ethan's immediately suspicious and I don't blame him. "Just like that, he's going to help us?"

I hand him some clothes I got from Tyler since Ethan's clothes are ruined. He eyes the T-shirt and hoodie but doesn't say anything about them or ask where they came from.

"This has gone further than he thought it would. He thinks we're better off to stay here, but he agrees that it should be our decision. And he feels especially bad about Teeny—he didn't know she would be involved. If we want to leave he'll help us, but we only have a short amount of time to do it."

It's weak but I'm hoping that, in his half-concussion state, he goes with it.

"You don't have to ask me twice," Teeny says, then moves toward the door. "But where are we going? That man is still out there."

"He's going to drop us off near the club where hopefully Will is still hanging out. Then we're getting out of town."

"No, I don't buy it."

I sit beside him on the bed. "I'm playing him. He thinks I trust him. He's trying to act like a hero for me."

And there is some truth to that, but Ethan will probably never speak to me when he realizes I'm lying to him, again. At least he will be alive. And hopefully out of this mess.

I help Ethan get his arm inside the hoodie and I can tell it hurts him. A lot.

Once he's ready, I stare at the potted plant. I need the gun.

I grab it quickly and try to shove it in the pocket of my jacket, but it's too long and sticks out.

"Unscrew the silencer," Ethan says as he walks toward me. "If we need to fire this, we definitely want people to hear it."

I do as he suggests and the gun fits perfectly in my pocket.

"You've come a long way with this. I'm really proud of you."

I smile at him and pray he forgives me when this is all over.

We leave the room through the balcony doors and head down the outside steps.

"Where's Thomas?" Ethan asks.

"He just left but won't be gone long," I answer. I'm sure he's actually watching us from one of the windows on the other side of the courtyard.

The same car Tyler picked us up in is idling near the double wooden doors.

He gets out of the car and opens the backseat.

He and Ethan stare at each other for a long moment before Ethan finally slides into the car.

"You have to duck down like before. I'm willing to help you, but I can't let you find this place again."

Teeny and I follow behind him.

Once Ethan gets in a somewhat comfortable position, Tyler opens the wooden doors and we drive away from the house.

Chapter 25

NEW RULE BY ANNA BOYD:
Sometimes you just gotta wing it.

WE'VE been driving for about five minutes, all twists and turns, before Tyler says, "You can sit up now."

We're at a stop sign near the busiest section of Bourbon Street. If memory serves me, the club where Will is waiting is a couple of blocks away.

Tyler doesn't get out, just watches us exit from the rearview mirror.

Just before Ethan shuts the door, he knocks Tyler in the back of his head and says in a quiet voice, "If you come around Anna again, I will kill you."

Tyler doesn't say anything, just pulls away from the curb the second the back door slams shut.

"Let's get moving," Ethan says as we join the flow of traffic down the street.

It's so much more crowded tonight than it was last night and I can't help but wonder if there is someone out there taking pictures of us and sending them back to Thomas. I'm taking a huge risk that he won't swoop in and take all of us, including Will, back to the house, but I try to remember—this is not about me. This is a power struggle between very ruthless people. He needs bait and I'm willing. Hopefully that will be enough.

"Do you think it's the weekend?" Teeny asks. "I can't believe how many people are walking around."

"Who knows? I'm not sure what month it is anymore," Ethan answers.

I can see the Barely Legal doorway up ahead and the girls are back outside. One by one, these girls are plucking men off the street and shoving them through the smoky doorway.

Ethan stops when we reach the door to the Blues Club.

"We're not going to be able to walk in; we don't have IDs," Ethan says. "And they're sure as hell not going to let Teeny inside."

"How's Will in there then?" Teeny asks.

"Last year, we had fake IDs, but Will's eighteen now so he's in there legally. Here, you only have to be eighteen to get in but you can't drink until you're twenty-one."

All three of us look through the front door but all we see is a set of stairs going up to the second floor.

"Hold on, let me see if I can't get in long enough to look around," I say, then move Ethan and Teeny to an empty doorway next to the club. "Y'all need to get out of sight for a minute."

Ethan backs Teeny into the corner then stands in front of her, blocking her from sight. "Just hurry. If he's in there, y'all come out here."

I jog up the steps to where a bouncer is guarding the entrance.

"Hey," I say. "Where do I talk to someone about a job?" It's going to take a miracle for this to work.

The guy looks me up and down and I know what he's thinking. I'm dirty. My face is bruised and I probably stink.

"How old are you?" he asks.

"Eighteen," I say with a fake confidence I hope he believes.

The bouncer rolls his eyes and crooks his finger for me to follow him. "Come on, boss man is over here. You look like you been in a helluva mess. Hope you hit his ass right back."

I let out a nervous laugh and pray I find Will before boss man finds me.

I almost pass out the second we enter the smoky, blues-filled room. Not only is Will sitting at a back table but so is Catherine.

I push past the bouncer and throw myself at her.

"Oh my God! Anna! It's you. You're here!" Catherine screams over the music.

Will throws his arms around both of us and I can barely take it all in. The bouncer pulls me away from them and starts dragging me toward the stairs. "Girl, don't think I'm gonna let you stay up in here after you tried to play me."

Will tries to push him away but I say, "Stop. It's fine. We need to get out of here. Ethan and Teeny are outside."

Will throws some money on the table and they follow me down the stairs. The bouncer all but tosses me out of the front door.

Ethan and Teeny, hearing all the noise, pop out from around the corner. Before he can brace himself, Will slams into him.

"Man, you had me scared out of my mind!"

Ethan falls back, holding his arm. I rush to him, catching him before he hits the ground. The concussion already has him a bit unsteady and I'm sure the staggering pain doesn't help.

"What's wrong?" Will says to him then turns to me. "What's wrong with him?"

We're causing a huge scene, which is not good. I scan the crowd, terrified I'll see that string of cross tattoos.

"We need to get off the street." I point to a walk-in pizza place on the next block. Will steps in front of us and Catherine gets behind. We get inside and I help Ethan into one of the few booths in the back.

His face is pale and he's got a faint sheen of sweat over his top lip.

"Will, can you get him some water?" I ask.

I sit next to him and Catherine and Teeny slide into the booth across. Will heads to the counter for water.

"Are you okay?" I ask.

He nods but doesn't speak.

"What happened to him?" Will asks when he returns with a full glass.

"He got shot yesterday. In the arm. Also got kicked in the head and we think he has a concussion."

He's woozy. As much as I want him to get better, it will help if he's a little out of it right now.

Catherine's jaw drops and her eyes fill with water. Will takes a step away and kicks the booth in front of us. "That son of a bitch," he yells out and the guy behind the pizza counter hollers for him to shut up.

"Shouldn't he be in a hospital?" Catherine asks.

"Probably." I answer.

Ethan finally seems to catch his breath and asks Will, "Did you talk to Fred? Tell him about my family and Anna's dad?"

"Yeah. Ben was at Pearl's when I got there. He was hounding her about where Emma was. He was really torn up. Knew something was wrong but no one knew anything. He wouldn't leave until I told him what I knew. He left with Fred and they were headed to Arkansas just as Catherine and I were headed here. I told them someone may be there, watching them. They are gonna tell y'all's folks that we're picking you up."

I nod, biting my lip so I won't cry and say a silent prayer that nothing bad happens to any of them. "I'm so sorry to put everyone in so much danger. If it wasn't for me, you all would be safe and sound back home."

Catherine reaches across the table and squeezes my hands. "You didn't ask for this, either. I'm just glad you're okay."

I squeeze her hands back and say, "We can't stay here. Ethan needs to be checked out by a doctor, but we need to get out of New Orleans first. He can explain everything in the car."

Ethan looks like he's about to pass out. This was too soon to move him.

Once we're out of the booth, he leans on me more than he probably realizes.

Will holds him up on his other side. "We're parked around the corner. Luckily, we got here before the crowd."

"Yeah, what's with all the people? Is it a weekend?" Teeny asks.

Will answers, "It's Friday night. Dude in the club told us it's the

St. Joseph's Day Parade tomorrow afternoon. They'll throw a damn parade for anything down here."

I spot Will's Explorer up ahead as I scan the street for Mateo. The crowd works for us because it's easy to blend right in with the different groups of people meandering through the Quarter. After half a block, Will is almost entirely holding Ethan up. Seeing him like this, I know I'm making the right decision.

It takes forever to get Ethan in the third row of the vehicle but somehow Will and I manage it.

Ethan grabs Will by the sleeve just before he turns to get out of the car and says, "Man, you're a good friend. I owe you."

"You know I love getting your ass out of trouble. You're gonna owe me for the rest of your life for this one." Will lets out a loud cackle, then jumps out of the car.

There are some extra hunting coats in the very back and I use those as pillows, stuffing them around Ethan until he finds a spot he's comfortable in.

I'm crouched on the floorboard beside him and I take his hand, bringing it to my mouth so I can kiss his bruised knuckles.

"Are you going to be okay to ride like this?" I ask.

He smiles and says, "It will be a helluva lot better than the ride down here." His eyes start to droop. It will only be seconds before he's out.

I lean in close and kiss him softly on the lips. He's out before I pull away. My head stays bent toward him until my eyes feel dry. Now it's time for the ugly part.

I hop out of the SUV. "Um, I gotta run to the bathroom before we get on the road," I say to the group then turn to Will. "Can I talk to you first?"

"Sure."

We step away from the SUV and he asks, "What's wrong?"

"I have to do something and I can't do it unless you agree to help me."

His brow creases and I can tell he isn't looking forward to what I'm about to say. "I'm not gonna like it am I?"

"No. But you have to agree."

"What is it?"

I take a deep breath. This is the hardest thing I'll ever do but it has to be done. "I'm staying here. To finish this."

Will starts to interrupt me but I hold up my hand to stop him. Will is one of the few people who knows everything that happened to Ethan and me in Arizona. "Just listen. Ethan is hurt. He needs a doctor. And Teeny has no business being anywhere near this. This is the only way. It will be better if all of you are as far away from here as possible."

"I'm not leaving you here. Not only are you my friend, but Ethan will hate me for the rest of my life."

"Ethan almost got killed, Will. Dead. I want you to get him out of town, get him to a hospital or a doctor or something. Thomas has someone watching my mom. Call Fred and tell him to tell Dad she's not safe. If I don't go back, he's going to hurt her. I had to make a deal so Ethan and Teeny could be safe."

Will shoves his hands in his pockets and turns in small circles, muttering to himself.

"I can't do it. I can't leave you," he finally says.

"This will never end if you don't." I don't wait for him to answer, just hug him quick and whisper, "Tell Ethan I love him."

Before I can pull away, he shoves his phone in my hand. "At least take this with you. This is insane, Anna."

And then I turn and lose myself in the crowd. I can hear Teeny scream my name, but I don't stop running.

Tears stream down my face and I don't care what I must look like. I am a hazard to everyone I come in contact with and I can't let them get hurt just because they are near me. There's a real chance I won't survive this, but at least it will only be me—not Ethan and Teeny, too. And at least this entire nightmare that started with me will end with me.

I go two blocks and I'm back to the spot where Tyler let us out not long ago. And there he is, waiting for my return.

I power Will's cell phone off then shove it in my back pocket, readjust the gun in my jacket pocket before jumping into the back-seat of the car. Tyler pulls away before I get my door shut. "I thought you changed your mind," he says.

"I almost did. Do you really think I will walk away from this?"

"Yes. I do. And I will do everything in my power to make sure of it."

It's not comforting to know my life is in the hands of a lunatic stalker but it's better than being on my own.

He makes me duck down on the way back, which means he really doesn't fully trust that I won't tell where the house is. But it also means he thinks I'll live to tell the tale.

I feel guilty for not telling Ethan everything. Really guilty. And I'm sure he will never trust me again. But I truly believe I've made the right choice. If Ethan was well, I would have never tried this without him, but he's not. I know Catherine will take care of Teeny, and Will will make sure Ethan gets medical treatment.

It takes no time to get back to the house with the courtyard. Apparently we drove around in circles earlier.

Thomas is waiting in front of the double doors when we get back.

"Tyler," I say just before he gets out of the car. "I'm trusting you. Don't let me down."

He smiles. "Anna, I'm on your side. I swear."

He gets out of the car and I follow, crawling out of the backseat. Thomas is standing in front of us, arms crossed in front of him.

"I take it Ethan and your sister are on their way out of town." He's so calm and cold sounding. No trace of emotion.

"Yes," I answer.

"Do you need a reminder of what's at stake?"

Mom.

"No. We're clear."

As much as I hate them both, I need to play along right now, at least until this is over. "I was the original contract—not them. You don't need anyone else. Just me."

A flicker of something I don't recognize, maybe smugness, crosses Thomas's face before he hides it away.

Thomas takes a step in my direction and I fight the urge to take a step back. I refuse to look weak in front of him.

"I hope that brave front you've put up doesn't crumble. Why don't you go back upstairs for now." It's not a question.

I'm back in my room before I loosen the death grip on the gun hidden in my jacket. The bed is in the same shape it was when Ethan crawled out of it. I bury myself in the covers, pulling them up over my head, and make sure my head falls into the same indention on the pillow. I inhale the scent of him that's left behind.

Being here, in this bed, by myself, I can't fight the urge to call him and make sure they left New Orleans. I have to assure myself that we didn't fall headfirst into a trap. Using the phone Will gave me, I call Catherine. She answers on the first ring.

"Anna! Is that you?"

"Yes. Did y'all get out of town?"

"Yes. We're on I-10. Why did you go back?"

"It's the only way to end this for good, Catherine."

Silence. And then she says, "Well, I'm so angry with you. You better come back home in one piece. Ethan woke up a few minutes ago mad as hell. Here he is." And then there's a muffled sound before Ethan gets on the other line.

"I can't believe you did this." I sense worry in his voice and anger, too.

"I'm sorry I lied to you. Again. But I knew you'd never leave without me. You're hurt, Ethan. And this problem is not going away. We both know it. And Thomas has someone watching Mom. He showed me pictures. . . ."

I hear Teeny begging to talk to me in the background and Ethan promises her she can as soon as he's done.

"So, you're just going to trust Thomas? Walk right into whatever plan he has?"

My heart is breaking because I know my chances of surviving this are slim. I feel so alone and powerless and scared. More scared than I thought possible. But the only thing that is keeping me from completely falling apart is that Ethan and Teeny will be okay and hopefully my parents and the Landrys, too.

"This has to end, Ethan. I want nothing more than to be in the car with you right now, but then what? We've talked about this for hours—who do we trust? Where do we go?"

He's doesn't reply.

"I'm so sorry about everything. Sorry I lied to you. Sorry your family is stuck on an island in Arkansas. Sorry you got shot. Sorry Teeny has been traumatized. And if this all works out, I totally understand if you never want to see me again."

I'm trying to hold the tears in but am not succeeding.

"Oh, Anna. Please don't cry. Please. This is killing me. You are a victim of this as much as the rest of us. That's what's making me crazy—your need to let all of this rest on your shoulders. And you're not getting rid of me that easily. I may be mad about what you've done but you're still stuck with me."

"Are they taking you to a doctor?" I ask.

"We're headed to Baton Rouge. Catherine's uncle lives there. He's a doctor." I hear the pain in his voice.

"Please don't be mad at Will. I really didn't give him a choice. Is Teeny okay?"

"Yeah, she wants to talk to you. I'm passing the phone to her but I want to talk to you again when she's done. Don't hang up."

"Okay."

My heart is thumping by the time Teeny gets on the phone. I'm not sure if I can handle hearing her voice right now.

"Sissy, why did you leave us? You said we'd stick together. What if something bad happens and you're by yourself?"

And then my heart cracks wide-open. "Teeny, it's going to be fine. I'll be back with you in a couple of days. I promise. Can you help take care of Ethan?"

"Yeah. I'm really pissed at you right now. Catherine is, too. And Will. He's mad you put him in that position. You managed to piss off this entire car of people. Especially Ethan. He's the most mad. He tried to crawl out of the backseat and punch Will for leaving you. Will says he's gonna chew your ass out when he sees you next."

I let out a quick laugh. "Yeah, I deserve that. I'm sorry everyone is mad. And I love you very much, okay?"

"Okay. Here's Ethan."

"Will you keep this phone on?" he asks once he's back on the phone.

I look at the screen and there's only 45 percent battery left. "I'm gonna have to power it off if I want the battery to last."

"Teeny's gonna stay at Catherine's family's house until this . . . is all over. Once I get checked out by the doctor, I'm coming back to New Orleans." And then he pulls the phone away and yells to everyone in the car, "And if anyone tries to stop me, I will beat the shit out of them with my one good arm. I'm talking to you, Will."

He gets back on the phone. "Promise me you'll try to get out of there. Don't stay and go through whatever Thomas has planned. I don't trust him and I don't trust Tyler, either. Get out of there in the morning then call me and tell me where to come get you. Don't do this, Anna."

"He'll hurt Mom if I leave. Try to get to you and Teeny, too. I promise I'll be careful. I really wish you'd stay in Baton Rouge but I know you won't. If you come back, stay out of the Quarter until you hear from me. Mateo is still here somewhere."

He lets out a heavy breath of air. I know he's upset that I didn't tell him what he wants to hear. "Do you still have the gun?"

"Yes."

"God, I wish we could have gotten some more practice in. Listen, there are plenty of bullets and I put one in the chamber. A Glock doesn't have a mechanical safety. If you pull the trigger, it will fire, so be careful. Keep the silencer off; you want people to come running when you start firing. You don't have to do anything for the next bullet to load, just keep pulling the trigger."

"Okay. Pull the trigger. Keep firing."

"And Anna, when you shoot a gun because you're in danger for your life, you shoot to kill. Hold it steady, aim for the chest, and keep your eye on the target. Do you understand? Use all of the bullets if you have to."

I swallow hard and realize my hands are shaking. "Okay." I didn't tell him I stood over Mateo's body and couldn't pull the trigger.

"I love you, Anna. More than you know. You gotta come back to me, okay? We'll figure the rest of it out later, but you have to come back to me."

"I love you, too. That's why I had to do this. I can't risk you getting hurt or dying. That's the only reason I lied was to keep you safe. I hope you know that."

"I'm scared to death to get off the phone with you," he whispers.

"Me, too. But I don't want to use up too much battery. I'm going to power off the phone but I'll call you in the morning."

"You promise?"

"Yes, I promise. I love you."

Then I end the call. And cry myself to sleep.

A slamming door has me jumping up in the bed. It's still dark out but I can tell it won't be long before the sun starts to rise. I tiptoe to the French door and crack it open. It's cool out, and windy. The plants in the courtyard are doing a rhythmic dance back and forth.

I catch a glimpse of Thomas walking across the courtyard toward a small wooden door in the corner. He opens it but doesn't move away. By his hand gestures I can tell he's talking to someone.

I move out on the balcony for a better look. The person on the other side of the door steps through the opening but I can't make out any details.

Then I hear a door open and close below me. It's Tyler, heading to Thomas and the unknown person. The other person moves deeper in the shadows while Thomas meets Tyler halfway across the courtyard. He passes a cell phone to Thomas and I hear a one-sided phone call in muffled tones, but can't make out the exact words. Tyler takes the phone back once Thomas is finished.

Thomas leans in close, talking quietly to Tyler. Tyler nods then heads to where the car is parked and I hear it crank.

I don't know what time it is but it's got to be close to dawn. Where is he going?

Thomas waits until the car is gone before he moves back to the door. Whoever is there waiting, Thomas doesn't want Tyler to see him.

I move down the balcony but keep my back to the wall. Thomas finally moves aside and lets the other person step inside, light from the courtyard falling across his face. My knees go weak the second I see him. He's got a scarf wrapped around his neck but I know what's underneath it.

Cross tattoos.

Chapter 26

NEW RULE BY ANNA BOYD:

They're all foe. Don't trust anyone. There are no exceptions to this rule.

OH my God, I was so stupid.

Stupid. Stupid. Stupid.

They stop walking close to where I'm hiding on the balcony above them, then I hear faint steps coming up the outside stairs.

As quickly and quietly as I can, I shut the door and dive into the bed, faking sleep. I sense a shadow move across my window and it takes everything in me to relax my body.

As soon as I hear Thomas making his way back downstairs, I slide out of the bed and creep through the door. There is no way in hell I'm about to miss what's going on.

Once Thomas is back in front of Mateo, he motions him to sit down in one of the chairs.

Are they friends? What is going on?

So this is why he wasn't worried about me making noise in the convent or taking Ethan and Teeny out of here. He knew there was NO ONE out there trying to kill us.

I peek through a gap in the balcony floor and watch them. Mateo's posture might be relaxed but his face tells a different story.

Whatever they are, I don't think they're friends.

"So tell me, where are they now?" Thomas asks Mateo.

"At a private residence in Baton Rouge. Records show the house belongs to a Dr. Patrick Alexander."

Oh, shit. He knows where they are.

"And the boy's injuries?"

"He hasn't left the house. I'm assuming if the doctor thinks his condition is serious, he'd get him to a hospital."

And there's a drastic change in Thomas's personality. He looks much more like the man I knew in Natchitoches when he was trying to gain my trust as a federal agent. From what I can tell, he even seems to be smiling.

Not only is he a sociopath, he must have multiple personalities. Or is this part of the game? Is he making Mateo feel comfortable just like he did with me in Natchitoches?

"And why exactly did you shoot him? That wasn't part of the plan—you were just supposed to locate them. I wanted them back unharmed."

Mateo comes halfway out of his chair when he answers, "That son of a bitch kicked me! Twice. And then he rushed me. He's lucky I didn't pop him in the head."

"No, you were the only one popped in the head," Thomas says with a chuckle.

He actually chuckled.

Mateo doesn't crack a smile, just pulls his hair back showing a row of stitches. "When this is over, I intend to repay the compliment."

I almost vomit.

"They should have never had that much time on the outside," Thomas says. He looks back to the balcony and I press myself farther into the wall.

"You shouldn't have lost them. And if you would have put a tracker on them that was easy to follow, I would have found them a helluva lot sooner."

Tracker? He put a tracker on us? This was a big mistake. I knew something else was going on, but this is so much worse than I thought!

Thomas stiffens. "I wouldn't have lost them if it wasn't for you. I told you not to come to Ursuline."

"And I told you before, be careful how you talk to me," Mateo replies. "I was coming here, and it's hard to do that without passing the convent. I stopped to see if you needed help when I saw the crowd."

We're close to Ursuline. Really close.

"Anna made a spectacle of herself. The rumors worked against me. And Tyler freaked out like a five-year-old girl. I could have beat him to a pulp for being so stupid."

"How'd you get them back?"

"Anna called Ty. Apparently the lovesick bastard kept the same number just in case she called. It's almost pathetic but at least it worked out for us."

Mateo stands up and pulls a package out of his pocket. "I retraced their steps to a pawnshop. Once I made it clear I wasn't leaving until I got what they pawned, the greaseball who owns the place finally turned it over. This is how they had the money for a hotel room. And by the way, that tracker only told me they were in the building . . . It didn't give me a read on the room."

Thomas opens the package and pulls out the letters, picture frame, and the pocket watch. "What is this?"

"Some old shit from the convent. Dude nearly pissed his pants when I took it from him and destroyed the footage of the kids from the security cameras. I know you hate leaving any sort of trace behind." Mateo gets up and paces near the table. I push farther back, praying he doesn't spy me up here.

"One problem," Mateo says. It looks like he's struggling with what he wants to say. "When I woke up after she cracked that bottle over my head, my gun was gone."

Thomas puts everything back in the bag and asks, "What do you mean gone?"

"The gun is gone," Mateo bites out.

The difference between Thomas and Mateo are obvious. Whatever Mateo is feeling shows in his face, his movements, and his voice. But Thomas is completely different. Right now, he looks calm and relaxed but I know it's not real. I wonder if Mateo knows that.

Thomas waits a moment before changing the subject. "And what about Williams? Where is he?"

"In Mandeville. Didn't think you'd want him in the Quarter just yet, but he's close enough to be here within a few minutes. He's about to blow a gasket trying to figure out what's going on and where the boy is. The last message I sent said that he would get instructions today about where to meet. And as far as I can tell, he hasn't called anybody yet. Too scared about what will happen to the boy." Mateo laughs and I instantly feel sorry for Agent Williams. He must be in hell wondering how his grandson is doing.

"And how is the boy?" Thomas asks. "You're not to touch him, remember?"

"He's fine, but I think you're making a mistake there. Just think how *useful* he could be if we kept him a while."

It's the way he says *useful* that makes my skin crawl. Thomas may be a cold-blooded killer but Mateo seems pure evil.

"This is my show so my call. Don't touch him," Thomas says in a relaxed tone. I wish I knew what he was thinking. "And what about Riley?"

Who's Riley?

"Yeah. All set."

"And no problems with the group in Arkansas?"

I slide down the wall. Is he talking about our families?

"It's getting pretty tense but they're still on the island. Checked the webcam a few hours ago."

Mateo waits a moment before saying, "I'm surprised you let the other two go. Seems like you're getting soft."

There's a threat there that even I can see. "Again, not your concern. I will clean up those loose ends. You don't need to worry about them."

"Everything that happens here is my concern."

I can't breathe. I can't believe how stupid I was. Ethan and Teeny aren't safe . . . not at all.

I'm waiting for one of them to throw a punch but Mateo finally relaxes. "So, it's still on for this afternoon?" he asks.

"Yes. Three p.m. Everything has to be ready by then. And Hammond, where is he?"

"Close. Still in the Quarter. He still thinks he's communicating with Williams instead of yours truly. Said he saw the kids near Café du Monde and they ran from him. He couldn't understand why." Mateo pulls a pack of cigarettes out of his pocket, offering one to Thomas.

He accepts the smoke and says, "Good. For this to work, he needs to be killed at the site. We'll bring him in after we've finished with Vega. Once they find the pictures and reports, Hammond's guilt will be sealed."

Hammond isn't the mole? He chased us but he wasn't trying to hurt us. God, we were so naive. Thomas just wants the agency to *think* he's the mole. So who is it?

"When do you want Williams to show?"

"By three thirty it should be done. We just need to make sure it's laid out just right." A thin stream of smoke drifts up from Thomas and hangs suspended in the air in front of me.

"And Anna?"

"I promised Ty she wouldn't get hurt."

Mateo chuckles and shivers race down my spine. "She's going to get hurt, no doubt about it. I'm not risking everything for her to run back home and spill her guts to anyone who will listen. There will only be three people who know what really went down here—me, you, and Riley."

Thomas takes a long drag. "I'll get him out of town before any of this starts. He's so overemotional where she's concerned. I should have trusted my instincts and gotten rid of her in Arizona. He's always been weak, but I've protected him for too long. Maybe if she gets caught in a little cross fire it will toughen him up."

I was so stupid.

"Yeah, but if he wouldn't have screwed up, we'd still be waiting for the right time to make our move. We just bumped this takeover up a few years thanks to him." Mateo crushes his cigarette out and scoots closer to Thomas. "And how do I know you won't try to screw me over when the dust settles?"

Thomas laughs. "You don't. But what I'm offering you is worth the risk. Am I right?"

"I won't be so easy to get rid of," Mateo says. They're both smiling at each other but it's the sick kind of smile that is just for show.

"I wouldn't expect anything less." Thomas waits a moment before continuing, "We'll meet back here when it's done and settle up. The door off the kitchen will be open. You can wait in there if you beat me back."

"No problem."

Even though I thought I was being so clever, I've just played right into his hands. We all have—me, Agent Hammond, Agent Williams.

They start talking about random sports stuff now like they're just two guys shooting the shit. I crawl back to my room but leave the door open so I can hear if someone else comes or goes.

I yank the phone out of my back pocket and power it up, calling Catherine's phone.

She answers on the third ring and I can tell I woke her up.

"Anna?"

"Yes. How's Ethan?"

"He's sleeping but he told me to wake him if you called. My uncle said the wound looked good and that whoever fixed him up did a really good job. He cleaned it really good and started him on some antibiotics but that was it. Ethan is refusing a pain pill, says he needs to be alert. With the concussion, he just needs to rest. He's hell-bent on heading back to New Orleans this morning. Will told him the only way he would take him was if he got some sleep first. How are you? I'm worried sick about you. We all are."

"I'm okay. I'm so sorry you're in this mess, Catherine. I'll make it up to you . . . when I can. I hate to wake him, but I really need to talk to Ethan. Can you get him up?"

"Sure. Hold on. Oh, and be safe, Anna. Don't do anything stupid. Anything else, I guess I should say—leaving us was already pretty stupid!"

It's quiet on the other end for a few seconds so I poke my head out of the room to make sure they're still down there talking. I hear their faint murmurings so I slip back in my room.

"Anna," Ethan says, his voice groggy from sleep.

"Oh God, Ethan. Are you okay?" I'm nearly busting with wanting to tell him what I've learned.

"Tired but better. Room isn't spinning like it was yesterday. Did you get away? We can be on the road in ten minutes, Anna. Tell me where you are."

"It's so much worse than that. We've been played. I've been played. Mateo is here, outside talking to Thomas like they're old friends. And he knows where you are. He told Thomas you're at Dr. Alexander's house in Baton Rouge. Is that Catherine's uncle's name?"

"Are you kidding me?" Ethan asks.

"No. He mentioned a tracker. I think we have something on us. And I think someone is watching the house."

"I've been wondering why he only shot me in the arm if he took the contract to kill me."

"Yeah, he wasn't supposed to shoot you at all. He was supposed to find us and call Thomas. But he was pissed you kicked him in the head."

"Oh, just wait. I'll kick that son of a bitch until I bash his head in."

"Ethan, I need you to promise me something. Don't come back here. It isn't safe. They are so far ahead of us, you'll end up getting hurt. Take Teeny and run."

"Hold on." And then I hear a muffled sound and Ethan's gone from the phone for a few seconds. "Sorry, trying to get dressed. That's bullshit. I'll be there in a couple of hours. I talked to Catherine's uncle. He's meeting a lawyer buddy of his at the police department here in Baton Rouge this morning and they are going to try to figure out what to do. The dude is smart when it comes to medicine but he's scared shitless about getting involved with this."

"If the guy watching the house sees this, he might go for Mom!"

"I'll tell him the house is being watched. Truthfully, I think he's looking for a way out of helping us. Do we have any idea if Agent Williams is on our side or theirs?"

"I think ours. Sounds like Noah was taken to keep him quiet. Agent Williams is here. He's in Mandeville, wherever that is."

"A town right outside of New Orleans. Is Tyler in on this, too? Can you get out of there? God, I wish you would have come with us."

"It wouldn't have made a difference. They would have gotten me back somehow and maybe someone would have gotten hurt in the process. They also talked about somebody named Riley but I don't know who that is. Tyler was out there with them for a few minutes but Thomas sent him on some sort of errand before Mateo showed himself. He's using Tyler and Tyler has no idea." I still hate Tyler for what he's done and for what he's doing but a very small part of me feels so sorry for him. He must really look up to Thomas to be involved with this and Thomas is making a puppet out of him, too. I totally believed him when he said he would make sure we were okay. But now I know that's not a promise he can keep. "Whatever they have planned, it's for three p.m. today. Agent Williams will be led in when it's all over. Hammond isn't the mole either, but Agent Williams will think that."

"Why do they need you? I don't get this."

I quickly tell him about Mateo's and Thomas's plan to kill him.

Ethan lets out a deep breath. "The best thing we've got going for us is that they don't know we're on to them. Check everything you have for a tracker, especially your shoes. It will be small and fit into a tiny space. I'll figure out how to get out of this house without being followed. You stay put until I can get there. Keep the phone powered on but put it on silent. I'll be there in two hours."

"Ethan, don't come here. Go get Mom. Make sure she's safe. Find a way to get in touch with Agent Williams and tell him what's really going on. Tell him to come to the Quarter and to keep his eyes peeled for me. And tell him about Hammond. But you stay away."

"I'll make sure someone gets your Mom and I'll get Catherine's uncle and his buddy to find Williams, but I'm coming back for you right now. It'll be hours before they're even talking about a plan. If I wait for them, it could be too late. I love you. Keep the phone on."

He ends the call.

I could scream! He's so stubborn! Why is he risking coming back? He's hurt and is no match for what's happening here. There may be no stopping him from coming back, but I will do anything in my power to keep him out of this disaster, so I power the phone off. Tiptoeing back out on the balcony, I listen for anything else I can find out about the plan for today.

The wind picks up again, blowing through the small trees planted in the courtyard, and the door I left open to my room slams shut.

Both men stop talking and look toward my room. I throw myself against the wall and I don't think they've seen me. I crawl back to my room, opening the door just enough to slip through, just as I hear steps coming up the outdoor stairs. I can't let them have any clue I've seen Mateo or know anything they've said.

Racing to the bed, I shove the gun and the phone under my pillow and get the covers over me just as I catch a glimpse of Thomas's shadow fall across the window.

I fake sleep. Let every muscle relax and concentrate on even breathing. I'm not sure how long he stands there because I am terrified of opening my eyes, but after what seems like an eternity, I inch my lids open.

He's gone.

I'm still lying in the bed an hour later. I can't quit thinking about the conversation I overheard.

There's a knock on the door and then Thomas's booming voice asking, "Are you up?"

I'm still in the bed, mostly buried under the covers mainly because I can't find the will to get up.

"Come in," I call back.

Thomas walks in and looks around. He's here to find the gun. "We'll be leaving here in a few hours."

"Where are we going?" I ask.

He shakes his head and answers, "You'll know everything all in due time."

Oh, I'm sure I will.

"I'm here. I know you have someone watching Mom. Please tell me so I can be prepared."

He paces around the room, eyeing every surface. As if I would leave the gun out in the open.

As I watch Thomas open drawers, I still try to process what is going to happen today. Mateo will double-cross Vega. Thomas will take over Señor Vega's position and Mateo will take over Thomas's. Win-win for them both.

"So who will be the big boss after today? You?"

He doesn't answer but I see a small grin on his normally emotionless face.

"Is it that easy? The other cartels will let you just slip into his place?"

I need him talking.

He smiles a little bigger and my stomach turns. "I'm not sure easy is the word. Let's just say I've spent a number of years preparing for this day. In the end, it should be a smooth transition."

He walks to the dresser on the far wall and peeks in each drawer there. When he goes into the bathroom, I slide off the other side of the bed and crawl to a set of drawers he's already checked. Slipping the gun inside, I pray he won't check this area twice.

I make it back in the bed and under the covers just as he comes out of the bathroom.

"Get up."

"Why?" I ask, hoping my voice sounds confused. "What are you looking for?"

He doesn't answer, just motions for me to get out of the bed.

Once I'm out, he throws back the covers and searches the bed, the pillows, and even underneath.

"You aren't worried about Mateo being there?" Even knowing what I do, this plan is dangerous but I'm hoping to distract him.

"No. Mateo is an amateur. I will kill Señor Vega. And Mateo. And anyone else in the room." He shoots a glance in my direction. He's come up empty and I try not to smile. "Stay here until I come get you. I'll have Tyler bring you some food."

And then he's gone.

Chapter 27

NEW RULE BY ANNA BOYD:

Never involve innocent people if you can help it. Just because you're fighting for your life doesn't mean they should have to as well. Plus, it's just rude.

THE second Thomas leaves the room, I hop out of bed. I could tell he didn't want to leave without finding the gun, but unless he was going to come out and ask me about it, there wasn't much left he could do.

I've got a few hours to get control of what's happening or I could very well be dead. I think he fully intends for me to get caught in the cross fire. I will be nothing but a loose end at that point.

And then he'll go after Ethan and Teeny.

First, I need to find the tracker. I grab every single item I brought with me from Ursuline and throw it into a heap on the floor. Starting with my clothes, I inspect every inch of them, paying close attention to the thicker areas like collars and pockets.

Nothing.

I grab my tennis shoes. They are the only shoes I've had since the island. Taking the soles out, I dig around the inside of the shoe until my finger runs across a hard part in the toe of the left one. It takes forever to get it out but once I do, I know I've found it.

It's small, not even as big as the tip of my pinkie finger, and looks almost like a button battery.

So this is how Mateo followed us to that souvenir shop. This is how Thomas has known every single thing we've done since we left the convent.

I stare at the tiny thing in my hand. What to do with it? For now, I'm going to keep it on me so I don't alert him as to what I know, but at some point I'll have to figure out the perfect way for it to help me disappear.

Thomas is sending Tyler away but I've got to get to him first.

I checked the doors in my room and they're not locked. That doesn't mean I can make it out of this compound, though—there are still the double wooden doors that lead to the street and the small door Mateo came through the night before. I'm not sure if there's any other way out of here.

I need to find Tyler.

I retrace the steps that lead me downstairs. Searching the rooms I've found him in before, I come up empty. I don't know where he sleeps in this place but that doesn't stop me from looking.

The fifth door I open is a jackpot. Tyler is there, throwing clothes in a bag, and doesn't seem very happy about it.

He looks up when I open the door and I say, "You can't leave."

"I have to. It's part of the plan. The plan to make everything right."

I inch inside the room and shut the door behind me. I need to do this just right. To say what I need to say just right.

"So you just blindly follow whatever he tells you to do, and you believe everything he tells you no matter what? I'll be right in the middle of a confrontation between him and Vega and Mateo and you really think I'm walking out of there alive? Excuse me if I think that's the stupidest shit ever."

"The only reason I'm going along with this plan is because he promised me that this is the only way to keep you alive." He drops his hand and looks toward his bag. "You have no idea how much I hate that I had any part of drawing you back into this with the journal and flowers."

"Why did you do that? You knew I would think it was Thomas the way you signed it. You knew there was a good chance the suits would find out about it. What were you thinking?"

"When Thomas came home with the journal, he threw it on the table and said, 'I guess you did make an impression on her after all. She feels bad for leaving you behind in Florida.' I know it was wrong but I wanted to read what you wrote." He finally looks up at me and says, "I missed you."

"So you and Thomas both read it," I say it more as a statement than a question.

"Yes. I read it. And then I felt terrible. I'd been checking in on you after you left Florida." He holds his hands up when he realizes how bad that sounds. "Not in a creepy way. Everything looked fine on the outside. I had no idea how it was for you, or how bad things really were. That's when I decided you needed it back. I could tell how important it was to you."

I don't say anything so he keeps talking, swaying back and forth. "The note was a mistake, I know that now. But at the time, I just wanted to tell you in some way that I hoped things were better for you. That I hoped the nightmares were gone. I know I couldn't sign it with my name and even if it was left unsigned, you'd assume it was from him. In some way, leaving it with just a *T* meant it was possible you might think of me. I know that sounds stupid."

"But why the flowers?" I ask.

He gives me a crooked little smile and says, "Because they're your favorite."

I can't look at him without my stomach turning. Something is so very wrong with him that he can't see this for what it really is. But I truly believe he is the only reason I am still alive.

"If you leave, there won't be anyone here to make sure I survive what's happening this afternoon. He plans on killing me. And my family."

This gets his attention.

"No. He promised me you would be safe and he promised he would let you go when it's over."

"I think there's a lot about this plan that you don't know. I was on the balcony early this morning when you brought Thomas the phone. There was a man, hiding in the shadows. Then Thomas sent you away."

The pair of jeans he's holding fall back to the pile of clothes he just picked them up from.

"He sent you away so you wouldn't see who he was meeting with. It was the assassin, Mateo. The one 'after us.' The same man who shot Ethan in the arm. The one Thomas is supposedly trying to kill. He was here and they weren't acting like enemies. Not at all."

He's shaking his head, looking confused. "No. That's not possible. All this that we've done is to stop him from killing us. And you. He wouldn't lie to me." He storms toward me, grabbing me by my upper arms, lifting me off the ground. "You're just saying this to turn me against him. But you can't. We're all we have. We only have each other."

"Is that what he told you? Is that how he talked you into going along with such horrible things?"

He drops me to the ground and I fall on my butt. He returns to his packing just like before.

"Tyler, listen to me. I heard him talking to the other man. Did you know he put a tracker on us?" I pull the small round device out of my pocket and hold it out in my hand for him to see.

He glances over but is still quiet.

"He told Mateo that you were pathetic for keeping the same number just in case I called. He said you were stupid for freaking out like a five-year-old girl when the crowd formed at the convent. He said he was getting you out of town before any of this starts just in case I get caught in a little cross fire. Maybe if I got killed, it would toughen you up."

His eyes pop to mine and I know I nailed it. He's heard this before.

"And I'm not the only innocent person who will get hurt by all this. He said they would go after Teeny and Ethan when this was over. Clean up the loose ends. Did you know that? And Hammond isn't the mole. Thomas is setting him up. Do you know who the real mole is?" I ease down on the bed next to him. "Tyler, you're better than this. Help me. Be on my side."

He drops his head in his hands and starts crying. It's so incredibly awkward, I'm not sure what to do, so I put an arm around his shoulder and give him a there, there, kind of pat on the back.

He sits up abruptly, wiping his eyes quickly. "We need to get back to Ursuline. There's something there I want to see."

He grabs a dark hoodie and baseball cap out of his bag and throws it at me. "Put this on."

There's no car or ducking in the backseat this time. No, this time we're on foot as we slip out a side door that puts us in a narrow alley that dumps out on a narrow street.

I'm afraid to push Tyler too hard right now because I think he could flip either way. We left the tracker inside the house, buried under some clothes. From what it sounded like when they were talking, the tracker gives a general area of where it is, but not the specific location.

"What's at Ursuline?"

We're walking fast. I wasn't wrong when I thought the Quarter felt small. In the few times I've been out of these streets, I keep seeing the same groups of people walking around. The bride-to-be from the first night, the group of guys Ethan nearly puked on. We all seem to be roaming the same streets over and over.

"Thomas tries not to keep any records. Nothing to prove what he is or where he goes or anything that can be used against him. But sometimes there's just no way around it. He fell in love with New Orleans, the French Quarter especially, years ago. This is one of his favorite spots to hide out in. He loves the craziness of this town and the history.

"Anyway, there's a room on the third floor of Ursuline with nothing but filing cabinets. I saw him walk in there with a large envelope and come out empty-handed just after we arrived. It was something he didn't want me to see. And he's been going over there a lot in the last two days. Something is going on over there."

We walk two blocks to the convent. I didn't realize just how close the house was to Ursuline. It's so different seeing it in the light of day. It looks nice. And harmless. It's hard to believe that's where he was keeping us.

"Come on, we can get in through the back."

It's not empty inside like the night we fled. There are two tourists here, being led around by an elderly guide.

"I can't believe he held us here when there are random people coming in and out."

Tyler walks to the end of the hall to a narrow staircase. "He says the best place to hide is where no one will think to look. The second floor is nothing but storage and no one ever goes up to the third floor. And with an old building like this, you can't hear anything down here."

"So do they think he's a priest?" I ask.

Tyler lets out a laugh. "Yes. And they love him here. This is where they keep records for this whole area and any priest can come in for research but none of them ever do. He talks to them in a French accent. He tells them what they want to hear and they do whatever he wants no matter how stupid it is."

And then he stops. We're halfway up and he leans against the wall.

"Just like me. He talks to me like a brother because he knows being part of a family is what I want more than anything. And I do whatever he wants, no matter how stupid."

It's almost like I can see the lightbulb going off over his head.

"At least you know now. At least it's not too late to change things. You can help me and my family and that means something. You mean something to me. No matter what, you protected me and for that I will always be grateful." I may still think he's crazy, but I'd rather he be crazy on my side.

He grabs my hand and squeezes it softly. "Thank you for that. And thank you for being here with me now. I don't think I could stand up to him alone."

"You can. You're way stronger than you think."

"Let's hope so." And then we're bounding up the rest of the stairs.

He flips the lights to the room with the shower and I stagger back.

The bed is gone, as is the nightstand, but the desk remains. Above the desk is a large corkboard—and it's what's on the corkboard that makes me want to vomit. It's the last year of my life played out in pictures and maps and notes.

"What is this?" I ask.

"It's how he tracked you while you were in the program, using the information he got from his sources. He must have printed everything out and brought it here." He pauses a moment before saying, "This must be how he's framing Hammond." He points to a stack of correspondence, notes with Hammond's name all over it. "There's a lot he hasn't told me. I never knew he had so much information until now."

I walk to the wall slowly. There's so much stuff there my eyes have trouble focusing.

Then I realize there is some sort of pattern. The grouping at the top are pictures of us in our first placement—Hillsboro, Ohio. There is a picture of Teeny and me in the small backyard, a picture of Mom coming out of the front door of the small house, and one of Dad and Agent Williams talking through the window. There's also a sheet of typed paper, just like the one the suits gave us when we got to a new placement, summing up our new identity.

I read the familiar words:

Family name: Holmes.

Parents: Charles and Elizabeth

Children: Madeline and Hayden

My eyes follow a small line drawn to the next grouping—our second placement: Springfield, Missouri. A few more pictures here since our stay there was longer. Same typed sheet. But there is also a grainy black-and-white image of the suits picking me up from Charlotte's house the night I got on Facebook and screwed up our placement there.

My stomach drops to think he was just outside. Or if not him, someone working for him. Right there, the whole time.

I glance back at Tyler and he's watching me nervously, the way you watch an animal you're not sure about and that you're hoping isn't about to attack you.

I turn back to the board. It's sickening to see, but I can't ignore it, either. I leave Springfield and follow the line to Florida.

The images there are much closer. More intimate. There are even a few of me and Tyler on the beach the first night we kissed. What I thought was a sweet, romantic night on the beach, under the stars, just me and Tyler, was a total lie.

"I didn't know until after you left that those pictures were taken." He's behind me now and it's disgusting, standing here in this room with him, seeing this.

"That doesn't make any of this okay. At all."

He takes a step closer and I can feel his breath on the back of my neck. "I took you to the beach that night, to the most secluded part, thinking we would be alone. I swear, I never knew exactly when he was watching. Thomas doesn't tell me everything. Still doesn't. He believes the only way for a plan to work is to make sure no one knows the entire plan."

He thinks we're having a moment, me and him, looking at these pictures of us making out on the beach. And in this moment I know Tyler is seriously sick in the head. And it's probably Thomas's fault.

"So something will tip off the suits to come here and they will find all of this. But Hammond will be dead and there will be no way for him to defend himself and they won't even look for the real mole."

"He's a genius," Tyler says, his voice full of awe.

I move away from the Florida pictures and the images get more and more painful. Mom at the liquor store buying bottles and bottles of gin. She's out in public, hair a mess, and no makeup at all. And Teeny. She looks physically different in these pictures than she did two placements ago: slumped shoulders, pale complexion, sad eyes. God, I remember those sad eyes. They ate at my soul.

I skim over the pictures from Kentucky and South Carolina, instead wanting to see us in Natchitoches.

And there we are in that crappy little cottage. There is image after image of me going back and forth to Pearl's, sometimes walking with Teeny and sometimes riding in Ethan's truck. I take a step closer so I can make out the grainy black-and-white images: the house in the country where the party we were at got busted, me running from the laundry room, and Ethan and me on that dock down by Cane River.

"I can't even tell you how sickened I am by this," I say.

"Would you believe me if I told you I am too?"

No, the voice inside me says.

I turn away from the wall and look at the desk. It's covered in papers. It looks like reports from the people watching us—everything about us all laid out. And other things, too. Bank statements and ledger forms. Stuff that reminds me about the ledgers we found in Arizona that Thomas was desperate to recover. I pick up another sheet of paper; it's a phone number, and then written above it: *Hammond*. I shove it in my pocket.

"Come with me to the other room," Tyler says. "There's something else I'm looking for."

Going down the hall, I peek inside the room where Teeny and I were kept just a few days earlier and it's empty. Completely empty. No mattress. No card table of snacks. And the shutter and wall have both been repaired. You would have never known we were here.

Now we're in the room with all the filing cabinets that I saw from the air conditioner duct. It's inching toward noon and there's no telling if Thomas is looking for either of us yet.

Tyler starts looking through drawers and I step back out in the hall. I power on Will's cell phone and stare at the keypad. I can't call the hotline number for the suits because I still don't know who the real mole is. I don't have Agent Williams's number, but I do have Agent Hammond's. I quickly dial his number and he answers on the second ring.

"Agent Hammond. It's Anna," I whisper in the phone, hoping Tyler won't hear me.

"Anna! What's going on? Agent Williams keeps sending me these crazy messages telling me to come to the French Quarter, but don't tell anyone. Are you in trouble?" You can't miss the stress in his voice and I hate more than ever that we ran from him the other day.

"I'm at Ursuline. The third floor. Thomas is setting you up. It's a trap to make it look like you're a mole in your agency. Agent Williams is close by but his grandson is being held hostage. You're not getting those messages from him, they're from one of Thomas's men. I can't talk long. Please come get me!"

"I'm on my way!"

I end the call and go find Tyler.

He's searching for something so I open a drawer and flip through the files. The problem is I don't know what we're looking for and I can't get the images from the next room out of my mind. All I've found is church document after church document.

"Here it is," Tyler says and I run to the cabinet where he's standing.

"What is it?"

He drops down on the floor and spills the contents of a brown manila envelope. Four bundled stacks of hundred dollar bills, a handful of papers, and two passports are on the floor between us.

I can't help but squeal. "That's forty thousand bucks." I don't know that I've ever seen that much cash in one place.

Tyler goes for the papers while I go for the passports. They're blue with a gold crest, very similar to the U.S. passport, but it says REPÚBLICA FEDERATIVA DO BRASIL. I open the first one and it's Thomas's picture but the name is listed as Rafael Costa. I hold it up to show Tyler, "Look, meet Rafael."

He glances at it quickly but seems more concerned with the papers he's reading. I lean over so I can see what it is, but he hands it to me instead.

I start reading but I don't know what it is.

"Those are wire transfers. From five or so different banks into five or so different accounts under the same name on the passport."

I read the papers again and see lots of different names all transferring money to the same person: Rafael Costa.

"I don't get it," I say.

Then Tyler hands me another sheet. It's written in Spanish. Or Portuguese, I guess, if this is from Brazil.

"I can't read this."

He points to the top and says, "I can read some of it. It's a deed for a piece of property. In Rio."

I look down at the second passport, but Tyler grabs it before I can. He opens it up and I can tell immediately it's not for him since his face drains of color.

"He's leaving you behind, isn't he?"

He's got a death grip on the passport. "There has to be another one in here. He wouldn't leave me behind. He wouldn't!" He searches the brown envelope but it's empty.

There's nothing else inside so he moves back to the file drawer, throwing papers out as he searches, still clutching the second passport.

He's doing that crazy back and forth swaying thing again.

He's losing it. Fast.

Tyler slams the file drawer closed and screams, "I can finally see just where I fit. Nowhere!"

He throws the passport down and it lands near my leg, but all of a sudden I'm scared to pick it up.

"Go ahead. Look."

I pick it up and open it to the page with the picture. Agent Parker's smiling face is staring back at me. Or should I say Mariana Costa's.

Chapter 28

RULES FOR DISAPPEARING
BY WITNESS PROTECTION PRISONER #18A7R04M

~~It's risky hanging out with a bunch of amateurs.~~

NEW RULE BY ANNA BOYD:

It's riskier hanging out with your psycho ex-boyfriend and his assassin brother.

I see her face but I can't process what it means. She's dead. Thomas killed her in the woods and left her body there.

"She's the mole," I say, and the moment it leaves my lips I know I'm right. "And they're leaving town—new identities, the money, the property. . . ."

He nods and shoves the money, papers, and passports back in the envelope. "Yes. Looks that way. Apparently he's *not* taking over once Vega is gone. And it doesn't look like I'll be traveling with them."

"But . . . but . . . I don't understand," I stammer out. "She was in the back of the van. Her face was a wreck. She was so scared."

"She must be a very good actress."

"You really didn't know she was involved with this? I'm sorry if I find that hard to believe." I'm seething.

Tyler stiffens and says, "I told you, he doesn't tell me everything."

"You really had no idea?"

He slams the filing cabinet drawer closed and says, "No. I saw her on your detail but I didn't know she knew Thomas. I thought he killed her and left her in the woods. He let me believe that and I was okay with it. How sick is that?

"He told me he was overthrowing Vega. That he would be running the cartel. He promised me a place there. We would be together. Like a real family. But that's not what he's doing. He's getting out. He said they never let you out when you work for the family so I guess this is how he's doing it. It's all a lie. All of it."

Tyler stands up, shoves the envelope inside his jacket, then leaves the small room. I follow him out. There is so much rage in me that I'm afraid I can't contain it. It sucked when I thought Hammond was the mole. That someone could get that close to my family and betray us at the same time is shocking, but for some reason finding out it's *her* is even worse. It's like a punch in the stomach. She had the nerve to go through the charade of making me change my appearance when all the time she was the one I should have been hiding from. How could she have shown up at my house after I got my journal back full of concern and worry?

What a bitch.

And then in the van. Her swollen eye and busted lip. That look of fear etched across her face. Her screams when he pulled her out of the back of the van. All a lie.

And that bitch cut my hair.

My knees buckle and I fall down a few of the steps. I drop my head in my hands. "I've never felt more stupid in my entire life."

Tyler pulls me up. "We've got to get out of here."

We make it to the bottom floor and back out on the street without incidence. I wonder what Tyler's going to do with the envelope. Or what Thomas is going to do when he finds it missing. I should have brought the gun with me when we left, but I just wasn't thinking straight.

"So what are we going to do now?" I ask as I scan the street for Agent Hammond. I don't know where he was when I called, but hopefully it won't take long to get here.

"We're leaving town." He stops walking and looks at me. "We'll find a cab to take us out of the Quarter, then we'll figure out where to go from there. It's just you and me, now Anna. I will protect you." And then he smiles.

Oh God. This is wrong. So wrong.

His forehead scrunches up. "You do want to come with me, right?"

It's hard to find the words I need to make him stay on my side when obviously my face is showing the disgust I feel.

"We need to concentrate on getting away from Thomas before we make any long-term plans, okay?"

I reach for his arm to give a reassuring squeeze but he moves it just out of reach.

I walk slowly, giving Agent Hammond time to get here. The house and Ursuline are so close that it doesn't take long before I can see the alley we came out of from earlier. Tyler scans the street for a cab and I pray one doesn't show. I may just have to make a run for it. We're both so focused on our personal goals that neither of us notices Thomas until he's right in front of us. I jump the second I see him.

"I've been looking for you," he says to Tyler. He's got that really controlled voice thing going on and I know he's pissed we left. And then he looks at my feet. Oh, crap. He probably tried to find me with the tracker and it didn't work because I left it at the house. God, please let him think it broke.

"Anna needed a little air. We just took a walk so I could say good-bye to her. I didn't see any harm in that."

Tyler is different. Everything about him: his voice, his posture, his steady eye contact with Thomas. And if I'm picking up on it, I know Thomas is, too.

"It's my fault," I say. "I begged him to let me get out for a minute. I was going crazy in there."

Thomas glances around the street then back at us. "We need to get back." He extends his arm, gesturing for us to go first. We start walking and I hate that he's behind us. Now, I'm scared for Agent Hammond to show. He doesn't know what Thomas looks like but Thomas for sure will spot him.

Once we're back in the courtyard, I turn to Tyler and pull him in for a hug so I can whisper in his ear. "You gotta act like you don't know anything. He'll know something's different." I pull away and say in a regular voice, "Thanks for the walk."

He gives me a hard look and I'm afraid I've lost him.

I run up the stairs and back to my room.

What do I do now? What do I do now? runs through my head.

Grabbing the gun, I lock myself in the bathroom and turn the water on to help drown out the sound.

Powering the phone on, I call Agent Hammond's phone.

"I'll be there in less than two minutes," he says instead of hello.

"I'm not there anymore. Thomas found me. I'm down the street in a private residence about two blocks away. I'll try to get out. Just be on the lookout for me."

"Be careful, Anna."

I end the call and then call Catherine's phone. I need to make sure Ethan isn't in the Quarter.

He answers on the first ring.

"What's going on? I've been trying to call you for hours. I'm here. Are you okay?"

"It's bad, Ethan. Agent Parker is the mole. Everything in the van was fake."

I've stunned him because it takes almost thirty seconds before he says, "That bitch. We're not far away—within a few blocks of you. Can you get out?"

"You know where I am?" I ask.

"Yeah. When we pulled back into town, Will remembered we could track his phone with one of those find-my-phone apps. As long as the power is on, we can see where it is. Right now, it's showing you're in the middle of the block between Chartres and St. Philip. Okay, we're driving around your block now, but it's a big block. I can't figure out which way to get in. Nothing but stores and bars and six sets of those wooden doors he drove through the other night. All painted green."

"Do you see an alleyway?"

"Yeah, there's at least one on every side. It's really crowded out here. . . . Something weird is going on. . . ."

And then someone's banging on the door.

"I gotta go. I'll call you right back," I whisper in the phone before ending the call. I don't power it off but I do put it on silent.

I crack the door and stick my head out. Thomas is on the other side. He's wearing a tuxedo, with a red bow tie. What the hell?

"We're moving this up a bit." He slides a white garment bag through the door to me and I take it from him. "Slip that on and be ready to go in five minutes."

He stares at me a few seconds then says, "I'll wait right here for you."

I slam the door and lock it again.

Oh my God.

I hang the bag on the hook on the back of the door and unzip it. I don't know what to expect—but it's surely not a white evening gown with full-length gloves and a jacket.

I stare at the dress for half the amount of time he's given me to get it on. I don't even know what to think about this, so I crack the door open to see if he's really waiting for me.

He is.

"I don't understand? Why do I need to put this dress on?"

"You'll understand in a moment. Please get dressed."

I shut the door and stare at the dress again. He's completely insane, but if dressing up will get me out of this house—I'll do it. I'm hoping I spot either Agent Hammond or Ethan on the street and can just jump in the car with them. I strip out of my clothes and take the dress off the hanger, checking it for a tracking device before stepping into it. If there's one there I can't find it. It's long and fitted but still a little big. Turning around to the mirror, I look ridiculous. My cheek is still bruised and my hair is a mess. I look like someone tried to do a makeover but the only thing they did was put a dress on me.

I crack the door open again. "Am I supposed to wear my tennis shoes with this or what?"

He shows me a pair of white flats but doesn't hand them to me. I feel certain there is a working tracker in there. He knows something is up but he doesn't know what.

I shut the door again and try to figure out where to put the phone and gun. All I have on under the gown is a pair of panties. No bra since the gown is strapless. I try to stick the phone in the bust area and it slips down and hits the floor. I've lost so much weight I can barely keep the dress up much less hide a cell phone in there.

And the gun is bigger than the phone. Where in the hell am I going to stick it?

A knock on the door has me jumping.

"Time to go, Anna."

The coat has one small pocket—the gun and phone can't fit in there together and I refuse to leave either behind. The gloves! Once I have the coat on, the top part of the gloves will be hidden. I can stick the phone in there and hide the gun in the pocket.

I type a quick text to Agent Hammond:

Chartres and St. Philip . . . Leaving . . . fancy white dress . . . find me.

And then I text the same message to Ethan, minus the street location, but tell him Agent Hammond is close by, too.

I shove the phone inside the glove where it sits near the upper part of my inner arm before I open the door.

Thomas hands me the flats and sure enough, the second my toe gets to the end I feel something hard there. A tracker.

He eyes me up and down and clearly agrees that I look horrible in this dress. "Let's go."

We leave out of the front door. He's okay with me seeing where the house is and that's a bad sign. I thought I would totally stick out in this ridiculous white evening gown in the middle of the afternoon. That is until I see all the other girls in white evening gowns walking through the Quarter. And with them, men in tuxedos. And every single one of them with red bow ties. We blend right in. Thomas and I are on foot and I scan the streets for any sign of Agent Hammond, Ethan, or Will. Traffic is getting heavier and heavier and most cars are at a standstill. We're all headed in the same direction, but I'm not sure what's up ahead, and the farther we go, the more crowded it gets.

God, I hope one of them can find me.

I don't know where Tyler is—I haven't seen him since I ran up the balcony stairs. He must have known there was no hope for us as a couple. It's just me and Thomas now. He's got a death grip on my wrist as he pulls me down the street like he knows how easy it would be for me to just disappear in this sea of white.

"What's going on?" I ask him. I'm dragging my feet, making it hard for him. And giving Ethan or Agent Hammond time to find me before we are totally swallowed by the crowd.

"St. Joseph's Day Parade. The girls in the dresses like yours will be presented as debutantes tonight after the parade. The men in tuxes are fathers, brothers, and other male relatives."

"But what's the point of this? I don't get it."

"It's tradition."

Whatever. I don't care why they do it—it's still weird.

"So why are the men carrying the towers of really bad fake flowers?" And they are really bad. The flowers are red, white, and green but I'm mostly trying to distract him with all the questions. And slow him down a bit.

"The men will pass them out to women on the parade route in exchange for a kiss."

Thomas is clever. I can only imagine after we're all dead he'll just rush out in the crowd and lose himself.

"Where is everyone going?"

"To the parade staging area. It's just ahead. And stop dragging your feet."

Most of the streets have been closed off, so unless Ethan and Will are on foot, there is no way they'll find me. I think really hard about ditching the shoes and making a run for it but I don't know where to go. And I don't know how far I can get barefooted, with no money.

And then I see Agent Hammond. He's on the other side of the street, scanning the crowd. He got the text!

We're still walking fast. And I don't think Thomas has seen him yet.

We're moving away from him with each step and I feel like it's now or never.

"Agent Hammond!" I scream at the top of my lungs. And even though it's loud with all these young girls in white filling the streets, the sound carries down the block.

He stops and his expression changes the second he hears his name. As he charges across the street, Thomas pulls me in an open brick alleyway, similar to where Tyler parked the car at Thomas's place.

Hammond barrels through the door but stops when he sees Thomas pointing a gun at my head.

"Don't come any closer."

Hammond doesn't move a muscle but his eyes dart to mine. "Are you okay?"

I nod slowly and the barrel of the gun scrapes the side of my head.

"What do you want, Thomas? Whatever you want, I'll help you get it—just leave the girl here."

I can feel the gun dig into my temple a little harder. His movements are jerky and he's flustered.

"You will help me get it, but Anna stays with me. We're going to walk out of here, nice and slow. I'm putting this gun in my pocket and it will be trained on her the entire time. Start walking and I'll tell you where to go."

Thomas sounds nervous. It's not a sound I've ever heard before and I'm glad this is screwing up his carefully laid-out plans.

We start walking. Just before we leave the alley, Thomas whispers in my ear, "You weren't supposed to know the truth about Agent Hammond. I'm afraid you just signed your own death warrant."

Chapter 29

NEW RULE BY ANNA BOYD:

Routines aren't bad. At least people will know where to find you if you're always doing the same thing over and over.

I need to get Agent Hammond alone.

The fingers of my left hand stay close to the small opening of the coat pocket where the gun hides but I don't feel confident enough to use it while Thomas has his own gun trained at my back.

We're back on the street, close to the Riverfront, where all the floats are parked and ready for riders. There are girls in white dresses everywhere.

Thomas is on his phone. He's talking softly, and in Spanish, so I don't catch a single word he says.

Agent Hammond seems to be as confused as I am as to why we're here. I still haven't seen any trace of Ethan or Will.

"Thomas, you don't need her. You've got me. Let her go."

"Keep moving."

We move down the line of floats, weaving in and around the crowd until Thomas directs us into the side door of a small hotel.

Once we're inside, Thomas stops. "Hammond, please remove your weapons."

Hammond waits a few seconds then pulls a gun from his holder.

"Drop it in the plant over there," Thomas instructs. "Come closer to me."

Hammond obeys and Thomas pats him down for any other guns he could be hiding but finds nothing.

"Go straight down this hall. We're going to room 105."

Thomas drags me through a narrow hallway, bumping along the wall. Agent Hammond is ahead of us and stops abruptly in front of the door.

"Knock on the door."

This is bad. I take a step toward Agent Hammond and Thomas jerks me back. "You will stay right by my side."

A large man opens the door, letting us in. Just past the entry-way, the room opens up into a spacious living area. There are two other men in the room, one standing and one seated in an over-size arm chair. From the look of his clothes, this must be Señor Vega.

"Pat him down," Vega tells the man who let us in.

Oh, crap! What happens when he finds the gun in Thomas's pocket? And will he pat me down, too?

I cringe, waiting for the moment the gun is found. And then nothing. The man moves to stand behind Vega and says, "He's clean, boss."

What?

Thomas pushes me farther into the room. Agent Hammond

inches closer to my side. Then I realize the guy who opened the door must be working for Thomas, too.

"You're both quite dressed up this afternoon," says Vega.

"It's always best to blend in. This is what was called for given the events of the day."

The two men behind him have guns drawn but they keep them pointed down by their sides.

"What have you brought me?"

"As requested, Miss Anna Boyd," Thomas says, his clipped tone echoing through the empty room.

Vega lights a big, fat cigar and blows a huge cloud of smoke in our direction. "Very interesting. And who's her friend? Surely, this is not the boyfriend. He is too old!"

"Agent Hammond of the U.S. Marshals Service," Thomas answers.

I'm trying not to panic. I don't see Mateo here but I know he's here somewhere. Vega looks put out with this whole charade and keeps glancing to a room on his left. Is he signaling Mateo to come out? The room is big but not that big. It will be hard NOT to get caught in the cross fire. I've got to turn the phone off. I can't let Ethan walk into this. I should have left it behind.

Agent Hammond is surveying the room. I wish I knew what he was thinking.

"Interesting," Vega says, "so I assume you wish to be back in my good graces. I'm not sure there is room for you when there are so many eager to take your place."

"Señor Vega, I was disappointed to hear you lost faith in me so quickly. Especially after so many years of loyal service"—he pauses briefly, then continues—"and the many years of loyal service my father gave before me."

Vega laughs and his two companions follow suit as if on cue. "Your father was a good man. I never once questioned his loyalty." He takes another long pull on the cigar before saying, "You, on the other hand, seem to be more ambitious. Those who are ambitious only look in one direction, and that is up."

Chills race down my spine. This is not going well at all.

Thomas lets out a sharp, quick laugh. "You're right. That was my father's biggest complaint about me as well. And as much as he tried to beat that out of me, I'm afraid he failed. The problem is, I always think I can do it better. And I'm usually right."

Before I can grasp what's happening, Thomas pushes me to the side and lets out two quick shots. The henchmen behind Vega fall to the ground dead before they have a chance to raise their guns, including the one who just gave Thomas a pass in the doorway.

The gunshots barely made any noise so it's unlikely anyone else heard anything.

Agent Hammond dropped down to a crouching position when Thomas started firing. But now he stays that way, his hand inching toward the gun one of Vega's men had been holding moments before. When he fell, the gun landed under the side table, near Agent Hammond. God, please let him get it before Thomas sees him.

Vega screams, "Mateo!"

Mateo waltzes in from another room, his gun drawn.

"What are you doing? You are here to kill him!" Vega screams.

"I'm sorry, I can't do that. He's made me an offer I can't refuse," Mateo answers back.

Vega is terrified.

Thomas levels the gun on Vega. "Señor, you are right to feel concerned."

Vega holds his hands out in front of him and stutters out, "You must think about what you are doing . . . my death will not go unpunished!"

"Well, you may be right. I'm afraid you'll never know, will you?"

And then Thomas shoots him in the head. Vega falls backward, dead before he hits the ground.

Holy shit.

Thomas spins around, leveling the gun on Agent Hammond. "Sorry, but he's right. They will be looking for someone to blame for this but it won't be me."

"Stop!" I scream. The gun is out before I finish the word. Ethan's instructions are flying through my head. I stare at Thomas's chest and try to get my hands to stop shaking. I'm close to him, just a few feet away. Surely I can't miss at this range.

"Well, well, well . . . there is the missing gun." Thomas keeps the gun trained on Hammond, but his eyes dart between the two of us.

I'm outnumbered. I've got to try to turn Mateo.

"Mateo, do you know he's leaving for Brazil?" My voice is shaky and I hate how weak it makes me sound but I can't help it. After seeing Thomas shoot the man who let him pass through with a gun, I know whatever deal he made with Mateo was a lie.

"She's lying," Thomas says, coolly. And convincingly.

Mateo doesn't answer me, but I can tell he wasn't expecting that.

"He's got money. And a passport in a fake name. And a deed for some property in Rio. Did you know all that? He's not planning on taking over the cartel. He's planning on getting revenge then disappearing. I wouldn't be surprised if you're the next on his list to die."

Mateo now has his gun raised and he's moving it between Thomas and me.

"If you let this girl outmaneuver you, then you will be a great disappointment."

"She's smarter than you gave her credit for, my friend," Mateo says.

"We have a deal, Mateo. Think about what you will lose if you make the wrong decision today."

Mateo's head nods to one of the dead henchmen and he says, "I'm sure poor Miguel wishes he would have taken that gun from you."

Thomas looks frustrated. "You knew that was part of the plan. You didn't seem too concerned for poor Miguel when you mentioned how open he would be to flipping sides."

And then the room is quiet, both men weighing the other. Mateo's gun slides in my direction. I'm losing him.

"This gun is loaded. I know y'all are better at this than me but my finger is on the trigger and it won't take much to fire off a round. He may get me but I'll get you, Thomas."

Mateo puts one hand on his waist. "Maybe I should let her kill you. Then I won't be worried about if you're double-crossing me or not."

The one thing neither of them is doing is paying attention to

Agent Hammond. I can't tell what he's doing but he's been making slow, steady movements ever since Mateo raised his gun.

Thomas takes a tiny step toward me, the gun still pointed where Agent Hammond is crouched on the floor. "I didn't give you enough credit."

I have to keep them talking. "So you plan to frame Agent Hammond for this?"

"Everyone in the Marshals Service is looking for the mole. Everyone in the cartel will be looking for Señor Vega's killer. I've given both groups their answer."

"And no one is looking at you," I finish for him.

"Precisely."

Agent Hammond explodes off the floor, shooting Mateo in the chest, then yells for me to get down. I scream and fall to the ground the second before Thomas turns his gun on me. The wood in the wall behind me rains splinters on my head. I raise the gun up, keep my eyes open, and focus on pulling the trigger, but Thomas is already falling to the ground in front of me.

Agent Hammond got to him first.

Thomas and Mateo are on the floor, dead. My ears echo with the vibrations and my nose burns from the smell of gunfire. I look around the room and see nothing but dead bodies and I sink to the floor. Agent Hammond moves to me, making sure I'm okay.

"I can't believe you got them both," I say. I collapse and Agent Hammond drops down beside me.

"Anna, it's over. They can't hurt you."

"I don't know if I could have done it," I say in a ragged breath.

They're dead. They're all dead. I can't bring myself to look at the bodies. "I wanted to shoot him. I wanted to protect myself but I don't know if I could have gone through with it."

I loosen my grip, and the gun rolls onto the floor.

Chapter 30

NEW RULE BY ANNA BOYD:
Original rule still in effect.

HAMMOND reaches into his pocket and takes out his phone. "I called Agent Williams after I spoke to you earlier. It shouldn't take him long to get here."

When he starts replaying the events over the phone, I drag myself off the floor. I can't handle hearing that right now. I get up and walk to the tiny bathroom. There's blood all over my white dress and coat. After scrubbing my hands raw, I finally walk back into the other room. I can't look at the floor littered with dead bodies.

"It's over, Anna. For good. There's no one else to worry about."

But that's not completely true. "No. Agent Parker is still out there."

He shakes his head. "Agent Parker? We found her remains not far from that island where Agent Williams took you. I'm sorry, Anna. She's dead."

I shake my head, slowly. "I'm not sure what you found, but she's not dead. She's the mole. And Thomas's girlfriend. What I said about Brazil was the truth. There was a passport with her picture and a new name."

Agent Hammond looks stunned. "Riley?"

Riley? "Is that her first name?"

"Yes."

That was the one person I couldn't figure out the night I heard Thomas and Mateo talking in the courtyard. "I think I know where she is. What time is it?"

Agent Hammond glances to the clock on the wall. "Just after three."

I move to the door. "Let's go."

"Where are we going?"

"Ursuline. She won't wait long. Thomas is meticulous. When he doesn't show on time, she's gone."

Agent Hammond calls Agent Williams again, telling him the change in plans.

The sun has gone behind the buildings, leaving the streets in semidarkness. Most of the girls are on the floats and they're moving slowly down the streets.

Agent Hammond puts his coat around me, probably to hide all the blood, and we make our way through the crowd.

Most of the other men in tuxes are already drunk and this event hasn't really even started yet. They're trying to kiss my cheek and hand me plastic flowers, but I just push through them.

"So how do you know all of this? Is there something you're not telling me?"

"Thomas's brother, Tyler, figured it out. I just happened to be there when he did."

"There seems to be a lot of this story I don't know."

Once we're a block from the convent, we leave the parade crowd altogether. We stop across the street.

"Where will she be?"

"Probably on the third floor, looking for the money and passports that aren't there anymore."

Agent Hammond pushes me into a side alley. "Stay here out of sight until I come back for you." Then he sprints across the street.

I dig the phone out of my pocket and dial Catherine's number. It barely rings before Ethan picks up. "Where in the hell are you? There are girls in white dresses everywhere! And this damn app just narrows it down to a single block."

God, it's so good to hear his voice. "Come back to Ursuline. It's over. Or almost over. Thomas is dead. And so is Mateo. Agent Hammond has gone in to get Agent Parker—then it will be over for good."

"Thank God." Ethan chokes out on the other end of the line. "I'm close. Stay put, I'm coming for you."

I end the call and feel something against my back. "You've made a very bad mistake."

I turn around quickly and that's when I see her. Agent Parker.

She grabs my arm. "Let's walk."

"Don't touch me! You betrayed me. You betrayed my family. I cried for you when I thought you were dead!" I try to jerk my arm out of her grasp but her claws dig in deeper.

"Agent Hammond!" I scream at the top of my lungs. "Help!" She pulls me deeper into the alleyway then pushes me down to the ground.

She moves closer and I cringe with each step she takes. I can't believe how normal she looks—no bruises, no busted lip, nothing.

"Where is it? Where are the money and the passports?"

"I don't know."

She is furious.

"Get up. You're coming with me."

I don't move.

She cocks the gun and says, "You come with me or I leave you dead here. Your choice."

I didn't come this far to let this bitch kill me now. Agent Hammond won't be long so I just have to stay alive long enough for him to get back.

"You shoot me and you'll never find the money."

"Tell me where it is and I'll let you go."

I press my lips close together.

"I took a peek at dear ol' Mom. Looks like she's all dried up. Wonder if she'll stay that way after she finds out you're dead?"

That one question is all it takes to knock the breath out of me. She's the one who took the picture of her at the treatment facility. I refuse to answer her. I refuse to give this woman any power over me.

The problem is, she won't stop talking.

"I can't say I miss those tearful calls from her at all hours of the day and night. I mean, you'd think a fifth of gin would last more than twenty-four hours, but no. She always needed more."

I crumble on the ground. I could never figure out how Mom, with our limited resources, could have an endless supply of booze. Now I know. After everything that has happened today, this is what does me in.

Agent Parker points the gun at me, yelling for me to get up—then she's tumbling down to the ground, headfirst. The gun still in her hand.

It's Will! He's holding her down with his knee pressed in her back as she struggles. "Knock her gun away, Anna," Will says.

Once I have her gun, Will and Ethan, using his one good arm, yank her up to a standing position. I take two steps until I'm face-to-face with her, then slap her across the cheek with everything in me.

"That was for Mom."

I hear heavy footsteps and it's Agent Hammond charging down the alley toward us.

"Anna! Are you okay?" Agent Hammond takes Agent Parker from Ethan and Will and throws her against the brick wall, twisting her hands behind her back.

"Find me something to tie her hands together," he says to Will and Ethan.

Will grabs an old piece of rope near a Dumpster and Agent Hammond binds her hands together behind her back.

Ethan and I both run to each other at the same time. I throw myself at Ethan and he grunts in pain. He hugs me back with his one good arm while the other is tucked away in a sling.

"Sorry! I just didn't think I would ever see you again."

He digs his hand in the back of my hair and says, "Me, too. God, Anna, when I saw her pointing that gun at you, I didn't think we would make it in time."

"Okay, Ethan, move back. My turn." And then Will hugs me tight. "I'm still mad at you."

I laugh. "I'm okay with that."

"Okay, give me my girl back," Ethan says.

And then I'm back in Ethan's arms.

"It's over. Finally. Forever."

Agent Hammond starts walking a very pissed-off Agent Parker back toward Ursuline. "I need to call Agent Williams," he says. "Tell him we got her."

There is a crowd surrounding the convent and lots of speculation of what has been going on inside here. They would all be so disappointed to know that it had nothing to do with the supernatural or vampires or any other crazy thing they will try to come up with. There are local cops and federal agents all over the place. Thankfully, Agent Parker has been taken away.

"Anna, we're going to have to go back to that hotel and walk them through what happened," Agent Hammond says.

I shiver at the thought of seeing all those dead bodies again. "Is it . . . like it was when we left?"

He nods. "I'm sorry you'll have to see that again, but you won't have to stay long. I promise."

"And I'll be with you," Ethan says and looks at Agent Hammond like he dares him to say any different.

A few hours later, all the loose ends start coming together. Agent Parker is spilling her guts hoping for some leniency. She said Noah was kidnapped so they could control Agent Williams. He was also told to go to a specific hotel in Mandeville and wait to be contacted. He did exactly as he was told. The plan was for him to be led to the scene where Vega and Hammond would be dead. Thomas would have planted something there to lead him to Ursuline for further proof of Hammond's guilt. Or so they hoped.

Agent Williams is beating himself up for trusting Parker. I thought he was going to kill her when he got here, but he settled down rather quickly once Noah arrived. Someone made an anonymous call to the New Orleans Police Department telling them where Noah was. I'm pretty sure it was Tyler, but we'll never know for sure.

Tyler is gone. Really gone. I told them everything I knew, including the names on the fake passports. An agent went to the airport and sure enough there was a Rafael Costa who left the airport. The problem is, the records showed him leaving on five different planes, in five different directions. Maybe I didn't give Tyler enough credit.

Ethan, Will, and I are sitting on the curb of the back parking lot, waiting for them to let us go. Dad and the Landrys should be here any minute. I'm sure they drove like bats out of hell from Arkansas.

There was no sign of anyone watching the island, but they did find several webcams scattered throughout the campground.

We've been getting all of our information from Agent Hammond. He's been back and forth all evening, relaying information, and it's twisted how deep Thomas's plan was. Some agents went to Baton Rouge earlier and were able to use one of the trackers to flush out a man there who was watching Catherine's family's house. They are questioning him now, but it seems he was hired just for that job and doesn't even know by whom. Dad picked up Catherine and Teeny on the way here.

I watch Hammond talk to Agent Williams, and I say to Ethan, "I feel sorry for Agent Williams. Do you think he's going to get in trouble for not telling anyone what was going on?"

Ethan shrugs. "I don't know. I'm sure there will be some sort of internal investigation."

One of the cops walks to where we're sitting—he's holding a small bag in his hand. He hands it to me and says, "This was found inside and we're not sure what it is. Agent Williams asked me to show it to you to see if you knew."

He hands me the bag and I open it. It's the letters, the pocket watch, and the framed photograph of Henry. "These are my sister's things."

The cop waits, like I'm going to give it back to him, and when he realizes I'm not, he finally walks away.

"Teeny's gonna be thrilled when she sees this," Ethan says. "I was already prepared to lose a fortune buying it back."

Not caring who's looking, I pull Ethan in for a deep kiss. "I love that you would have gone back for that stuff for her."

"I would do anything for her. And you."

"Y'all are gonna have to get a room," Will says.

Hammond is back with more info to share. "Agent Parker and Thomas have known each other for years. Her older brother was a friend of his growing up. They're all from some little town in South Texas near the border."

"But she didn't get on our detail until Natchitoches. How did she know all that stuff?" I ask.

Hammond shrugs, "They'll have to look into all of that when they're done here. But Agent Williams said she was in the main office—almost everything went across her desk. She was in the perfect position to tell Thomas whatever he wanted to know about any case the Marshals had. He feels guilty since he always assumed it was one of the field agents."

"Did she say what his real name was?"

He laughs. "She did. John Diaz."

John Diaz. I don't know what I was expecting, but that wasn't it. It's very . . . anticlimactic.

I stare at the convent windows on the third floor and try to wrap my brain around everything.

Agent Williams walks over and stops in front of us. "Anna, Ethan—I can't tell you how sorry I am about what happened." Then he looks directly at me and says, "Noah said you and your sister were really nice to him. That means more to me than you'll ever know."

"I'm just glad he's okay."

"Me too. Our guys just got back from that house you all were in and it was rigged to blow. Not the whole thing, just the kitchen."

Will looks confused "Why would he have done that?"

Agent Williams shrugs. And I remember what Thomas said the night he was talking to Mateo.

We'll meet back here when it's done and settle up. The door off the kitchen will be open. You can wait in there if you beat me back.

"It was for Mateo."

Will gets up and says, "This is some crazy shit. I'm gonna walk over and get a Coke. Anybody want one?"

"No," I answer. "But I won't turn down some regular clothes."

The white dress is a disaster—stained and torn—and I would give anything to get out of it.

When Ethan and I are finally alone, he puts his good arm around me and I burrow into his side.

"I know you saw both of them get shot. Do you want to talk about it?" Ethan asks.

"When I was in that moment and I knew it was them or me . . . I was really glad it was them."

He squeezes me and says, "I'm really glad it was them, too."

"When I talked to Dad, I asked him if we could stop in Baton Rouge on our way home to see Mom. Are you good with that?"

"Of course. We can do whatever you want."

"Well, I know you love New Orleans, but I don't know if I ever want come back down here again."

He chuckles softly. "You may feel differently later on. We'll give it some time."

And then I think about what that means. Time. We have all the time in the world now, and I can't help but smile thinking about it.

Epilogue

"ON the count of three, we're jumping!"

I'm so excited and terrified that I can hardly stand it. "Are you sure it's going to be okay?" I scream my question over the roar of the waterfall.

"Yes! You can do this."

After what happened in New Orleans, we don't want to waste a single second of our lives. We're in Costa Rica, where we've spent the last week hiking and river rafting and basically having a really good time. Our high school graduation had barely ended before we were jumping on a plane, headed south. "Look, everyone else has done it and they all survived. You're the bravest girl I know."

And that's all I need to reassure me.

"Okay! On three!"

Together we count, "One . . . two . . . three!"

And then we're falling fast. We're in the deep pool of water within seconds.

Ethan breaks from the water, yelling, "Hell, yeah! Let's do it again!"

I laugh and splash him.

"Anna! Ethan! Over here!" Catherine and the others swim toward the rocky bank. Ethan and I let the waves take us to where they are.

The water flows in between the crevices of the large black rocks, making little coves. The sand is not like any I've ever seen, dark gray and spongy-feeling. And the water is so gorgeous; the deepest shades of midnight blue and emerald green swirl and mix with each crashing wave. This may be the most beautiful place I've ever seen. So far, at least.

I look around at everyone here—Catherine and Will, Emma and Ben, and especially Ethan—and say a quick prayer of thanks that I'm alive and here in this moment with them.

Ethan swims up beside me, his hands running across my waist. "Come explore with me," he whispers.

We float through the shallow water, deeper into the rocky coast, until we find a secluded little corner. Ethan pulls me into his lap and we soak up the warm sunshine.

We can still hear the splashing and laughing of our friends, but for all purposes, we are alone.

I twist around until I'm facing him. Both of my hands are on the sides of his face and I pull him in for a kiss.

The water is warm and our hands slip and slide over each other. I could stay here, like this, forever.

"I'm not ready to go home tomorrow," Ethan says between

kisses. "We'll be back to our own beds and your dad's eagle eye."

"My mom's, too. And I think she's worse than him!"

Mom has been home for a month and it's been good. Really good. We were all a bit nervous around each other for the first few days but it didn't last. She's not back to her old self—she's actually better than her old self. I don't know if it will last forever, but what I learned after New Orleans is to enjoy every day for what it is.

Ethan trails kisses down one side of my neck and back up the other. "Maybe we can go backpacking through Europe until it's time to start school this fall? Just me and you weaving our way through France. Doesn't that sound better than the summer in Natchitoches?"

"Ummm . . . yes, it does. But there's no way we could go to France and leave Teeny behind. She'd never speak to us again. You know she's trying to convince Mom and Dad to send her there for boarding school."

Ethan pulls back from my neck and I'm sorry I distracted him. "What?"

"She's obsessed with Francesca. She's dying to find out what happened to her, and she thinks she needs to start at the beginning."

"That's crazy."

"No, it's probably more that she thinks Francesca saved us and she just wants to make sure things ended well for her."

Ethan frowns. "I thought she was doing better? She seems like she's back to her normal self."

Normal self would be full-blown crush on Ethan and total brat to me.

"She is, for the most part. That picture and those letters are really important to her. She's just having a hard time letting it go."

We hear the group getting closer and it's only a few seconds more before Will's head pops into view. He climbed on top of a large rock near where we are. "Who wants one more jump before we head back?" Will asks.

Ethan grabs my hand, bringing it to his mouth, and kisses it slowly.

"You ready?"

I smile. "Always. Let's go."

Acknowledgments

SO many thanks to . . .

Sarah Davies, my amazing agent, for her continued support and encouragement. Greenhouse Literary feels like a family and I'm so honored to be a part of it.

Emily Meehan and Laura Schreiber for being rock star editors. You helped me dig deep to make this story the best it could be and I'm so fortunate to have you both on my side. I'm one lucky author.

The entire team at Disney-Hyperion including: Elizabeth Holcomb and Mark Amundsen for their meticulous copyediting, Dina Sherman and Jamie Baker for getting my books into readers' hands, Marci Senders and Theresa Evangelista for blowing me away with this beautiful cover, and everyone else behind the scenes—I'm truly grateful for everything you do.

Elle Cosimano, Megan Miranda, and Moriah McStay Lee—you are not only phenomenal critique partners but also treasured friends. This journey would not have been near as much fun without you.

My parents, in-laws, family and friends for being beyond supportive and excited and the basically the best fans a girl could ask for. A special shout-out to Nicole Guidry Earl—you're friendship has meant so much to me over the years. And to Elizabeth Pippin for patiently listening to every single story idea I have (usually while we're in line for carpool).

And always the biggest thanks to my husband, Dean, and our sons, Miller, Ross, and Archer. Every day is an adventure and I'm so glad I get to share it with you. I love you all so very much.